GOD REVEALED MY HUSBAND WAS LEAVING

LEWISA DeBLAKE

GOD REVEALED MY HUSBAND WAS LEAVING

This is a work of fiction. All of the characters, names, incidents, organizations, and dialogue in this novel are either the products of the author's imagination or are used fictitiously.

Cover Painting by Yvonne Krajenbrink Hulin

iUniverse books may be ordered through booksellers or by contacting:

iUniverse
1663 Liberty Drive
Bloomington, IN 47403
www.iuniverse.com
844-349-9409

ISBN: 978-1-6632-2673-0 (sc)
ISBN: 978-1-6632-2674-7 (e)

Library of Congress Control Number: 2021919597

Print information available on the last page.

iUniverse rev. date: 09/21/2021

This book is dedicated to God for being my rock during the storms in my life; my mom for giving me life and later, after God gave her peace in her heart, encouragement on my spiritual journey; my siblings for being my first friends; and my children, Candace, Christopher, and Eion, because while I was walking by faith, you all believed me when no one else did. I also dedicate this book to Bishop T. D. Jakes and the other ministers God has used to help encourage, motivate, and push me into my destiny and to the late Johnny Foote for the public one-on-one prophecy during a confusing, frustrating, and low moment in my life (RIP). I am grateful to my ex-husband for the good times and our children, though our lives diverged in different directions, and to my future husband because God said so. I thank Yvonne Krajenbrink Hulin for the cover of this novel and for being a kind and caring friend. Last but not least, this book is dedicated to everyone going through various forms of life's storms. God is not a respecter of persons. This story is about the good, the bad, and the ugly from my life. If you are walking through the valley of the shadow of death, God will see you through to the other side. With this novel, I am allowing God to use my pain for his purpose.

ONE

I must tell Jesus all of my trials; I cannot bear these burdens alone; In my distress He kindly will help me; He ever loves and cares for His own.

—Elisha A. Hoffman

JUST CALL ME Joseph. God did. Did you know following God can sometimes cause your life to spiral out of your control down into a dark, hard, and lonely hole? That was part of Joseph's story in Genesis 37-50 KJV in the Bible, but the hole I encountered was figurative. Still, it was a cold, isolated, deep pit as a result of a private spiritual battle. My *Leave It to Beaver* lifestyle and portrayal of a modern-day June Cleaver came to a screeching halt. My title of stay-at-home mom was relinquished. Making sure dinner was served just slightly after six o'clock and greeting my husband as he walked into our house became a fleeting memory. Life as I once had known it was over. The life my family once had enjoyed together was torn apart like tiny pieces of paper. *Hmm. Joseph. Dark. Lonely. Hole. Oh! Yes, that's right. Okay, I see it now.*

I lost my husband recently because I chose to believe God had a plan for my life and decided to follow Jesus. Unfortunately, the idea of walking by faith and not by sight to follow what God called me to do overwhelmed Yury because he wasn't interested in living like that. Therefore, my husband secretly found comfort and support in the company and arms of other women, which made him lose my trust. I guess no one told him that once you get married, pouring out your disappointments and sorrows to women of interest undermines your marital relationship.

Outside of sex, my husband never truly got to know me. Yes, in body, he was with me, but I didn't know his heart and soul were a hundred thousand miles away. I had no idea my husband was a slick Willie, a country Casanova, a player, or a smooth operator—you know, like Sade's song. The fact that it was one of his favorite songs should have been a clue for me regarding our future. I didn't know telling a lie was as normal to him as breathing. He refused to accept the call of God on my life and my invitation for him to be a servant of God with me. He despised my resolve to be committed to the things of God and went around behind my back, calling me crazy, a zealot, a pious nut, a Jesus freak, and a Bible-believing fanatic.

I would have accepted my husband's rejection and betrayal better if I hadn't loved and cared for him so much. I genuinely liked him too. To be fair, he reciprocated the same emotions toward me. I gave him my love, my heart, and my trust. He couldn't see what I offered him, nor did he care to invest time in trusting or listening to me. Instead, he bruised and crushed my heart, and he had the nerve to think he hadn't done anything wrong.

He never tried to tell me he was unhappy. Although when I first told him God was communicating with me through dreams and prophetic words, he told me if I didn't stop talking like that, he was going to divorce me.

I sat beside Yury on the couch, and while looking at him tenderly, I said, "God has been telling me through dreams and prophecy given through ministers that he wants me to go to Dallas, Texas, because he wants to use me there."

Yury narrowed his eyes and slowly shook his head, saying sharply, "No, God doesn't do or say things like that. If you keep talking like that, I'm going to divorce you!"

Those words from his lips pierced my heart like a pin puncturing and deflating a balloon. They crumpled my hope for an everlasting marriage, one that could survive every kind of storm imaginable. He lost respect for me, and I had no idea. I wanted his love to be so strong that he wasn't able to bear the idea of losing me. Thus, he'd become a willing participant in going where God was leading me. I wanted my husband to show me that I was valuable enough to him to fight for our marriage and that it was a top priority for him to fight for me and keep our family together. I wanted to be so important to him that he considered it worthy to examine what was driving me to go where I normally would never have gone and do what I ordinarily would never have done. I wanted him to at least weigh the fact that God had been a huge part of my life before he entered it and during all the years we had been together. He didn't recognize God was real to me.

I was taught not to force or push accepting God on Yury, so I didn't. I'll admit that since following God and walking by faith were new to me, it took a long while and a lot of mistakes before I received a clearer understanding about what God was showing me. I didn't understand it. I heard some ministers say the things God shows you are like pieces of a puzzle. God gives one piece at a time. When you put the pieces together, the puzzle becomes a picture and sheds understanding on God's plan for your life. Maybe in his own way, Yury did his best to try to be supportive, even though he didn't understand what I was facing. Or I thought that was what he was doing.

I wanted to please God and complete God's will or assignment for my life. I'd heard ministers say God had one for everyone's life. I was praying for God to touch Yury's heart and open his eyes. Even though I waited on Yury hand and foot and kept him sexed up, our polar-opposite beliefs and endeavors contributed to a devastating blow that destroyed our home life. Years later, when his dirty laundry was exposed, it was like receiving a swift sucker punch to the gut. My world unraveled before my eyes as years of hidden lies shook me to my core. Our lives took on the role of the good, the bad, and the ugly.

God warned me nine years before the truth screamed for attention, but he didn't give me the details before the crap hit the fan and smeared all over our marriage. I'll admit I wanted to give my husband a one-way ticket on the train to glory to meet his Maker. I was close to being charged with SHS—shaken husband syndrome— but with time that feeling slowly passed. Hey, afterward, I would have asked my pastor and church family to pray with me for God to raise Yury back to life again. Nothing is too hard for God, right?

I know that doesn't sound godly, but unless you have actually felt the sting of that kind of betrayal, it is hard to understand the emotions it drags up. It never occurred to me that I would be the one who would ask for a divorce. However, divorce is better than murder; at least we can still be friends if he is still alive. The motive behind my telling my story is not to disgrace or hurt my ex-husband. Even though he made some bad choices, he is still a good, responsible, and hardworking person and father. I too made plenty of unwise choices before and after accepting Jesus as my Savior.

God already knows our future. Also, we can't hide our secrets from God, because he knows everything. My story taught me this: never think you are smarter than God and can keep deceitful things covered, because when you least expect it, he will allow the truth to be heard and seen. First, let's go to my childhood and life with my mother.

I was five years old when Mama and Daddy separated after twenty-one years of marriage. He not only was verbally abusive toward her but also began physically abusing her. Things escalated, and one night, things got dangerous. I believe he was drunk, because that was what he did on the weekend: drink.

If my brother William hadn't been home that night to step in between them and fight for Mama, Daddy, who was six foot one and medium built, with pecan-colored skin and a full head of hair cut low, would have possibly taken her life. A short, pudgy, hairless brown cab driver held Daddy with one arm around his waist and one arm around his neck and walked him to the front door. He knocked, and Mom opened the door. Mama was short, with pale skin, sandy-brown hair, and jade-green eyes.

She asked, "Where is the car?"

Dad jerked from the cab driver's arms toward Mom and, in a hateful tone, yelled, "Don't worry about my car! You didn't pay one penny for it!"

Mom dodged to the right of Daddy, and he landed on the floor.

The cab driver said, "I don't know the answer, ma'am. I just drove him home."

Mom said, "OK. Thank you!"

The cab driver asked, "Miss, are you going to be all right? Are you going to need help getting him up?"

Mom shook her head and said, "I'll get our children to help me with him. He'll sleep it off."

He said, "Well then, have a good night."

Mom replied, "Good night." Then she closed the door.

Daddy jumped up, teeter-tottering on his feet, and belted out, "How you gonna throw yourself at another man right in front of my face?"

"Ryder, I wasn't flirting with him. You should know what kind of woman I am," Mom answered softly.

"I know what I heard! Do you think I'm stupid?" he said as he staggered toward Mom.

She backed up. "No."

His legs swung unsteadily. "Desi, you know you are planning to leave me one day, so do it now!" His eyes raged.

Mom's face turned red as she backed away. "That's not true."

Slurring, Dad thundered, "Are you calling me a liar?" He leaned forward and swung at her, but she ducked and swerved clear of Dad's reach.

Mom screamed, "No, Ryder, don't do it! Our children need us!"

Hearing the commotion, William, age sixteen, with a sturdy body, stopped playing his guitar in his room down the hall and dashed into the oversized foyer. He stood in front of Mama. Facing Daddy, he warned him, "Don't you hurt my mama!" Then he told Mom, "Lock yourself in the bathroom."

Dad reached into his dark blue jacket and pulled out a revolver. "No other man is going to have my wife! Not alive, that is!"

Mom backed up, turned around, and ran to the bathroom down the hall.

Dad shouted, "Boy, you don't tell me or my wife what to do! So do you think you are a man now? That you can take on your own old man now?"

With steely eyes, William said, "Daddy, I don't want to hurt you, so put the gun down!"

Daddy snapped, "Back down, Son, or you are going to meet your Maker tonight!"

In the blink of an eye, William careened across the floor, slid on one leg through the opening between Daddy's legs, and ended up behind Daddy's back. Before Dad knew what had happened, William did a fast, fancy karate move to remove the gun from Daddy's hand.

The gun fell to the floor. Mom ran from the bathroom into the kitchen to call the police. Then William did a karate takedown on Daddy. Once Daddy was on the floor, William pinned him there until the police came.

Daddy's violence was ruthless. Without any warning, he would pull out his gun. When a sober person handles a gun, it makes a situation critical, but when a drunk person tries to use a gun, it becomes a catastrophe. Fortunately, William's brawny size and karate skills helped him subdue Daddy until the police could lead him away. William played the tuba in his high school marching band, took karate classes, and played the bass guitar with a musical group in the evening sometimes.

It was an act of God for William to be home that night in the first place. By God's love and mercy, the band's gig scheduled for that night had been canceled. That night, I didn't understand what was happening, but I felt pain when I heard the next day that Daddy wasn't going to be living with us anymore. It felt as if my heart were severely bruised and seeping blood.

During Mom and Dad's separation process, Mom took Donna, age eleven; Wanda, age seven; and me, age five, with her to live with her sister, Aunt Naomi, in Jacksonboro, South Carolina, a.k.a. the country. She had many acres of land. We were surprised when we were introduced to our cousins and other family members who lived next door (a few acres away). They lived down the road and around the corner from each other, all on dirt roads, including Sally Mae, Betty Sue, Daisy Lou, Emma Jean, Bobby Lee, Leon Earl, and Parker Ray, to name a few. They used their first and middle names together all the time. Aunt Naomi and her children didn't follow that tradition.

We were city slickers, so our transition to country life was choppy and alarming. We felt we were in hell on earth for six long months. In the city of Charleston, we'd grown up with indoor plumbing and toilets in the bathrooms. In Jacksonboro, we were introduced to an outhouse for the first time. It was in the middle of a cleared field on Aunt Naomi's property, in view of her house.

I felt horror when we were given instructions to take a flashlight and toilet tissue with us and, most importantly, listen and watch out for snakes, rats, frogs, and spiders. Of course, they never told us what to do if we encountered said creatures. Snakes automatically knew to stay away from the city, but we were in their territory now. It was the first time we had been put into a position in which using the bathroom could turn out to be deadly. You can only hold it for so long; then nature's call turns into a bully. Times like that will teach a nonbeliever to call on the name of Jesus each time he or she needs to take care of business.

Mr. Jim, Aunt Naomi's beau, built Mom a brand-new house of her own within walking distance behind Aunt Naomi's house, and we had a bathroom, but it still didn't have a toilet. It did have a sink, a bathtub, and a mirror on the wall. What animosity did those people have against toilets? Mom came up with the wise idea for us to do our business in a sturdy basin half filled with water. Then we would travel to the outhouse, only during daylight, to dispose of the waste. It was a lot better than sitting on a wooden hole while knowing that a larger, deep dirt hole was underneath us. Plus, we had heard stories of critters coming up from the hole while someone was in there.

Mr. Jim built the house as a favor for Aunt Naomi because sometimes it's hard for two grown women to share a house together when both of them have strong personalities. It was a single-story house with a long front porch that had three evenly spaced small square columns. Our house was made of wood and painted white. It was about eleven hundred square feet, with three bedrooms, one bathroom, a kitchen, and a living room. We lived there for three or four months.

Even though the new house was cute, having it didn't compare to living in Charleston. Many people there treated us as if we were immigrants who had crossed enemy lines. They didn't trust outsiders. Even some of the children asked me how many times I had gone to jail. My answer was "Never, because I'm only five." They wanted to know if I sold drugs, to which I responded, "Mom doesn't let me handle medicine." I guess they transferred the stereotypes they saw about city folks on TV onto me because I was from the city.

The children also gave Donna, Wanda, and me a hard time because we were three different shades of color. Wanda was a few shades lighter than I, and Donna was fair-skinned like Mama. Sometimes we endured cruel remarks just because they thought our coloring was strange. We were Neapolitan ice cream. I was chocolate, Wanda was strawberry, and Donna was vanilla. Country life was quite an adjustment for us.

On the school bus, a thirteen-year-old boy with a frizzy Afro and legs like a bow pulled Donna's hair and said, "How can y'all be sisters? You three look nothing alike. Who's your daddies?" He frowned.

Donna struck his hand and said, "Get your hands off me, and it's none of your business!"

He teased, "Don't get mad at me because y'all turned out looking like Neapolitan ice cream. That makes you vanilla flavor, Donna. Your sister Wanda is strawberry, and that makes Lewisa chocolate." He laughed.

A bucktoothed boy with ashy hands laughed and said, "That's right. That means your mama had a baby for a white man, a Hispanic man, and a black man." He paused and thought for a moment. Then he said, "Yuck! That's just nasty." He laughed again.

Donna raised her voice and said, "Y'all better stop talking about my mama! You don't know her! And for your information, we all have the same mama and daddy!" She flared her nostrils in anger.

The bus driver, a lady in her sixties with gray hair, eyebrows, and lashes, looked to the rear of the bus and drove slower. She called out loudly, "Hey! Do I need to talk to your parents?"

The boys said together, "No."

She continued. "Well, if you don't sit down, keep your hands to yourselves, and leave her alone, I will do just that!"

The boys sat down and talked quietly to the person next to them.

I still remember all too well the day we thought a group of men were killing somebody. It was a sweltering, sunny day with a faint hint of breeze dancing and dashing through the trees. People young and old gathered outside in front of the pig pen as if they were waiting for the main event to start. Children played together and ran around as some adults conversed in both audible and inaudible chatter. However, we were shell-shocked. From our observance, none of the natives were unhinged. Our hearts were beating fast when the screaming and hollering started. It sounded like a human being. A group of about six men, some with ropes, surrounded what we thought was a person.

"All right, men, spread out, hold your rope steady, and move in when I give the word," a pale, thin man with a scruffy salt-and-pepper beard said.

The other five men did just that. There were three black men, who looked like linebackers; one Asian man with long bluish-black hair, chewing on a straw; and an older ivory-skinned man, whose skin resembled tough cow hide.

The man with the tough skin said, "All right, men, you heard what the boss said, so move when he say move."

We discreetly watched the commotion from the window of our house. Someone owned a pig pen across the field in front of our dwelling place. Our view was blocked by the crowd of people who had gathered to see the strange form of entertainment. We didn't have cable. It wasn't available there at that time. Also, it seemed most people didn't watch television there anyway, because many of them sat outside for hours either talking to each other or watching the sunrise and sunset. We were beginning to wonder if they killed people in that town for sport.

Mom exclaimed, "You mean to tell me we left danger of a different kind in the city just to run into it here in the country?" She left the window. "I'm going to call Naomi." Naomi was the shade of cinnamon, slender, and taller than Mama. After Naomi answered, Mom said, "Naomi, what on earth is going on in front of my door? There is a man hollering, and people are crowded around him, watching whatever is happening to him." Concern ran through her voice.

Naomi laughed. "No, those men are catching a hog to take it to be slaughtered. The hog is making the sound you hear."

Mom took a deep breath, let it out, and said, "Whew! Thank God! Now I don't have to move again right now. I don't know where I was going, but I wasn't planning on staying here."

After Mom ended the call with Aunt Naomi, she told us the men were trying to catch a hog to take it to be slaughtered. It seemed the word had gotten out to the hog, because he was fighting for his life as he resisted being loaded onto a truck.

Then we were granted a serendipitous gift. Our brothers and oldest sister, Tabitha, who looked like a female version of Daddy, came to see us from time to time. We missed them and enjoyed having them in our new space. The weekend Big Mama, who was as tall as Daddy and looked similar to Lena Horne with glasses, came to visit us was meaningful. It was good to see familiar faces in the midst of the new foreign land we found ourselves in. We became even more pleased when Big Mama said she felt like having fresh fried chicken for dinner. I thought she was going to the food store to buy fresh chicken, but that was not what she was referring to.

I asked, "Big Mama, are you going to the store to buy chicken?"

"No, child. We don't buy chicken from a food store in the country. City folks come here to buy the best chicken on earth. We are having farm-raised, fresh fried chicken for dinner tonight," Big Mama said.

Cousin Ada, a plus-sized woman who always walked with a large stick for killing snakes, had live chickens, and Big Mama wanted to catch one to prepare it for dinner. I couldn't believe it. I'd thought Cousin Ada's chickens were her pets because she was unable to get a dog or cat.

Once Big Mama changed out of her dress into a loose shirt, blue jeans, and tennis shoes, it was game time. When she entered the huge grassy area with the chicken coop, the chickens went berserk, trying to flee. When Big Mama chased after them, the chickens started ducking, dodging, and zigzagging around her whenever she got too close to them. They gave her the slip many times, but Big Mama wasn't getting winded. She was prepared for the challenge, as if she had done this before. She lost her balance one time while running and ended up on the ground.

She roared, "Phooey! You are not getting the best of me, you peanut-brained, ground-pecking, tiny-feet chickens!"

That was when the chickens underestimated her and relaxed for a split second. They were gathered in a small group of seven. As Big Mama stood up, she paused for a while. Then she sprinted with all her might at the chickens in the group. To my surprise, when she turned to face us, she had a chicken in her hands. She gloated and said, "I've still got it! We are having chicken tonight!" Then she looked at us with a wink and said, "Children, that's how you catch a chicken."

From there, she started doing the most barbaric thing I had ever seen. It traumatized me. She took the chicken by its neck and flung it around in a circle again and again until its neck broke. Then, once the chicken's neck was broken, she set the chicken down for a moment so she could use a butcher knife, which was on a chopping block outside. I was stunned and grossed out after I saw the chicken with the broken neck trying to run away from the chopping block. Its head was cocked completely to the side, hanging, and trickles of blood were falling from its injured neck. This time, it didn't run as fast, but it was still determined to get away. The scene was like a zombie show on TV.

Finally, Big Mama grabbed the chicken, placed it on the chopping block, and gave it a good whack. She went on to pluck the feathers, cut the chicken into quarters, clean it, and fry it for dinner. My little mind was blown. Before that day, I'd thought the meat we bought from the store magically materialized in the store. I'd had no idea the animals came from farms and had to be killed and distributed so we could buy them.

That night, I didn't have an appetite for chicken after what I'd witnessed. It took a while before I could eat chicken again.

We probably asked Mama more than a thousand times, "When are we going back to Charleston?"

The day Mom told us we were moving back to Charleston was reminiscent of God speaking from heaven after John the Baptist baptized Jesus: "And suddenly a voice came from heaven, saying, 'This is My beloved Son, in whom I am well pleased'" (Matthew 3:17 KJV). We gladly left that new, modern house for our much older house built one hundred years before. The day we arrived back in Charleston was melodious. It was as if a melody filled the air. Our sentence on death row with the snakes was pardoned.

"We're home! Yay, yay, yay!" my sisters and I exclaimed as we jumped up and down.

Mama said, "It's good to be back home." She raised her hands toward the ceiling, saying, "Thank you, God!"

Once our dog, Joe Joe, a black beagle with white fur on his neck under his chin, saw Mama and us, he was happy. He wagged his tail, wiggling his body and making a crying sound. Then, when Mama rubbed his belly, he started peeing into the air as he continued wiggling.

Mama didn't get angry. She just laughed and said, "Well, look at that. Even the dog is expressing how much he missed us." She reached down and rubbed his belly and told him, "You are such a good boy, Joe Joe." He never had peed in the house before.

Time marched on. Then came 1979. I was ten years old. I didn't wear the latest fashions or spend a whole lot of time on my appearance. No, Mom didn't have me looking like Buckwheat from *The Little Rascals*. She bought everything at a bargain price, and we wore hand-me-down clothes—you know, clothes that once belonged to other people, such as siblings. Occasionally, when needed, Mom would buy us new shoes from a store in downtown Charleston called Edward's. It was a five-and-dime store long before Walmart existed. She'd buy us cheap tennis shoes from Edward's. The children in our neighborhood teased us about our shoes and made up a song about them. They would sing, "Bobos, they make your feet feel fine. Bobos, they cost a dollar ninety-nine."

During other times, Mom would put our shoes on layaway at the House of Shoes store in downtown Charleston. The owners, Mr. and Mrs. Goodwin, were good, caring people who worked with struggling families so they could have good, quality shoes. We didn't have a lot of money, but we were rich in family connectivity and love. Mom would say, "You don't need designer or name-brand products on your body to be somebody. Be proud to wear your own name, because somebody else's name doesn't make you who you are. Be a leader, not a follower, and be willing to stand for something, or you will fall for anything."

In Mama's house, the only rights we had were the right to breathe and the right to stay black. Mom would tell us everything else we needed to do or know. Mama taught us that our character was more important than what we looked like or wore. The way some of the children at school viewed me worsened the day Mom paid me an unexpected visit in my classroom. When she slid in through the open door, the conversation of Mrs. Keller, my fifth-grade teacher, and Mrs. Simmons, a visiting teacher, came to an abrupt stop.

"Can I help you?" Mrs. Keller asked with confusion etched on her face.

Mama smiled and said, "I'm Lewisa's mother. I apologize for interrupting your class, but the principal told me I could share with her the important information I need her to know for when school ends."

Mrs. Keller gave me a bewildered blink. "Lewisa, is she your mother?" she asked.

"Yes, that's my mom," I said proudly, beaming with joy.

Flashing a weak smile, Mrs. Keller told Mom, "You are welcome to talk to Lewisa outside the door if you like."

I followed Mom into the hallway. I don't remember what she told me that day, but it must have been important, because Mom never had come to my classroom like that before. Afterward, I returned to my class, and Mom left. Mrs. Keller and Mrs. Simmons were still standing together, talking softly.

"Um, Lewisa?" Mrs. Keller said, beckoning me to her.

I went to her desk and said, "Yes, Mrs. Keller?"

She adjusted her glasses on her nose and then, out of curiosity, asked cautiously, "Um, Lewisa, sweetie, is your mom your natural mom? Or is she your adopted mom?" She spoke softly.

"She is my natural mom since I wasn't adopted," I answered.

If black people's faces could turn pale, hers would have. Leaning in with her face inches from mine, she asked in a low tone, "So, sweetie, is your mother white?"

Shaking my head, I answered, "No, she is only half white."

As I took my seat, all my classmates stopped talking and watched me as if I were a scaly purple alien girl from Neptune who had just infiltrated the classroom. I went to an all-black or African American school in the inner city at that time. We had only two white teachers and no white, Hispanic, Asian, or other ethnic students.

Mrs. Acox looked white, but whenever she was given a chance, she would tell us she was a woman of color. She was convincing too. She had the sassy savoir faire many old-fashioned older black mothers endowed with a combination of tenderness, toughness, and godly wisdom possessed. She went on to share some of her historical background to inspire us to reach higher. She had either a black parent or a black grandparent. She genetically possessed the full traits of a Caucasian, unlike my mother, who hadn't gotten the full hair texture.

Mrs. Acox would say, "Don't let this white skin fool you. I know what it's like to struggle to get through school and about some of the struggles you all face in life. If I can make it, you can too."

After I returned to my seat that day, a few of the bold boys in the classroom frowned and said, "Lewisa, you got a white mama?"

I stayed silent.

"Your skin looks just like mine! Lewisa, how can your mama be white?" They continued while the teachers were still talking.

I didn't know how to answer them, so I stayed silent. It was time to go to music class. I sat where I usually did. Then some of the bold boys and a few girls came over to examine me, as if they were looking for something that stood out. They were checking for something Caucasian. I didn't know why they thought I was suddenly different just because they had seen my mother for the first time.

Mr. Crogan, our music teacher, came in. He was tall, slim, and in his thirties and had a goatee. Around ten or fifteen children ran up to his desk to spill the beans. Mr. Crogan gestured for them to quiet down and speak one at a time.

A boy who wore thick black glasses and had braces on his teeth said, "Mr. Crogan, Lewisa's mama is white!"

"How is it that she can have a white mama?" another boy, the smallest fifth grader in the class, and a girl with cornrow braids with pink-and-white beads at the ends asked.

A small group consisting of a boy with a snotty nose, a boy whose breath reeked of garlic, and a girl with silky, crimpy dark hair spoke up. "She looks just like us!"

A boy who huffed often when he talked and had a body like a beer barrel said, "No wonder she likes to follow the rules and is stiff and proper."

The way they were carrying on made me feel as if I had committed a crime I was unaware of. Yes, I had to follow the rules, because Mama had said she would cut my transmission if I didn't. I hadn't even known humans had a transmission, but wherever mine was in her eyes, I didn't want it cut. It sounded painful and too important to be severed.

Mr. Crogan calmed everyone down and said, "Take your seats, children. There's nothing wrong with having a parent who doesn't look like you. There are all kinds of people and families in this world. I know you might not think so now, but when you get older and go to a different school in another part of this city or one day go to college, you are going to see a variety of people living and interacting together. You all need to continue to treat Lewisa the way you want others to treat you. She had no control in choosing her family. You didn't choose your family either. You were born into it just like she was born into hers."

Although the lecture gave everyone peace for the moment, including me, many of my classmates started calling me *white girl*. At first, just a few people used that term. Then it managed to grow to a few more. It was mainly the boys who had to let me hear them use those words.

My mother was no joke. The kind, sweet, mild lady who had appeared in my classroom was an imposter, because at home, Mom was gladiatorial when she needed to be. The consequences for disobeying her included having a shoe or whatever else was in her hand at the time thrown at the perpetrator or receiving a whipping with her shoe, a belt, an electrical cord, or any kind of stick. Mom would wrestle, box, or have a karate match like the fight scene between Sergeant Emil Foley and Naval Officer Zack Mayo in the movie *An Officer and a Gentleman*.

My mom was an OG (original gangster), though I didn't even know what that was at the time. Mama could have been used as a secret weapon for the Scared Straight jail prevention program. Of course, for me and my sisters, Mom only had to use her booming, penetrating voice to correct us. I never had a bout with peer pressure, because I knew I would have to face my mama. That was a consequence too high to face. Mom was no joke. She could have been a drill sergeant in the marines.

Once, when my brother Jack was a teenager, he momentarily lost his mind and had the nerve to talk back to our mother after she told him to do something. Personally, I think the devil made him do it, because normally, he wasn't that stupid. Out of nowhere, the music that usually plays in western movies when a duel, gunfight, shootout, or showdown is going to take place began to play in the atmosphere. Mama stood with her hands by her sides. Then, with the speed of the best gunfighting cowboy, she managed to break a wooden leg off a small pool table my brothers had gotten for Christmas.

She gave Jack a chance to regain his senses, but somehow, unknown forces had taken over his mind, so the moment was a lost cause. My brother wouldn't back down. At first, Mom's back was facing Jack. Then, before he could blink, Mom turned around and started using the wooden leg as if she were Bruce Lee. Let's just say my brother never traveled down that dusty road again. Now he is cockeyed, drools uncontrollably, and walks with a limp. Just joking! He is still alive and well.

Jack was intelligent academically but ignorant when it came to staying in Mom's good graces. During another one of his and Mom's run-ins, he decided to use his wit and started calling on the name of Jesus in the hope that the name would save him from getting a whipping. But that evening, Jesus didn't step in to help him. He not only called Jesus but also called on the Lord, God the Father, and the Holy Spirit, but to no avail, because Mom was determined not to spare the rod and spoil the child. Jack ended up saying whole the Our Father prayer, hoping the power of God would intervene. He cried out, "Our Father, who art in heaven, hallowed be thy name. Thy kingdom come. Thy will be done on earth as it is in heaven. Give us this day our daily bread. And forgive our trespasses as we forgive those who trespass against us. And lead us not into temptation, but deliver us from evil. Amen."

Mom struck Jack with a switch every time he paused between each stanza in the prayer. She wanted to laugh because the scene was a bit comical to her, but she had business to take care of first. I think Jack might be the only human being who has nine lives, but that story is for another day.

In 1979, at ten years old, I went with Mama to meet her siblings at a church that was having a wake for their father. I was nervous because I had never seen a dead person before. Once we arrived, we met with two of Mama's sisters. We entered the church, which already had the casket open for viewing the body. For some reason, I was looking for the person lying there to have some kind of resemblance to Mama. On the contrary, I saw an average-sized man who had the darkest black skin I had ever seen in my life. He could have passed for someone from Senegal or Micronesia, where skin tones are so dark that they take on a blackish-blue pigmentation.

Mom's sisters said, "That's our daddy."

"Wow! That's our daddy?" Mom asked.

I just stared at the man in the coffin and thought, *That can't be your daddy, Mother. He doesn't have your skin color. He doesn't have your green eyes. You are not an albino, and under normal circumstances, two black people can't make a baby who looks like you.* Since Mom believed children should be seen and not heard, I couldn't say anything out loud, or Mother would have backhand-slapped me in my mouth.

Mom's view on life was shaped not only by how she had been raised by her adopted family but also by how some of the people in society treated her because of her skin color. She was a white sister in the black community and a colored woman in the white community just because she was related to black people. Moreover, for decades, Mom was exposed to some of the recurring negativity that plagued the country's grotesque history known as racism.

Ever since I was a young girl, I had seen Mama take a stand to bring justice to her immediate world. She declared that no white man was going to come sit in her house and date her daughter, when her black sons weren't allowed to go to a white woman's family's house and weren't welcomed with open arms to date their daughter.

My mother got married in 1952. Mama and Daddy met when he came to visit Mom's much older adopted brother, Gabe White, at their house. Mama called Gabe Bubba, perhaps because she couldn't say the word *brother* clearly when she was a young child. Her brother was an independent contractor who had sort of taken Daddy under his wing. Also, he was a pastor. Gabe had graduated from Avery Institute, a college that catered to colored people many years ago.

Daddy served six years in the navy as a cook. He also worked at the naval hospital as a cook. Later, he ended up retiring with more than thirty years accredited to his name.

Once Daddy laid eyes on Mama, he was smitten at first sight. Since he knew Gabe was a pastor and Mom's mother was an evangelist who had passed on to glory by that time, he told Mom he was a Christian, attended church regularly, and sang in the choir but once in a while drank a little bit of alcohol. Unfortunately, the only true thing about Daddy's statement was the alcohol part, but then again, that was just slightly true.

Gabe wasn't home that night, so Daddy went back the next night too. After he attended to the business he had with Gabe, he asked Gabe if he could court Mama. Gabe told Dad and Mom he was against their getting married, but Mom married Dad anyway. Since Gabe loved Mom, he tolerated the marriage—and bought a gun in case things went awry. In Mama's day, men were placed on a pedestal by most women and society in general. It was normal for men to be looked upon to financially take care of the family and make major decisions. In healthy families back then, men were treated as the kings of their castles.

My mother was a combination of Edith Bunker from *All in the Family* and one of the characters on *The Stepford Wives* with the way she served my dad, except she didn't run around the house like Edith Bunker did, and she didn't wear high heels or dress in her Sunday best like a Stepford wife. She believed in waking up early to make breakfast for my dad before he went to work. Then she would get the children up and ready for the day. After we were taken care of, she would start her daily chores around the house, and she made sure dinner was ready before Dad came home from work. Mother served him dinner with the same honor a chamberlain served a king or queen.

About five years after Mom and Dad were married, Dad made Mom sell both houses her mother and brother had left her after they died. Even though he was an experienced jack-of-all-trades carpenter when he wasn't hanging out with Jack Daniel's, Dad told Mom it would cost too much money to keep both houses in good shape. He insisted on a quick sale. They ended up getting just pennies on the dollar.

One of the houses had fifteen rooms, including bathrooms, a kitchen, and a living room. The second house was slightly smaller. It had a total of ten rooms. Once both houses and the money were gone, Dad laughed and told Mom, "You don't own shit now." All he wanted in life was a tiny shack with a roof, so whenever he felt like it, he could piss alcohol against the wall. Mom had her share of troublesome times in their marriage. She knew Dad was seeing other women while they were married. She figured that out when he sometimes came home intoxicated with empty pockets on his payday. In his drunken stupor, every once in a while, Dad would tell Mom about the other women he was seeing. She never told us about it, though, not until many years later.

Mom always quoted the Bible verse Mark 10:9 KJV: "What therefore God hath joined together, let no man put asunder." To her, marriage was serious. She didn't like Daddy's extracurricular activities, but she was determined to stick it out because of the vow she'd made to God. There were plenty of times when Mom had to ask for an extension on the rent and for credit at the grocery store so we would have a roof over our heads and food in our bellies. Soon after Dad's behavior became repetitious, Mom implemented a strategy to intercept the household funds before Dad could squander the money away. She started sending a few of my older brothers to the bar Dad frequented. Since Dad was about putting on airs in front of other people in an attempt to make them think he was doing better financially than he really was, my brothers began asking him for the rent and food money after Dad had a few beers. It worked. Dad graciously handed them the money with a smile because an audience of people were watching him. That tactic allowed Mom to pay the bills on time for a few months.

However, once Dad returned home and discovered he had been outfoxed, he was livid and used a torpedo of spicy words sailors used, plus additional words he made up. Sadly, Mom was forced to pawn many of the items she'd inherited from her mom and brother, plus her wedding rings, to put food on the table until she was able to find employment. Mom believed family was important and should stick together through thick and thin, through the good times and the hard times.

We were one large unit working together to make the household operate smoothly. We all had our assigned chores. The older siblings with jobs were taught to contribute something toward expenses to learn about responsibility and help out too. Mom loved saying that blood was thicker than water, meaning that family came before strangers.

Loyalty was supreme. It was similar to the way the Mafia views family loyalty: you only exited the family by death. Okay, that's just a little joke, but it is also true if you think about it. In her eyes, marriage was an iron-clad contract. Once you got married, the only way to get out was by natural death or if your spouse tried to kill you or beat you black and blue. It was a promise you and your spouse made to God, which was a serious step and not to be taken lightly. Mom emphasized that breaking a promise to God was like cutting off your limbs. It would leave you helpless and in desperate need of hope and a prayer.

"Don't rush into marriage. Take your time. Watch and pray, because getting the wrong person will make you curse the hour and damn the minute you said, 'I do,'" she would say.

Mom also was passionate about teaching us about etiquette. She would say, "When you have good manners, people will go out of their way to help you when you need it. Having good manners is sometimes better than having money. Young ladies don't put their elbows on the meal table. Young ladies always excuse themselves from the table or an occupied room and go to the bathroom to pass gas."

Young ladies passed gas, and men farted. Passing gas was feminine, and farting was masculine. Young ladies were polite, kind, and never too loud, as if they never had any home training. The thought of a lady spitting sickened her and made her react with disdain. Ladies sat with their legs closed and never under any circumstances chased a man.

She would say, "It is a man's place to choose the lady he wants to be with." She told us to hold ourselves up with respect for ourselves and for others. Then a man would see those good qualities in us. She used to say, "A man may go to a nightclub to find women he can have fun with. Those women are considered his good-time girls. They are his playthings. When he is ready to settle down and find a wife, he won't go to the nightclub to get her. He is more than likely going to go to church, meet her through people he knows, or go to some other respectable place to find her."

I thought Mom's views were extreme, but I didn't trust defying her.

She would say, "A man is not going to want a woman who has been with every Tom, Dick, and Harry. He is not going to carry a fast woman home to meet his mother." So in essence, she wasn't going to have her daughters known as loose women. That meant no minidresses, miniskirts, or short pants that revealed anything. No cleavage could be exposed. We were not permitted to wear anything that showcased the form of our bodies or showed our shape, as Mama used to say. Last but not least, we were told not to wear red lipstick, especially not to church. Mom thought it was disrespectful to wear it there and would make us be perceived as Jezebel harlots.

Of course, Jezebel wasn't a harlot in the Bible, but sometimes Mother liked to string certain words together because it sounded good.

Mom would say, "Carry yourself like a lady." Whenever I heard those words, I pictured myself sticking my chest out, pulling my shoulders back, lifting my chin up, and moving gracefully like a model across a catwalk. Other times, after I heard Mama say those words, a more playful image would emerge in my mind. I would still imagine steps one through four, but I would include a fifth step: reaching down with my hands and picking myself up like a groom did his bride when he was carrying her over the threshold.

Mama raised us to be respectable young ladies—wives. It seemed that in Mom's eyes, reaching the status of wife was a higher honor than winning a Nobel Peace Prize or even being invited to sit among presidents. Actually, in light of the seriousness she placed on that role, I believe to Mom, it topped being crowned queen. She acted as if it were a privilege to be a wife, and once we were married, she believed it was our duty to keep our husbands happy. We were to keep our houses running properly and never let our houses get too hot for us—that was Mom's way of saying not to be a busybody. She didn't want us to go around getting into people's business.

However, Mom would say to my brothers, "You'd better shop around." I guess she was inspired by Smokey Robinson's song with the same title.

TWO

I GREW UP in the city of Charleston, South Carolina. I had a chance to see firsthand how some black men in that area shopped for women. Whenever a woman passed by in our neighborhood, some of the men would try to get her attention by calling out in a loud voice, "Hey, baby, what's your name?" or "Girl, you sure are fine! Can I get your number?" Sometimes they'd say, "Hey, sweet mama, can I walk with you?" or something corny but creative, such as "Your name has gotta be Eve, because I'm definitely your Adam! Baby, once you get with me, you'll never have to worry about a snake again!" If a woman ignored the unwanted catcall, the man or group of men would say the same things to the next woman or group of women passing by. Being exposed to the loud, aggressive, don't-take-no-for-an-answer way of picking up women the men in my neighborhood displayed made me cautious. It was a huge turnoff for me, even though I was young. I thought it was tasteless and lacked trueness of heart. It made me put up my guard to protect myself from people with superficial motives.

Even though I loved God and enjoyed being in his presence, I made a lot of unwise decisions. Besides my being trained to respect my mother's version of virtue, many of my views were shaped by what I watched on TV, especially when it came to relationships, including what a relationship should look like, how to interact, and things men and women did together. Darn those girl-meets-prince stories! Just joking.

It was a constant struggle as I wrestled between what was godly and what was secular. After graduating high school, I went to work at a fitness center. I started out as a receptionist. Then I graduated to assisting people with various exercise routines, depending on their fitness goals. Last, I was dragged into teaching two aerobics classes I was unprepared for when one of the aerobics instructors called in sick. It was a disaster. Half the class left after ten minutes because they were impatient and irritated with my level of experience. Then a handful of kind ladies took turns doing new aerobics moves to assist me. I appreciated their help. The class lasted about twenty-five minutes instead of an hour, as it was supposed to.

The fitness center was where I learned how to get my body in the best shape ever. A few of the bodybuilders taught me to increase my protein intake, reduce my carbohydrate intake, and exercise every day. It worked marvelously, turning my body into a fat-burning machine. When I first started working at the fitness center in 1987, I weighed 136 pounds. Six months later, I weighed in at 130 pounds, but many people thought I was 110 pounds, because muscle weighs more than fat but takes up less space.

Due to my new and improved athletic body, I started attracting men from many different ethnicities and races. It was a huge change from how the so-called good-looking, popular guys had responded to me during my school days. I had grown up hearing my mother tell me and the rest of my siblings we were beautiful. Around that time—I believe the late 1970s or early '80s—the "Black is beautiful" campaign was being echoed in magazines, commercials, and TV shows that catered to black viewers.

Seeing positive images and hearing that black people were attractive regardless of what shade our skin was heightened my self-esteem and gave me permission to look at myself in a new light. Those words were quickly pressed down and toppled over, however, by the unfavorable things some of the boys at school said about me because I didn't fit their ideal standards.

Nevertheless, in July 1988, by age nineteen, I had a fit and toned body, which sort of opened a Pandora's box for me. Unfortunately, it caused me to make a lot of thoughtless choices. I'm not saying I became promiscuous—no, nothing like that, because my mother would have killed me—but I did a lot of dumb things. Undoubtedly, I turned down all the married men who approached me and offered to make my life easier if I spent time with them. But then there was Ted, a firefighter I met in the bookstore where I worked. He passed by the store a few times one day. Then he decided to come in. Ted was a tall, lanky, friendly fellow who had a thin streak of sleek, satiny gray hair above his right ear.

During checkout at the register, Ted asked, smiling widely, "Hey, didn't I see you at that *Rusalka* opera at the Spoleto Festival last night?"

I answered, "No. I've never been to an opera before."

He said, "It would be an honor if you let me take you."

I smiled and said, "OK, you can."

I learned early on, after we went out a few times, our friendship wasn't going anywhere meaningful. That fact became obvious to me each time we walked together toward his car in the mall parking lot. As long as no one walked toward us or around us, he was confident and at ease; however, if anyone saw us together or came in our vicinity, even just to pass us by, Ted would take off running as if he were training for a marathon. I thought, *Wait a minute; he doesn't have to respond to a fire. He's off today.* We never made it to the opera. It didn't take long to figure out he wasn't a good match for me, and my mom would have rejected him anyway. I think he only wanted to experience jungle fever.

When I was still nineteen, as I stocked the candy shelves in the front of the store, Calvin passed by the bookstore. He was clean cut and shaven, wearing a flamboyant black blazer with dark blue paisley print on it, black slacks, and black Stacy Adams loafers. Moments later, he moonwalked back to tell me hello. Amused, I laughed at his attempt to impress me. He was cute and funny.

He came to the register where I was standing and let out an energetic "Hello. What's your name?"

A smile covered my face as I said, "I'm Lewisa. What about your name?"

He shifted his head from side to side and said, "I'm Calvin with a C. I won't waste your time if you get with me."

I laughed.

After we talked for a few minutes, he said, "I'm thirsty. I'm going to the Cookie Factory to buy a soda. Can I get one for you too?"

I smiled and said, "Yes, a Diet Coke would be nice."

When he returned with our sodas, we talked, and I gave him my phone number. He seemed like a nice guy.

I was asked to speak at an insurance meeting in the office of a friend of our family because I'd gotten my insurance license at age eighteen. Since my family were coming to hear my speech, I figured that would be a good time for them to meet Calvin, so they could tell me what they thought of him. He was thrilled I asked him to come and about meeting my family too. My mother was happy to meet him because he passed the color requirement.

Calvin was a hit with my family. He carried himself well and impressed them and me too.

Beaming with joy, with a twinkle in her eyes, Mom said, "Calvin, are you from Charleston?"

"Yes, ma'am. I was born and raised here. My parents are both high school teachers," he answered.

Appearing proud, Mom nodded and said, "That's real nice. Are you planning on going into the same field?"

Calvin shook his head and said, "No, ma'am. I'm about to enter law school."

Mom's eyes lit up, and she replied, "That's wonderful. Keep up the good work." Then she looked at me and added, "He's an educated man. It's good to see him doing something with his life."

Unfortunately, after the meeting, things went south fast one night when Calvin called me on the phone.

"Listen here, girl. Let's cut out the bull and lay down all of that good-guy baloney. What I want is sex. That's what I'm interested in, and that's what I want," he said.

I removed the phone from my ear and stared at it. When I put it back, Calvin was still talking.

He said, "I don't have time for long, drawn-out, sissy get-to-know-you games. Let's just cut to the chase and get busy. What do you have to say about that?"

With tension in my face, I said, "Calvin, please don't call me anymore." I hung up, feeling disappointed and ticked off.

Then there was Liam. Again, I met him in the mall. He worked there too. He was handsome and five foot ten, with long, crimpy black hair and glowing brown skin. When I invited him to my house to meet my family, I was surprised to find out some of my brothers had gone to high school with him. They said he was nice, shy, and quiet. He scored two thumbs up in their book because he was an all-around good person. Mom was happy he passed the skin test, and she thought he was a nice-looking young man.

On our first date, Liam picked me up in his car, which was on its last leg in terms of both the interior and the outside body. I was fine with it because my mother had taught us not to be interested in people based on what they had. She wanted us to look at a person's character and heart. I liked Liam's mannerisms and enjoyed his company. During our second date, Liam picked me up in a new red Mazda Miata.

"I got a good deal on this car. I wanted to drive you around in a better car than I had before." He beamed with joy.

I placed my hand on my heart and said, "You bought this car to drive me in?" I paused and then said, "I don't know if you are the One yet, and you bought this car to drive me around?"

He tilted his head and responded, "Yes, I had my mind made up about you before I asked you out."

Honestly, I was upset that he would make such a big purchase while not knowing if things were going to work out between us. We went out a few more times. He was a gentleman. I was beginning to thank God for allowing us to meet. In 1988, we went to the movies to see *Big* starring Tom Hanks. We enjoyed it. It made us laugh. Liam opened the car door when he picked me up, after the movie, and at the end of our date. I was pleased when he graciously accepted a handshake after he walked me to the door.

"I had a good time tonight," said Liam.

I said, "I did too."

"I would like to see you again."

"I would like that."

Then everything fell apart one night when Liam called me on the phone. He was drunk.

He spoke loudly and slurred. "Hey, I just want you to know that you are my woman! You hear me? You are mine!"

"Are you drunk?" I asked, teed off.

His speech was garbled. "I just had a little bit, baby. It's not a big deal. Really, baby, you've got nothing to worry about."

I sighed and then said, "Liam, no, we can't do this. My dad used to drink alcohol and get drunk. I don't want anyone who gets drunk. I'm sorry, but this is not going to work out between us." I hung up.

Then I met Zach in my mother's kitchen. He was friends with Scott, one of my brother Conner's friends. They were visiting Conner that day. When I walked into the house and into the kitchen, my eyes did a happy dance when they landed on Zach's face. When his eyes locked onto mine, I could tell the feeling was mutual. He was one of those people I was convinced God personally kissed before they exited their mothers' wombs—people who tried hard to look bad but failed at it.

Zach was blessed with flawless good looks. He was a combination of Tom Selleck and Pierce Brosnan back in their heyday. His wavy jet-black hair complemented his hazel eyes and chiseled face. He had the kind of looks that would have made most women smile and be happy to have him in their lives. Immediately, he shifted into pursuit mode without any reservations. He showered me with attention as he got up from his seat at the table and followed me around the kitchen, living room, and hall.

Zach greeted me, asking, "Who is this lovely lady?" His voice was filled with excitement, and his eyes joined the party.

I snickered. "I'm Lewisa." As I walked around the house, putting my jacket and pocketbook away, he followed me. He flashed an intoxicating smile as he eagerly asked me questions about my likes and dislikes.

"I bet you are the kind of woman who likes plays rather than movies and being wined and dined instead of fast food. Just by the way you carry yourself, I can tell you won't settle for just anybody. Am I right?" he asked as he studied me.

Still laughing, I shook my head and answered, "I'm flexible regarding plays and movies and being wined and dined versus eating fast food, but you are right that I won't settle for just anybody."

He boasted, "See? I know what I'm talking about."

Zach boldly entered my personal space, my comfort zone, while talking to me as if he had a secret that couldn't wait.

He pinned me against the bedroom wall and whispered, "Go out with me."

I nodded and replied, "OK, that sounds good to me."

Normally, that would have made me feel uncomfortable, but I liked it. I liked it a lot. I got lost in his gaze. I was captivated by his beauty and charm, so I was thrilled. He brazenly allowed his eyes to freely roam from my head to my toes. That day, I didn't mind that the windows to his soul revealed he viewed me as a juicy, mouthwatering, savory piece of meat. His eyes projected fireworks in response to his private desire for me. Unfortunately, he didn't stay much longer than our short encounter. We exchanged phone numbers before Zach and Scott left.

Conner shook his head and said, "Lewisa, don't get caught up on Zach's looks. That guy is bad news. I've seen him in action. He doesn't respect his parents, so that should tell you he won't respect you either."

"Oh, that's not good. Maybe we can just be friends," I answered half-heartedly.

He said, "OK, remember we had this talk. You know Mom always tells us not to make our heads hard, because it makes a soft behind."

"OK, I heard you," I responded in a lackluster manner.

Zach and I planned to go out three different times, but each time, something came up that canceled our date. The first time, my car stopped working properly; the second time, his car got a flat tire; and the third time, the night before, he was pulled over and given a ticket for driving under the influence. Looking back at the situation later, I knew it worked out for the best for me.

Skylar was a senior in college, studying to become a podiatrist. He was hired part-time during the summer at the fitness center for extra pocket change. The hours between 1:00 p.m. and 3:00 p.m. were our downtime. No aerobics classes were taught in between those times. Rarely did anyone sign up for one-on-one weight training around that time either. Therefore, we used that time to clean the equipment and make the facility tidy. We would spend the last thirty minutes at the reception counter for easy access to the telephone.

"Lewisa, while I serve whoever walks in, why don't you sit in front of the phone today? Then we can switch duties tomorrow," Skylar said.

I raised my eyebrows and said with a laugh, "Skylar, you said that yesterday too."

He replied, "And I meant it too."

I said, "Yeah right."

At 3:30 p.m., Burke would join us like clockwork every day. He was a manager at one of the fast food restaurants nearby. He always came before his shift started at 4:00 p.m. He was five foot nine, with smooth, velvety chocolate skin and oodles of charisma. Skylar was about the same height as Burke and had sun-kissed blond hair and ocean-blue eyes. The three of us used to joke around and talk for nearly thirty minutes daily. That was our pattern for months.

Burke leaned on the counter and said, "Since you have brothers galore, Lewisa, I bet you like watching sports on TV."

Scrunching my nose, I said, "No, but thank God we have more than one TV."

Skylar said, "Dude, her brothers are a sports team. She doesn't need to watch anything like that on TV."

Since I had grown up with seven brothers, I felt comfortable talking to Burke and Skylar. They were friendly and funny. The time we spent together was strictly platonic. They had a brotherly friend vibe going on with me. That was why I was taken aback the day Skylar walked up to me and, without any warning, planted a kiss on my lips. Then he walked away without even saying one word to me. I stood there lost and confused with my jaw dropped.

That day, I left the receptionist counter and walked toward the sales office. Skylar was leaving the office, and we met each other in the middle of the lobby. He traveled the same path I was on, but before I could veer to one side, Skylar grabbed me with one hand around my waist and the other behind my neck and kissed me. Once he let go, he just walked away. I just stood there for a moment with my head in the clouds in a startled state of mind. Moments later, I continued to the sales office, which was unoccupied at that time, and went back to the desk again. I replayed that moment in my mind repeatedly.

As I studied it scene by scene, I tried to remember if Skylar had looked as if he'd accidentally tripped on something. He hadn't looked like he was falling. I wondered if the kiss possibly had been meant for someone else, but somehow, I unknowingly had gotten in the way. No one had been behind me, and I had never heard of anyone being accidentally kissed before.

As I wandered in thought, Skylar dashed off. He was nowhere to be seen for hours. He avoided the reception counter that day. As a matter of fact, so did Burke. I had no idea I would never see Burke again. I knew only that Skylar and Burke had talked privately outside the day before. I was clueless as to why Burke had walked away with his head hung low. I didn't get a chance to ask Skylar what had happened. Before our shift ended, I spotted Skylar in the spa area. He was hiding out. I approached him.

"You found me." He grinned. "I guess I should have asked you first, but I was afraid I would lose the nerve to let you know I like you."

I sighed and asked, "You like me?"

He nodded and replied, "Yes, I think you are a wonderful person."

I responded, "Thank you! You are very kind."

"Would you be interested in going out sometime?" Skylar asked.

I nodded and said, "OK. We can do that."

With a smile covering his face, he said, "Great! I need your number, so we can discuss the details."

After writing my number on a piece of paper, I handed it to him and said, "OK."

"I'm looking forward to talking to you on the phone. My girl— that's what I'll call you," he said.

Late that night, and many more afterward, we talked on the phone, and I managed to keep him away from our house. I had no idea Skylar was going to stop by Mom's house one evening on the spur of the moment. It was December. The Christmas tree was dressed in red, green, and blue blinking lights, which kept time with the Temptations' Christmas album playing on the record player. Also, sentimental ornaments from many years ago adorned the tree. There were Santa Claus–face ornaments, assorted-colored sparkly ornaments, and silver tinsel icicles. When the doorbell rang, I answered it. I did my best to conceal that his visit was a curveball for me. Skylar's face glowed with warmth as he showed nearly all his pearly whites. He had come by to give me my Christmas gift.

I said with widened eyes, "Hello, Skylar."

He said, "Hi, Lew. Did I catch you at a bad time?"

I grabbed his hand and said, "No, not at all. Come in."

Even though my mouth was saying to come in, my eyes were stretched wide and saying, *What are you doing here?* Then Mom came out of her room to see whom I was talking to. At first, she reminded me of a curious cat, but moments later, she backed out like a spooked one. Minutes after that, the phone rang.

Mom called out, "Lewisa, telephone!"

I picked up the receiver. "Hello?"

"Hi, Lewisa. This is Donna. Mom is on the phone with us," Donna said.

"OK, what's going on? Why are both of y'all on the phone with me?" I asked.

Donna said, "Mom said you have your company sitting in the living room, and you know how she feels about it."

I cleared my throat and addressed the situation briefly and in code. "I didn't know."

"Didn't know what?" both Mom and Donna asked.

I replied, "Coming."

"Well, Mom wants you to honor her rules. You need to ask your guest to leave," Donna responded.

I exhaled and said, "OK, I will."

I guess I didn't do a good job of muting and covering the crisis brewing on the other end of the phone, because I could see unease painted all over Skylar's face.

He stood up, walked over to me, gave me a hug, and told me, "I've got to go. I'll call you later."

I said, "I'm sorry. I'll be waiting for your call."

Once he left, I grunted and sighed because our first evening together had been disastrous. After that evening, we drifted apart. I saw Skylar once in a while, but things weren't the same as before. In the midst of that disappointment, at the bookstore one day, Mrs. Altman, part owner of the store, stayed past the end of my lunch break to talk to me.

She said, "Lewisa, it has been brought to my attention that you have been spending time with an older man here in the mall."

I tilted my head and responded, "You mean with my uncle?"

Mrs. Altman narrowed her eyes and said, "People are talking about you around here. They are saying it's a shame that a young girl like you has taken up with a much older man."

I said, "Mrs. Altman, that man is my uncle. Uncle Phillip. He started working at that prestigious men's clothing store a few months ago. He's a tailor there. We eat lunch together sometimes."

Shaking her head, she replied, "Lewisa, how can that man possibly be your uncle? He's so much lighter than you are."

I stared at her in disbelief and said, "He is my mother's brother, and my mother has light skin too."

I could tell she still didn't believe me, but she ended the conversation with "OK, I'm heading back to my other business. I'll talk to you later."

I told Mama what had happened. A few days later, my mother and Conner came into the bookstore a few minutes before my lunch break. It was a complete surprise. She hadn't told me they were coming. Their timing was perfect because Mrs. Altman was already there. When I introduced my mother and brother to her, her eyes just about popped out of her head. Mrs. Altman was stunned. As she faced Mom with a loss of words, they shook hands.

Mom said, "It's nice to meet you."

"It's nice to meet you too. So you are Lewisa's mother?" she asked.

Mom smiled and answered, "Yes, I am. Is she working up to your expectations?"

Mrs. Altman glanced at me and then back at Mom and Conner and said, "Yes, she is a dependable and hard worker."

Mom ended the conversation by saying, "Well, we came to the mall to walk for a few minutes. Now we are going back home. Again, it was nice meeting you. Now I can match a face with your name." She laughed.

"Yes, I agree." Mrs. Altman laughed too.

After Mom and Conner left, Mrs. Altman said, "Wow! Your mother's skin is the same color as mine."

I answered, "Yes, she's half white."

Mrs. Altman cupped her face with her hands and said, "I'm so sorry! I didn't know."

I said, "It's OK. I don't normally tell people that."

I guessed she hadn't watched Alex Haley's miniseries *Roots* when it aired on TV in the 1970s.

Also in 1988, at age nineteen, I declined an offer to audition to be in a music video. The lead singer of a music group was shopping in the mall before his concert. He was caramel-colored and dressed in a fancy teal-and-black smoking jacket with a white shirt under it, black slacks, and black Stacy Adams shoes.

At the counter, he said, "I'm Jeff Free. I'm sure you've seen my video on TV."

I shook my head and replied, "No, I haven't. I gave up watching and listening to secular music and videos."

He looked surprised and continued. "Well, I'm getting ready to do a new music video. Would you like to audition for it? We're having one night of auditions here in Charleston."

I said, "Let me think about it, but more than likely, I won't."

He wrote down an address and said, "If you change your mind, we will only be there for one night."

I looked at the piece of paper and said, "OK, thank you!" but I didn't go to the audition.

I didn't want to connect myself to any industry where I might encounter and be influenced by people who could possibly cause me to bring shame on my mother and God. I also didn't go out with anyone who got offended whenever I talked about God. The attention I was receiving became irritating to me. It took an unpleasant twist when I was offered a job to pose nude in a magazine. In addition to that, I managed to pick up a stalker. Both happened while I was working in the bookstore. I was restocking cigarettes in the storage structure hanging on the wall behind the cash register. My back was facing the entrance of the store.

A voice from behind me called out, "Nice ass!"

I turned around, startled. A white guy who looked around twenty-five years old, with long brown hair, stood there. He was wearing a cowboy hat, a dark leather jacket, a white T-shirt, and jeans.

"Have you ever thought about posing nude for magazines?" he asked.

I said, "No."

He replied, "You can make more money in one day than you do here all month."

At the same time, a customer I had never seen before, a black guy, walked into the bookstore.

I greeted him in a joyful tone. "Hey there, fella! How are you? I haven't seen you in such a long time! Where have you been? What have you been up to?"

I acted excited to see him. The poor guy's eyes were clouded over as he angled his head to the side when I entered his personal space. Then I touched his arms. He crinkled his forehead and pressed his lips together as he carefully and leisurely came back with his answers. He was a good sport and played along by answering my questions. I could tell by his expression he was trying to figure out how we knew each other.

Devoid of attention, the other guy watched us carry on and then left the store. At that point, I came clean with the new customer and explained what had happened before he came into the store.

He was understanding and said, "What a weirdo! I'm glad I could help you."

He browsed around the store. Then I went back to restocking again.

The bookstore sold dirty and nude magazines. I hated selling those magazines, so in order to help ease my conscience, I started inserting cute money-designed Bible tracts into the magazines. I figured it would be a good way for God to touch the hearts or spirits of the men buying the magazines to try to satisfy their sexual curiosities. Problem solved, right? Well, not exactly.

Unfortunately, my good deed was not received with the warmest of regard. As it turned out, a number of men called the distribution company to complain about the unwanted gift. Can you imagine that? I mean, who doesn't appreciate hearing that Jesus loves him or her? It didn't take long for the distribution company to narrow their investigation down to the small store I worked in. When the owners found out what had happened, they questioned me about it.

I confessed. "Yes, I did it because I don't feel comfortable selling those magazines since I'm a Christian."

"Well, I'm Jewish. I don't like the fact that we sell those magazines either, but this is a business, and people want them. Therefore, please don't put any more Bible tracts into the magazines," Mrs. Altman said.

I said, "OK, I won't."

The year 1988 turned out to be a year of unusual events in my life. I had no idea I would have a brush with a stalker. I thought only famous people were stalked. I met the guy in the bookstore. Yes, the bookstore again. I bet you never thought a bookstore could be an exciting place to work, right?

One day a man came into the small bookstore. He walked around the store, taking a glimpse at everything on the shelves. Then he came to the cash register where I was standing. He was tall, with light amber skin that appeared to have been dipped in bright honey. He looked as if he had been gently kissed by the sun. He was the color of perfectly golden fried chicken. His eyes were small and dark, with a slight slant to them, and he had short, wavy jet-black hair cut close to his scalp. I thought he was possibly of African and Asian descent. He told me he was a military vet and had just moved to the area. He stayed near the cash register as I rang up customers' purchases. When there was a break, he asked me out.

"I know of a mom-and-pop restaurant downtown that has the best food around. You should go with me. I'll show you a good time," he said.

I told him, "I'm talking to someone right now, but thank you for asking."

He said, nodding, "It's all good, but if that joker messes up, I'll be waiting."

I smiled. He seemed to have accepted my response. We shook hands, and he walked away. A few hours later, I walked to the opposite side of the mall to eat my lunch during my break. As I was eating, I saw him in my peripheral view. I turned my head.

He said, "Are you sure? I'm here if it doesn't work out."

I smiled and nodded.

The next morning, after I arrived at work and unlocked the door, I retrieved the four-wheeled cart I used each morning to bring in the large variety of newspapers from the delivery zone. To get there, I had to travel down a long, dimly lit corridor that led to the delivery door, which led outside. The delivery area was where trucks delivered products and supplies to the different stores in that particular delivery zone. There were many delivery zones around the mall building. That was also where I and others traveled to put trash into a large dumpster outside.

Each delivery zone had its own dumpster. I saw the man I'd met in the store pass by on the opposite side of the semienclosed delivery-zone wall, but I didn't think he saw me.

Day after day, for twenty-one days, he came to the store and said, "I'm still waiting."

I began changing the location where I ate lunch, but he still managed to find me. After three or four weeks, one day I was putting trash into the dumpster, as I did every day, when he came up behind me and said, "I'm still waiting."

He scared me so much that my heart seemed as if it were beating out of my chest. With wide eyes, I responded, "I can't! What are you doing back here?"

He walked closer and said, "I just want to talk, but I think I want a kiss too."

I held some flattened boxes between us and replied, "No! I'm not going to kiss you! I don't even know you!"

He went to put his arms around me. As I squirmed away, a delivery truck pulled up into the delivery zone. The man looked at the truck and then scurried away. Although I was fuming, I was relieved at the same time and said in my mind, *Thank you, God!*

That evening, at home, I told my mom and brother Conner what had happened. They asked me all kinds of questions about the guy. I answered them as best as I could.

Lost in thought, Conner said, "Oh really? Well, we'll get to the bottom of this! I'm going to work with you in the morning. If he shows up, I'll have a word with him."

I tried to talk Conner out of it, but he kept his word. In the morning, he went to work with me. I drove my small cinnamon-orange-colored Toyota Tercel. Her name was Faith because that was what it had taken for me to save up for the down payment. Well, faith and lots of hours of work, plus delaying other things I wanted to buy at that time too. Conner sat in the front passenger seat. As I drove through the mall's parking lot, I spotted the man walking across the parking lot toward the building.

I couldn't believe it. I said loudly, "Look, Conner—there he is!"

My brother hollered, "Stop the car!"

I said, "No! Why? What are you going to do?"

Conner shouted, "Girl, stop the car! I'm just going to talk to him."

I stopped the car so my brother could talk to the guy. I didn't know if Conner was going to get his tail kicked, which would have caused me to have to defend him. I wished I could make the situation go away.

Conner opened the door. "Hey, man, I heard you were bothering my little sister!" he said, facing the guy with one leg in the parking lot and the other still in the car.

The guy used some non–Sunday school words toward my brother and said, "What's it to you? You gonna do something about it?"

When I heard things heating up, I slowly started driving the car forward. Conner was still in the same position.

He yelled out, "Stop the car! Stop the car!"

When I stopped the car, Conner got out and rushed toward the guy. I was freaked out. I had not expected to see a *Rocky* movie reenacted before my eyes. Nevertheless, in a quick second, that was what happened. Fists were flying everywhere. Heads were bobbing. Fancy foot shuffles and body dodges were in full effect as Conner's suit jacket danced in the breeze. I had never seen a businessman dressed in professional attire engage in a good old-fashioned beatdown before. I was sure we were all going to jail that day. In the distance, I saw the mall's security vehicle heading our way. I pleaded for Conner to get back into the car.

After what seemed like a long time, because it was as if time came to a standstill, Conner returned to the car after the guy quickly ran away. Then I pulled up to the mall entrance closest to the bookstore. I got out. Conner drove off with my car. He planned to pick me up after work. As I completed my daily routine before opening the store to customers, one of the security guards approached me to find out what had happened in the parking lot. I explained to her what had led to the incident outside.

Then I told her my brother had already left with my car. "He only came to make sure I got to work safely."

A couple of hours later, three different girls who worked in different stores came together to visit me. They told me they'd heard my brother had beaten up the guy who was stalking me. Then they shared that he had been harassing them too. The four of us were all small and shapely. As we talked, the guy my brother had just whipped outside like a helpless baby passed by the store. With his hands in his pockets, he gazed straight ahead, strutting with purpose, as if he didn't know us.

One of the girls said, "That's right—walk away! If you mess with us again, her brother is going to kick your ass!"

For the rest of the day, people who worked in other stores came in to let me know they had heard what happened. Who knew drama took place in the mall, let alone a bookstore?

THREE

IN APRIL 1991, Yury DeBlake started shopping at the bookstore in the mall in Charleston, South Carolina, where I worked. He was five foot six, with a small build. His short, wavy hair was brown with flecks of gray, and he had jasper-green eyes. He wore glasses, looked studious, and could have been the poster boy for professionalism since he dressed in a suit and tie daily for his line of work. He was more on the adorable, nerdy side of the fence than the jock or stud side. At least he was a few steps above Steve Urkel. In fact, in all fairness, he was a few jumps ahead in appearance of what was considered a nerd. Thank God!

When he called on the phone, I thought his coyness was sweet. I'd had a chance to go out with a couple of so-called pretty boys, and it had been a complete waste of my time, because their looks attracted plenty of other females, and they were more than eager to take advantage of the situation. Before that experience, I had placed good looks as a top priority when considering a future companion.

I opened the nearly three-hundred-square-foot store in the morning on Monday through Saturday. I was the only morning employee. The owners had another business apart from the mall bookstore, providing medical transcription for various doctors' offices. On a daily basis, one of the owners would come to relieve me so I could take a lunch break. After that, he or she would go back to the other business.

When I noticed Yury coming to the store on a regular basis, about every day, I just thought he really loved to read books. As he fingered through the pages of books in the back of the store, he directed many starry-eyed glances my way. I wasn't alarmed, because he seemed harmless, kind, and intelligent.

At the register, he showed all his pearly whites as he asked, "How are you today?"

"Fine. Thank you. I hope you are too," I answered, not thinking anything of it.

Still smiling and looking into my eyes, he said, "Yes, yes, indeed. I am. So what's your name?"

"My name is Lewisa," I said.

His eyes lit up when he repeated, "Lewisa. I like that. I'm Yury."

I smiled and said, "Thank you! It's nice to meet you."

My belief that he visited only because he loved books changed in early April 1991, when he called me on the phone at work to ask me if I would go out with him. He said he was too nervous to ask me in person. In asking me by phone, he thought it would be easier to handle the rejection if I said no.

One afternoon, the phone rang in the bookstore. I answered it. "Books, Books, and More Books. How may I help you?"

A warm male voice said, "Hi. Is this Lewisa?"

I said, "Yes, who is calling, please?"

He laughed and said, "This is Yury DeBlake. Do you remember me?"

I answered, "Yes."

He said, "Good." Then he cleared his throat and spoke again. "I'm calling to ask if you would be interested in going out with me."

The question was unexpected, so I paused for a moment. Then I said, "Yes, OK. Let me give you my number. You can call me later when I'm off from work, so we can discuss the details."

After I gave him my number, he replied, "Good. I'll definitely call you later."

In April 1991, at the age of twenty-one years old, through trial and error, having faced disappointment time and again, I had come to the realization that I needed more than someone who was just attracted to my body, so it was refreshing for me to go out with a brainiac bookworm. Since I worked out on regular basis, I thought I could handle my new beau if he made any unwelcome advances.

My parents had eleven children. Mom was a strong believer that children should be seen and not heard. On top of that, since I was next to last in the birth order, Mom and my older brothers and sisters dominated the conversation in the house and at the dinner table. Mom did the most dominating. Eating together as a family at the table was mandatory. In our house, eating alone in another room was considered absurd.

Our house was filled with plenty of gleeful, loud talking and sometimes arguments; radio playing; TV watching; laughter; discipline; and love. As I got older, I learned to clown around and put my two cents in when the time was right. However, I was comfortable being quiet too. I liked the fact that Yury was shy. It made me feel safe with him. Plus, when he told me he'd never had a girlfriend before that really got my attention. I thought God had smiled on me and sent a gentleman my way. I felt I had won the man lottery. In my mind, he was my fairy tale turned reality.

Yury was white. I didn't think it was a big deal. He told me he thought black women were beautiful. He had since seeing Thelma for the first time on the TV sitcom *Good Times*, which aired in 1974. Her beauty had gone straight to his heart.

As Thelma's character appeared on TV, Yury, at age thirteen, had sat with his eyes glued to the tube. His heart had raced and skipped as he listened to and watched her in scene after scene. He'd said to himself, *Thelma, you are absolutely stunning. You are the most beautiful woman I have ever seen.*

I was sure she had the same effect on many boys and men, especially in the black community. I appreciated the notion that he found beauty in black women. I could tell he sincerely meant what he said, so I decided to give him a chance. I earned brownie points with Yury after I passed his feet test.

"Can you do me a favor?" he asked.

I said, "Uh, what kind of favor?"

He smiled and asked, "Will you take your shoes off so I can see your toes?"

With a perplexed beam, I asked, "Why?"

He answered, "I'm just curious and want to know what they look like."

I didn't take them off that day, but I promised to wear sandals the next day, and I did.

Yury peered down at my toes. "OK." He nodded. "They'll do."

I wasn't sure how to process his outlandish request or his satisfied reply. Was he planning on showcasing my feet in a trophy case or booking me to be a foot model? It never occurred to me that he had a foot fetish. I didn't even know what a foot fetish was then. I don't understand how someone can be turned on by feet, but some people are. Go figure.

Once we started going out together, Yury cooked dinner for me on a regular basis. It was always salmon patties, pinto beans, and seasoned buttered potatoes because that was the only meal he knew how to cook. It was pretty good, though. It made me feel special to know he was going out of his way for me. He was sure to inform me that if we ever got married, he expected me to cook dinner every night for him. I agreed to do that.

One evening, I cooked for him since he wanted to taste my cooking. I was strictly on a health food kick then. I had cut out carbohydrates, sugar, salt, and fatty foods. I mainly ate meat, vegetables, yogurt, trail mix, salad, and fruit. My typical dinner was drained dry tuna served on top of a rice cake with a few slices of cheese and a cup of grapes. I changed it from time to time. Sometimes I would have an apple, orange, or grapefruit instead of grapes.

I don't remember what I made Yury for dinner that night, but it was awful. We ended up going out for fast food. Maybe that was why my brothers got upset and begged our mother not to let me cook, I thought. They told me I needed to plan to stay single if I was going to continue eating like I did.

"No man is going to want to eat your tasteless Styrofoam meals. We want a good, hearty meal that's going to stick to our stomach. You'd better listen to the saying 'The way to a man's heart is through his stomach!'" they teased.

Yury and I mainly spent our time watching movies on VHS, TV, and DVD and listening to radio talk show host Bruce Williams. We asked each other the basic get-to-know-you questions most people asked on dates.

"How long have you worked at the bookstore? Tell me about yourself and your family," he said.

After answering him, I asked, "Where do you work? Do you like to read a lot? Who is your favorite author? What is your favorite book? What is your favorite movie? Where are you from? How many siblings do you have? Do you believe in God?"

Yury's answers seemed sincere. He was confident, and he answered my questions quickly, so I thought his words were coming from his heart, his core. Therefore, I vehemently believed him. I explained to him that I had a call of God on my life, so I was looking for someone who would serve God with me.

I'd accepted Jesus as my savior when I was eight years old while watching Judah and Tema Cook on the Glory to God (GTG) Channel in 1977. I was drawn to the love of God that permeated the atmosphere there and seemingly penetrated through the TV screen and saturated the whole inside of Mama's bedroom. Also, the bond and love for each other and for God that the Cooks and their guest couples displayed greatly influenced me. I prayed to experience the same kind of love once my future husband found me. I wanted to be in a relationship in which my spouse liked spending time with God by himself, time with God together, and time with just me, not counting the time we shared in the bedroom. I was looking forward to our being friends and doing fun things together that we both liked. I wanted us to have some of the same goals and to unify to accomplish them together.

I told Yury I wanted to raise my children to know and love God. He told me he used to be a child evangelist, and if we ever got serious enough to get married, he would be active in going to church with me because he wanted to be an example for our children. He didn't just want to send them to church; he wanted to take them. He also said he wanted his wife to stay home with the children. He wanted to make sure the children would be in a safe environment and be cared for. When I heard those words, I thought I had died and gone to heaven.

"I want to take our children to church because I want us to be an example for them," Yury said.

I agreed. "That's what I want too."

He continued. "I also want my wife to stay home and raise our children, so I know they are safe during their vulnerable years."

It was as if God had opened the windows of heaven and decided to smile down on me. He was showing me his favor. I didn't know of anyone in my immediate family who ever had had that opportunity before. I thanked God often for many years, and I am still grateful to this day. Also, I told Yury my dad used to run around with other women while married to my mom. I made it clear to him that I wouldn't stand for that. In return, he told me his dad had done the same thing to his mother, and he was not my dad or his dad. I felt comfort and hope after he shared that with me. He was matter-of-fact in his response, so I had confidence he was going to stand on his conviction.

"Yury, my dad cheated on my mom on numerous occasions. That's not going to happen to me. It's my deal breaker." I shared with him as I sat next to him on his couch.

Yury looked at me and said, "I won't. My dad did the same thing to my mom, but I am not him. I'm not your dad either."

My mother had taught us that our word was our bond, like a pledge, vow, or oath. "If people can't trust what you tell them, they won't trust you." She would threaten to beat us if we told her a lie. She would say, "If you lie, you'll steal, and if you steal, you'll kill." She was adamant about it and was not going to be responsible for us going to hell for lying.

I trusted what Yury told me when we were dating. He seemed sincere. Plus, he was able to look me in the eye while he spoke. I had been taught not to trust people who couldn't do that. Mama explained that was evidence they were shifty and had an ulterior motive. As far as I could see, he didn't show any signs of deception.

Time went on, and one day, when I visited him, he pulled out a large folder and said, "Look what my mom sent me in the mail today."

I asked, "What is it?"

He opened it. It was filled with old clipped newspaper articles. He picked up an article and asked, "Who does that look like?"

I smiled, laughed, reached for it, and said, "Is that you when you were a child?"

Yury grinned and said, "Yes, I was a handsome fellow. I grew older and got better, didn't I?" He looked into my eyes.

I nodded and agreed. "You are right. There isn't anyone more handsome than you," I answered facetiously. He urged me to compare his face to the articles. I studied them and said, "Oh, I see it. It's really you! Wow, you were really a child evangelist! What was that like?"

He replied, "I was a child. I didn't know any better, but during that time, I always knew what to say. I guess God told me, but I'm not sure. I didn't know what I was doing. I was naive, like children are."

He showed me a medium-sized advertisement from his hometown newspaper in Marshfield, Missouri, dated 1972. It showed him at about eleven years old, preaching at a local church, so I took what he told me to heart. I took his spoken words as promises. Yury's brown hair framed his face. He had a classic home-style bowl haircut that reached above his eyebrows. His jasper-green eyes were magnetic, and he had a small, warm smile and thin, cute nose.

Years later, after we were married, Yury explained why he'd stopped going to church and quit spending time with God. God called him to be an evangelist when he was eight years old. It all started when he was at a church with his parents. A visiting minister spoke to them about God wanting to use Yury's life. The only thing Yury remembered about that time was that he automatically knew what to say whenever he was called upon to preach in different churches.

When he was fifteen, he and his family left the church, and Yury walked away from evangelism. They'd encountered a number of disappointing unforeseen issues and broken promises from many of the leaders of the churches Yury was called to minister in. In particular, love gifts promised to his family were never received. Since his age made him a phenomenon, he drew large crowds. Since Yury was young, he had to face the usual annoyances regular young children and teenagers went through, such as peer pressure and bullying. Because he was a child evangelist that compounded the typical stresses young children and teenagers experienced.

He couldn't stand it anymore, so he distanced himself from God and put his Bible away. Around that time, he said, his father made plenty of unwise choices, or "went off the deep end," as Yury liked to say. Those choices caused his dad to become seriously injured after a card game went wrong and turned into a gunfight. The outcome was nearly fatal.

Those confrontations, especially the last one, led his dad to examine his life. He decided to turn back to God and allowed God to clean up his life. Even though Yury's dad had been walking with God for more than thirty years since, Yury only thought about the negative things his father had done before accepting Jesus as his Savior. He didn't see the transformation as genuine, not even after thirty years. It was one of the things that turned Yury off regarding Christianity. Whenever anyone asked Yury what it had been like to be a child evangelist, he always said, "I was just a child. I don't know what I was doing. I didn't know any better."

Missouri is called the Show Me State. I believed for Yury, the state motto was deeply embedded in his mindset, because he didn't believe anything easily. He was naturally skeptical and looked at situations from a negative perspective. There were many red flags I can clearly see now when I think back on our dating time that I completely overlooked. For example, even though he traveled for work to different states and other countries where his clients were and was in town two weekends out of the month, he never wanted to go to church with me. Red flag.

"Yury, I know you travel often for work, but will you go to church with me on Sundays when you're in town?" I asked.

He hesitated and then answered, "If we get married, I will, but right now, I just want to relax and enjoy my days off."

That sounded reasonable to me. I never pushed him or complained, because nagging your husband or, in my case at that time, boyfriend was a big no-no according to what I'd learned from my mother. Of course, for Mom, those rules only applied to husbands. Anyway, I had no idea at that time that Yury's disinterest in God and his not wanting to go to church while we dated was a precursor to our future together.

Since I knew he enjoyed reading books, I bought him and myself between eight and ten Christian books on sale for 75 percent off from the Christian bookstore. I figured it would be good for us to read together, so we could have something to talk about when we got together. I gave him the books before one of his trips out of town. I hoped he would take at least one of the books with him, so we could discuss it once he came back into town.

Once he was back, I asked if he was ready to choose a book, so we could read it and then get together to talk about it. He told me he'd misplaced all the books. I could have understood losing one, but all eight or ten books? He might as well have told me a hungover tap-dancing donkey had run off with them. Red flag.

I asked him about the books on several occasions, but he never found them. Back then, I was blind to the fact that he had a collection of books and that books were precious to him. I wanted to believe the best about him since we were still getting to know each other. I pushed aside the notion that someone, especially a book lover, could lose that many books at the same time. I found that a bit peculiar.

Then, early in our dating relationship, Yury's friend Eddie came to visit him from Arkansas. Yury asked for a picture of me to show Eddie, since I was scheduled to work during the short time of Eddie's stay. I handed Yury a photograph that had been professionally done. Then I saw Yury the next evening.

He told me, "Eddie saw your picture and thought you were pretty."

"Did you put it in your wallet?" I asked, hoping.

Yury shook his head and said, "I tossed it into the backseat of my car, and now I can't find it. It has to be in there somewhere."

Widening my eyes, I said, "Why would you toss my picture into the backseat of your car?"

He shrugged and answered, "I was driving." Red flag.

Later, he decided he wanted to save money since he was out of town a lot. He lived in a town house, and at one time, he had a roommate, but she moved out shortly after we started dating. It was clear their acquaintance was strictly platonic, so once that was confirmed, it was never an issue for me. He found another roommate in the newspaper, a guy this time. He gave up his town house to move into the house of his new roommate.

Since he was moving, he placed an ad in the newspaper to sell some of his furniture. After the sale was over, I noticed he had two black females' names, La Diamond and Rashekala, and their numbers written down in his notebook. Red flag. When I asked him why he had the ladies' phone numbers, he said they'd bought furniture from him. He'd told them if he had another sale, he would call them.

I was uneasy about it, so I kept talking about how I felt about it, until he finally allowed me to scratch their names and numbers out with an ink pen. If he had had both men's and women's names and telephone numbers written down, I would have been more at ease with his wanting to notify them about future items. I never imagined that was a telltale sign of our future.

I glowered over their names and numbers and said, "Who are these ladies, and why do you have their numbers?"

He said, "Nothing is going to happen between them and me. I just want to let them know about my next furniture sale."

I blinked a few times and said, "I'm not comfortable with this at all. If you had a whole list of both men's and women's names and numbers, I would be more at ease. That's not the case here. It makes me think you have other things planned."

Yury huffed and said, "That's not true, but if you're worried that much, just scratch out their numbers."

I did and felt more at peace.

Six months after he moved in with his roommate, his roommate got married. The wedding was at their house. The wedding guests were mainly people the groom worked with and friends, including Yury and me. The groom was concerned about two of his guests who were planning to attend the wedding. One was a man, and the other was a woman. The problem was that they were having an affair with each other, but both of their spouses were coming to the wedding with them. The groom hoped the event would transpire without a commotion. I was shocked and turned off by the news. I couldn't understand why they wanted to bring their spouses to the wedding and pretend like everything was going well and on the level in their relationships.

In an attempt to calm me down, Yury said, "You don't need to get into their business. That has nothing to do with you. Just stay out of it and let them be."

I wasn't planning to confront them. I didn't know them. They were living the lyrics from the 1972 Billy Paul song "Me and Mrs. Jones." I was surprised Yury wasn't appalled by their actions. I thought about the fact that both spouses were coming into the same house and would be blind to the sad truth that their husband's and wife's lovers would be in the same room with them. That disturbed me. Red flag. It was another meaningful sign I missed.

The day of the wedding, my emotions were rumbling around inside me. I was happy for the bride and groom and sad for the two people being deceived. Plus, I wanted to spank the two people having the affair. All I could think was *God, please fix this and help the man and lady who are in the dark about their marriages.*

Also, there was another clue I missed: Yury had some pornographic videos of white men with black women. Humongous red flag. When I saw them among his video collection, I asked him about the tapes. He told me he only had them for entertainment, but if we got married, he would throw them away. I was trusting and didn't know about the damaging effects pornography had on those who dabbled with it. Once we were married, I immediately threw those videos away. In my eyes, the case was closed.

FOUR

EVEN THOUGH YURY and I dated for a year and three months, he was not allowed in my mother's house, where I still lived at that time. Mama taught us that God wanted us to love everybody. I thought she really meant that. I was thrown off when I found out she firmly opposed the guys who were attracted to me who were not black.

However, she decided she didn't like my black boyfriend either. Kent was five foot eleven, with a medium build and decent muscle tone. Also, he was serious-minded and humorless and didn't smile much. I met him at the fitness center I used to work at in August 1988, a few years before I met Yury. I was nineteen years old. I put Kent through an exercise routine recommended for men. Kent didn't want to start out slowly, as I advised him to. He insisted on doing more sets and reps than a person just getting started with exercising should have. I guessed he was trying to show me how macho he was. I tried to talk him out of it, but he wouldn't listen to me. His bad decision came back to haunt him. He came back to the fitness center a few days later, barely able to walk because he was so sore.

He said, "What did you do to me? I'm in so much pain!" He walked as if he were well beyond his age.

"You overexercised. I tried to talk you out of it. Just give it a few more days, and then you will feel better," I said. "Let's do some stretching. It will help too."

"You don't need to be training anybody! I'm in hellfire pain!" he grumbled as he hobbled away. He left the fitness center, frowning.

Then, a few years later, in 1991, on the same day my brother went to work with me to confront my stalker, I saw Kent and his sister in the mall. We were fortunate enough not to run into the stalker again during our time together. They were passing by the bookstore I worked in, but once Kent saw me, they came over to say hi. He was pleasant and smiling. We talked a little bit. He told his sister how we'd met, and we laughed about it. My brother had to work late, so he didn't pick me up after I finished my shift. Kent saw me standing by the exit as he and his sister were leaving the mall.

"Are you waiting for someone?" he asked.

I replied, "Yes, my brother is picking me up."

He coughed and said, "We can give you a ride home. Where do you live?"

I smiled and shook my head, "No, you don't have to do that. Thank you for offering!"

"Really, I don't mind. What street do you live on?" he asked softly.

I reluctantly told him.

His sister said, "We don't live too far from you. It's not a problem. It will save you from having to wait."

Kent added, "Yes, we are going past your house anyway."

I agreed to allow them to drive me home. As Kent and I talked, we found out both of us were Christians and were in relationships with unfavorable situations attached to them.

Kent started by asking, "Do you know God as your Lord and Savior?"

"Yes, I accepted him into my life at age eight," I said.

He nodded and said, "I accepted God at a young age too. My parents are ministers, and so am I. Are you in a relationship?"

I answered, "Y-yes."

He said, "That wasn't a strong yes."

I continued. "It's just because my mother won't accept him because he's white. It's a stressful situation."

Kent's forehead creased, and he said, "You should listen to your mom. She sounds like a smart lady. My relationship is strained too because my girlfriend has children who are not mine, and one child's father is still in the picture."

I was dating Blake, who smiled with his eyes, was sociable, and had an air of confidence. On his first day at work, we met in the bookstore I worked in. Yes, the bookstore again. He had just finished seminary school. Then he began working in the mall, managing a smoothie shop. While I rang his copy of *Sports Illustrated* magazine up on the cash register, I noticed he kept looking at my left hand.

A few weeks later, when Blake came into the store, he asked me, "Would you like to go out with me?"

I said, "Yes, I'll go out with you."

During our second date, he told me he wanted to marry me. On a sunny day in July 1990, we walked on Sullivan's Island Beach. The temperature was 88 degrees. The sky was painted the perfect shade of powder blue, and the atmosphere was exemplary. Then Blake got down on one knee.

He asked, "Lewisa, will you marry me?"

I cupped my face and said, "Yes." Then we embraced each other.

"We can look for a ring soon. I just started my new job, but I can tell you are special. I don't want to lose you," he said.

I nodded and said, "Yes, we can get my ring later."

I said yes because it just seemed like the right thing to say. I answered in an affirmative sense without giving it any thought. I handled it in a flippant way, like *I'm going to pencil marriage in on the calendar after my hair appointment this Saturday and just before I walk my dog.*

His marriage proposal created a dilemma for me. I was petrified to share the news with Mom. The only thing I could think about was how Mama was going to kill me before my wedding day. My mother didn't want to meet him. She didn't approve of him because he wasn't the right color. Blake was hurt by Mom's rejection, especially since his family welcomed me with open arms.

Then again, there were some theatrics that encircled our relationship. Blake was friends with a girl who was engaged to a guy in the military. She was living with Blake and his family and started working in the mall too. At one time, they were friends with benefits, but as Blake explained it to me, after she got engaged and he met me, they ended their physical involvement with each other. After Blake asked me to marry him, he asked her to move out. He didn't want the temptation of her being accessible to create a problem for us.

Based on the angry rebuttals from some people working in the mall who knew us, I learned she thought I was behind Blake's decision for her to move out. It was a stressful situation and time for both Blake and me.

Kent was dating June, a single mother with children. There was a lot of drama surrounding their relationship since one of the fathers was active in one of her children's lives. Kent suggested we get together for Bible study lessons.

After telling Blake about my encounter with Kent, I talked it over with him. Blake didn't see any harm in the Bible study lessons. The lessons went well. It was good not to have tension in the midst of our gathering. Then, later, Kent told me God had told him I was his wife. Therefore, we decided to go in the direction of God's leading. One evening, during our nightly visit at my house, as we sat on the couch, Kent reached over and took my hand.

He looked into my eyes and said, "As I was praying, I heard God say in my spirit that you are my wife."

I widened my eyes and replied, "Wow! Are you sure he mentioned me specifically?"

He did a double take, narrowed his eyes, and said, "I take this very seriously. This is not a game I'm playing. In God's eyes, marriage is forever, so I want to get this right."

I straightened up, swallowed hard, and said, "OK, then we need to do what God wants us to do."

So I broke it off with Blake, and Kent broke up with June. Even though Blake and I had dated for only two months, he was heartbroken. However, it was a rash decision that came back to bite me later.

My mother was ecstatically happy the first time I brought Kent home. He had one thing going for him: he was the right color. However, he got on her nerves because she thought he was too religious for her. Kent's parents were ministers. After he taught our Bible study as if he had been born to do so in Mom's living room on a Sunday afternoon, Mom served fried chicken, collard greens, rice, baked macaroni, corn bread, and tea in the dining room. After she blessed the food, she turned her attention to Kent to get to know him.

She said, "Kent, Lewisa said you are a minister. Please tell me about that."

Kent's eyes sparked with delight as he beamed. He responded by singing, "I love to praise him. I love to praise his name. I love to praise him. I love to praise his name. I love to praise him. I love to praise his name. Ooh, I love to praise his holy name."

He paused briefly. Everyone was somewhat unsettled by his unexpected singing. Then he raised both hands in the air and declared with exuberant gusto his love of God.

"I love God the Father, God the Son, and God the Holy Spirit! God has been so good to me! I have seen him heal the sick and make a way out of no way. God is almighty and wonderful!" He softly banged his hands on the table.

Mom's nostrils flared as she said, "It don't take all of that to serve God! You don't have to be overly religious to serve God!"

Kent dropped his head and eyes and finished eating dinner quietly. I shrugged, flashed a half smile, and mouthed the word *sorry*. He had been called by God to preach. He was passionate about God and got enthusiastic whenever he talked about Jesus. He had invitations to speak at different local churches in the area. He also went to nursing homes to share God's Word with the residents.

My mother thought he got a little too fired up whenever he talked about Jesus. She thought his excitement was bogus. The day Kent told me God had said I was his wife, I thought, *God, can we talk about this? He's not exactly what I had in mind.* He was a nice-looking guy, but he had a large nose and never had lost his bottom baby teeth. Then again, he did have beautiful feet. He could have been a foot model. Regarding foot fetishes, even though Kent's feet were beautiful, I didn't have a desire to make a move on him because of it. I told God I was going to trust him since he'd brought us together.

We dated for a little more than two months. Then, on October 31, 1990, on Halloween Day, he broke up with me in the bookstore I worked in. Kent made an unannounced visit to my job.

When I saw him, I said with a big smile, "Hi! What are you doing here?"

His face was expressionless. "Can we talk?" he said in a serious tone.

At that moment, two customers were in the store. I was restocking the shelves. I stopped for a moment.

"Yes. What are you doing here?" I said, giving him my full attention.

Kent cleared his throat and said, "I need to tell you I can't see you anymore."

I stood there frozen. I released my smile and mumbled, "What?"

Kent said, "I'm sorry, but I'm going to marry June." June was his previous girlfriend he'd been with before he and I started dating. Her father was a pastor of another church. She had five children by four different men, and she and Kent had broken up once because she was cheating on him. "We are getting married in two weeks. Please don't try to talk me out of it."

I just stood there fastened to the floor like a deer caught in headlights. I couldn't believe it. It was like a bad dream. Just a few minutes before Kent's arrival, I had been having a good day. My brain turned off, and my words dried up. My stomach sank. Time stood still.

Kent continued. "I didn't want to end things on the phone. My decision has nothing to do with you. You were good for me. I have to go now. Bye."

Then he walked out of the store to start his new life. The two customers left the store too. I slowly turned around and started restocking the shelves again. I was devastated. I tried to stay calm and professional. I was speechless. However, the more I thought about how and where he'd broken up with me, the more upset I got. I was more embarrassed than upset about the actual split. Couldn't he have waited until my shift was over?

Then the unthinkable happened: I broke down and started crying—in front of new customers. They had no idea my hopes and dreams about marrying someone God had chosen for me had just been smashed into zillions of pieces. At least I cried in a dignified way. It wasn't a loud, screeching, ugly cry. It was classy. Only dainty, ladylike tears rolled softly down my overwhelmed face.

Of course, I had to stay at work for hours after the big scene from the movie of my life ended. At least it was a calm and graceful scene, yet it was still a shameful and troublesome scene. At that moment, I could have used Edna "E" Mode, one of the characters from the movie *The Incredibles*. She was the little lady who slapped sense into Elastigirl when Elastigirl thought she was losing her husband, Mr. Incredible. Edna said, "Pull yourself together! What will you do? Is this a question?"

Throughout my remaining time at work, many people saw I was in distress. After inquiring about the reason, many shared some form of sympathetic words or thoughts. However, only one person went beyond sympathy and demonstrated empathy. One of the men who worked in the most expensive jewelry store in the mall at that time not only took the time to find out why I was crying but also hugged and held me. He didn't mind my tears getting on his suit as he comforted me. He told me he understood my pain because he had gone through a breakup recently with his boyfriend.

When Sid entered the store and saw my puffy red eyes, he touched his heart with his hands and, with concern in his eyes, said, "Honey, what happened? What's wrong, sweetie?"

In between sniffles and huffs, I said softly, "My boyfriend just dumped me."

He gasped, walked over to me, and said, "I'm so sorry, precious. All men are not like that. If a man decides he doesn't want to be in your life, don't try to make him. I learned that the hard way." He walked over to the side of the cash register and said, "Can I hug you?"

I nodded and said, "Yes."

Sid stood a foot shorter than a basketball player. His salt-and-pepper hair was combed back and kept in place with styling gel, and his tan skin looked hydrated. He wore light gray glasses and a black Hugo Boss suit with black shoes. He took my hand and pulled me into his body. My head rested on his chest, and he said, "I know just how you feel. My heart was broken two years ago by my boyfriend. I'm still recovering. Trust me. The pain will subside, and you will love again. Next time, only accept true love. If that man is willing to walk on hot coals to win your love, he is the man for you."

He didn't mind my tears getting on his suit, and I was grateful he took the time to care that much about what I was going through. By the time I got off from work, my eyes were puffy and bloodshot, and my face looked slightly swollen. Then, that same day, I had a job interview at a bank I wanted to work at. I had only an hour to go home, get ready, and drive to the bank. When I got to the interview, I still looked the same way, even though I'd tried to freshen up. Needless to say, I didn't get the job. I probably looked like someone who had just been beaten or was drunk or high on drugs to them. Plus, it didn't help that I was still crying during the interview. I don't remember how I answered the questions. I believe they were just delighted to get me out of their office.

The breakup was unexpected. I took it hard. On top of that, Kent got married two weeks later, just as he'd said he would. I was in so much pain, mainly because I was amazed that God had taken the time to choose someone for me, and then, in the blink of an eye, he was gone. Plus, I was mad because of how Kent had discarded our relationship. I spent all my extra time reading the Bible and listening to Christian music. I decided that secular music couldn't help me cope with the pain I was feeling. Ultimately, it didn't take long for God to reach out to me and truly give me hope and peace. He healed my broken heart. Then I had a dream one night. Kent appeared to me in the dream.

He said, "June's dad told me he would buy me a trailer and some land if I married his daughter. After the wedding, her daddy didn't keep his word. I found out he couldn't afford to buy a trailer or land."

I thought it was just a dream, but it felt real. Then my mother encouraged me to go to Kent's parents' house to thank them for being kind to me. Mom was ticked off with Kent; however, I believed that deep down in her heart, she didn't think he was right for me anyway. She probably did a "Thank you, Jesus" dance in private after hearing my unfortunate news.

His parents were pastors of a small church. Once, after the breakup, they called me up to say a prayer during one of their services. At that time, I hadn't seen Kent in three weeks, so I was filled with sadness. In church, before the service began, his mother approached me. Her long, thick black hair she'd inherited from her Native American mother moved from side to side as she walked.

"Lewisa, my husband and I are so glad to see you every Sunday despite what happened between you and our son. I hope you don't feel awkward around us now. You were the one we wanted our son to marry," his mother said in a caring tone.

I smiled and said, "Thank you for saying that."

She added, "I'm not just saying that. We would like you to say a prayer before church service ends today. Will you?"

My eyes grew wide, and I stammered, "I-I-I—"

His mother interrupted me. "You can do it. I believe in you. Please do this for me. If you do it today and don't like it, I will never ask you to do it again." She hugged me and said, "Trust me. You can do this."

I said with widened lips and clenched teeth, "OK, I'll do it."

My stomach churned for the entire length of the service. I sat there wringing my hands, hoping it would ease the dread I felt inside. Then the long-awaited moment was upon me. Kent's mother called me onto the floor toward the front of the church.

"Lewisa, please come up and pray for the congregation before we dismiss the service," she said, reaching her hand in my direction.

I stood by her. She squeezed my shoulder and told me, "You can do this."

I breathed in and out and started. "Our Father, who art in heaven, hallowed be thy name. Thy kingdom come. Thy will be done on earth as it is in heaven."

I felt as if I were talking for forever. Beads of sweat appeared on my forehead. When I finished the prayer, I was ecstatic and felt as if five pounds had been shed off my body.

After church, Kent's mother hugged me, rejoicing. "You were wonderful! I knew you could do it!"

Hesitantly, I said, "Well, thank you."

After the breakup, Kent's parents also encouraged me to participate in their Christmas program by reading a Christmas poem. It went the same as the first time I'd spoken in front of the congregation. In addition, they chose me to go to an orphanage to start a partnership with them. I went to collect some of the children's clothing sizes so we could get them something for Christmas.

When I visited Kent's parents, at first, I wasn't planning to tell them about the dream. Our conversation was pleasant. They were comforting and understanding regarding my sadness concerning the breakup with Kent. They didn't like how Kent had done things either, so I decided to tell them. Since his parents were pastors and knew God revealed things in dreams, I told them about the dream and repeated what Kent had said to me in the dream. As I spoke, his parents' eyes widened as they looked at each other. Then both of their mouths dropped wide open. Their reaction took me by surprise.

I asked, "What?"

They responded, "That's exactly what happened!"

I couldn't believe it. I was stunned and said, "Are you serious?"

His mother replied, "Yes! God has got his hand on you. You keep spending time with him. He's going to use you one day."

God gave me another dream during that time, which filled my heart with joy. I dreamed I was in my bedroom in my mother's house. I was playing hide-and-seek with a beautiful little baby boy. He had light caramel-colored skin and curly light brown hair with strands of blond highlights. He was running and laughing. He had the best smile. I was running behind him and laughing. I found the baby boy in my closet, where he was hiding.

When I opened the closet door and discovered him there, my heart filled up with happiness, hope, and joy. He looked up at me with a contagious laugh and bliss in his eyes. I didn't know what the dream meant, but I knew God had something special for me. At that time, I thought it was just a dream, but I learned later God had let me in on a little secret he had planned for me in my future.

FIVE

MEANWHILE, I FINALLY figured out Mom meant for me to love everyone figuratively, not literally. She meant I should love others from afar and not have relationships with people of a different color. I was baffled because my mother's skin was so light she could pass for being white. Plus, she had green eyes. Mama was five foot two. Daddy was six foot one. Although she had a heart of gold when a situation called for it, Mother, known as a little pit bull, was feisty and ready to fight anyone or anything that went against what she considered right.

With her hands on her hips, her eyes squinting, and the skill of a ninja, she swiftly belted out flaming, weighty words that took on the shape and feel of daggers whenever anyone dared to cross her with unsolicited annoyance. Yet on the turn of a dime, after she put people in their place, she would be the first one to lend them a helping hand.

Mama said to me, "I have seen this same scenario too many times already. How do you think people who look like me exist? That young man is just playing with you! When he gets ready to settle down, he is not going to marry you! He is not going to risk losing out on inheriting his family's money for you."

In May 1992, at age twenty-two, I found out I was pregnant. Perhaps I should have acted like Joseph and run from temptation, but I stepped into the trap of a smooth-talking, shy country boy. When I told Yury about the baby, he asked me if I wanted to get married.

I said, "I don't know."

He was surprised and responded, "What do you mean you don't know? You are carrying my baby!"

I told him, "I don't want you to marry me just because I'm pregnant."

"I love you," he told me.

So I decided to marry him. That same evening, we went shopping for my engagement ring.

Around that time, I turned down a chance to be a substitute model when the Ebony Fashion Fair traveling fashion show came to Charleston. I received an invitation from a lady who was an insurance agent for a family friend who owned his own insurance office. She was connected to the show and asked me to fill in for a model who had taken sick. I didn't do it, because I had recently found out I was pregnant. If the timing had been right, that would have been a dream come true.

My unexpected pregnancy had me imagining my mother turning into the Incredible Hulk, with green skin, a massive body, and a terrifying, beastly growl, and ferociously ripping me apart after discovering my pregnancy. I decided to get my sister Donna, Mom's clone, to help me break the news to her. She'd inherited Mom's complexion and height. She had brown eyes instead of Mom's green eyes, though. Many people who knew Donna found it hard to believe she was black. Some of them thought she was Jewish, of European descent, or a light-skinned Hispanic. Donna used to have my two other sisters and me go to the beach with her so she could get a tan, but we would come back two shades darker instead of her.

Donna planned to inform Mom of the news after church on Wednesday night. She believed Mom would be in a positive mindset then. She had me walk around in the church parking lot while she divulged the information. Maybe Donna thought God would step in and calm Mom down since we were still on holy ground. It worked, because Mama didn't try to lunge toward me, use any heated words capable of causing distress and mental injury, or take me out of the world, as many parents threatened to do whenever their children made a major blunder.

The only thing Mom said to me was "I knew something was up. I figured that something like this had happened."

That night, I told my mother Yury wanted to marry me and showed her the engagement ring he'd bought me. She was lost in her emotions, bearing a tense face and wild eyes. With her gaze locked on me, she slowly lowered her body into her La-Z-Boy chair. Acting as if the weight of the world were on her shoulders, she looked at the ring, then at my face, and then at the ring again, speechless that Yury and I were going to be married. Mom tried to talk me out of getting married by telling me I didn't have to get married just because I was pregnant. I assured her that wasn't the only reason.

"You don't have to get married just because you're pregnant," Mama said dryly.

I answered, "Yury said he loves me, Mama. The baby is a bonus surprise."

She said, "Just get rid of the baby. Have an abortion. Do you know what our family and longtime friends are going to think, knowing you are having a baby for a white man? Plus, people might try to hurt you two just because of your color. You are asking for trouble, and I don't want to get any bad news because of this."

It was a chilling moment when Mom suggested I consider having an abortion. I never had thought I would hear those words come out of her mouth. She was concerned about what her close friends and our family members would think about her if they found out her daughter was having a baby with and marrying a white man. Also, she was concerned about my safety.

I told her, "I don't believe in abortion. Yury is a good person. You'll see that too if you just give him a chance."

Mom creased her forehead, closed one eye, and shook her head as she searched for words. "You planned this," she said.

"No, I didn't. I wouldn't do that," I replied.

"You have gone out with a number of guys over the last four years, and you managed to keep yourself. Now, out of the blue, you're pregnant," she said. "I think you forced this just so I have to accept Yury."

I raised my right hand and said, "Mom, I promise you I didn't plan this."

She thought for a minute as she took stock of me from head to toe. Then she said, "All right, you can invite him here so I can meet him."

Before his arrival, on the phone, I advised Yury, "Just be yourself, and relax. Once Mom gets to know you, she is going to love you like I do."

He let out a nervous laugh. "I sure hope so, because you are carrying my baby."

They met for the first time the next night in Mama's living room.

While we waited for her to join us, I told him, "It's going to be all right, so don't be nervous."

Yury nodded with a serious stare and said, "I'm not nervous."

I squeezed his hand and said, "Good."

That evening, the atmosphere was calm and tranquil because Mama had spent all morning and afternoon reading her Bible. I thought we would have curious onlookers—my siblings—but they had their own life issues to tend to.

Facing each other, Mom sat on the couch, and Yury sat in a chair. Mom apologized. "I'm sorry I banned you from my house. It didn't have anything to do with you personally."

Yury said, "It's OK. Lewisa already explained it to me."

Mama said, "I'm glad she did. Since you are marrying my daughter, I just ask that you treat her well and do your best to protect her."

He looked into Mom's eyes and said, "Yes, ma'am. I promise to treat her well and protect her."

She nodded and said, "Thank you, because that's my baby girl, and I don't want to find out something happened to her. Plus, I don't want anything to happen to you either. I just have to say one last thing. If you and she can't get along, before you put your hand on her to cause harm, just bring her back home."

Yury's eyes widened to the size of oranges as he said, "Oh no, ma'am. I promise you won't have a problem with me ever hitting Lewisa. I don't believe a man should ever hit a woman."

Mom said, "Whew! I'm glad to hear that." She paused and then continued. "You have my blessing to marry my daughter."

The night ended harmoniously as she welcomed Yury into our family with a hug. We were married on July 11, 1992, in Mama's living room. Kent's mom and dad married us. God showed me favor and allowed me to find a short-sleeved, full-length, column-style white lace wedding dress at Marshalls for only twenty-two dollars. He knew I didn't have the money for an expensive wedding dress.

Our wedding was attended by Yury's two sisters. His parents weren't used to flying on an airplane, so they didn't come, and his brother was a farmer and couldn't take off at that time. We saw them in Missouri and Arkansas after the wedding. Yury's roommate and his wife came, as did two longtime friends from Arkansas. My mom, brothers, sisters, and cousin and some of my in-laws were in attendance.

The temperature was 98 degrees outside and about 115 degrees inside the house. Mom's air conditioner stopped working that day. She had fans whirling in just about every room, but they were no match for the heat. The house was sweltering. Therefore, we were all sweating. A few people's clothes were sticking to their bodies.

The most memorable part of our wedding for me was when everyone was outside taking pictures. Mom's house was on the highway, so as cars stopped for the red light, people honked their horns to congratulate us on our special day. It was an unexpected surprise, and it made me happy. I looked at it as if it were a gift to us from God. I thought to myself, *I have found the one. Therefore, I'll never have to date again.* In my mind, the hallelujah chorus was playing in the background.

We had our honeymoon at the Columbia, South Carolina, Riverbanks Zoo and Garden, a destination I chose because I wasn't used to asking for a lot, even though Yury said our honeymoon budget was $2,000. Donna confided in me later that my family made a bet after my wedding regarding how long they thought the marriage would last. Mother and my siblings participated in the wager. No money changed hands; the stakes were just verbal bragging rights. Some of them speculated that my marriage would last only one or two years, while others guessed it would end within two to four years. A few believed it would dissolve near year five. Their belief was brought on by how they thought of the unkind, harsh history in America between the white and black races.

I asked Donna, "Did you bet?"

She nodded and answered, "Yes."

"How many years did you think we would last?"

"I guessed four or five years." She smiled big. "We've never seen or known of a marriage between a white man and black woman in our family or among our friends before. Of course, we want your marriage to survive, but we were unsure if it would."

I said, "Wow! I can't believe it, but I suppose if I was in your shoes or their shoes, I would have done the same thing."

After we got settled into our new house in Mount Pleasant, South Carolina, I hung some Bible scriptures on a small section of one of the walls in the spare bedroom. We used the room as our office and exercise room. I used a variety of marker colors to write the scriptures on steno paper. I'd meditated on those Bible scriptures after my breakup with Kent. I'd had them on my bedroom wall in Mama's house. They helped keep my mind together. God and his Word brought healing to my pain. Those Bible scriptures were like precious gems to me.

One day, when Grant, Yury's friend from one of his previous places of employment, came to visit us, the visit turned sour. Yury and Grant stood glowering at the wall the scriptures as if I had spray-painted graffiti on a renowned piece of artwork.

Grant creased his forehead as he narrowed his eyes and scoffed at the wall of scriptures. "What child put those hideous pieces of paper on your wall?" he asked Yury.

Yury inhaled, tilted his head, and said, "My wife did that."

"And you didn't try to stop her?" Grant asked.

Yury shook his head and said, "I have to help keep our home in a harmonious state, so I keep my mouth closed. I don't think they should be up there either."

I interjected. "I know my scripture display doesn't look picturesque, but those Bible scriptures helped me recover from a broken heart."

Yury and Grant looked at me and then at each other with blank stares. I tried to explain how the scriptures had played a monumental part in my recovering from a broken heart. Sadly, they didn't get what I was saying.

I had made changes to my diet earlier after my brothers shared their wisdom with me concerning how to keep a man. Since I was pregnant, I abandoned the whole high-protein, low-carbohydrate lifestyle because I thought it would harm the baby. I indulged in all the delicious, fatty foods I'd avoided for three years. It was heavenly! I had no idea fat was going to be attracted to my body the way a magnet attracted metal or honey attracted bees. I gained seventy-two pounds during my pregnancy.

As I packed on the weight quicker than a sumo wrestler chowed down on a large twenty-four-ounce steak, the unwanted attention from men stopped. My hourglass figure turned into a beer mug. I refused to use the term *fat*, though. I was now pleasantly plump. Gaining that much weight was the best thing ever, a big relief. I hadn't enjoyed being ogled and having men leer at me with eyes kindled with hot desire while they drooled as if I were the last cup of icy water available to quench their thirst in the blazing, merciless desert sun.

My weight gain presented another uncomfortable issue. I heard someone say, "Once your baby starts school, you can't claim you have baby fat anymore." Well, I thought that person must have gained only fifteen pounds during pregnancy, or she had a high metabolism.

I found truth in the adage "Actions speak louder than words" when, after my weight gain, Yury told me during our intimate moments together he loved my body. As he and I sat on the couch, moments later, he inched over next to me, placed his right hand on my thigh, and massaged it. Then he lowered his head onto my shoulder and started kissing my neck.

In between kisses, he said, "You are so beautiful."

I asked, "Even with my weight gain?"

He replied, "Especially with your weight gain. I love you and your body no matter what you look like."

I chuckled, saying, "I find that hard to believe, because I don't see you trying to sneak glances at overweight women passing by outside.

And you don't make comments about the beauty of overweight women on TV either."

Yury said, "Trust me. You are a beautiful woman regardless of your size."

I smiled. Then he took my hand and led me to our bedroom.

One evening, we went to dinner in a fancy restaurant in downtown Charleston with some of the men who traveled with him and their wives. Our waiter accidentally dropped a bowl of salad on my back. It was embarrassing for both him and me, but I was grateful the salad didn't already have salad dressing added to it. I assured the waiter I was fine, and no damage was done, so he didn't have worry. As he was leaving our table, I could tell by his expression he still felt bad.

Later, when we were leaving the restaurant, Yury and I were walking with the wife of one of his traveling partners. She complimented what I was wearing. "I love your dress. It is such a pretty color on you," she said.

I answered, "Thank you! I got it on sale today at TJ Maxx."

Yury smirked and replied, "Are you serious? Look how fat she is!"

The lady looked at Yury and said, "Your baby is still young. It takes a while to get back into shape after having a baby."

I hadn't known her before I had my baby, but over dinner, Yury had shared the fact that we had a new baby. She just assumed I'd gained the weight because of the pregnancy, and she was right. It did take a while to lose weight after having a baby. I was embarrassed the subject had come up in the presence of a stranger. It caught me off guard. I also felt too exhausted and dazed to address the subject at home.

When I'd said, "I do," I'd understood I was making a promise to both my husband and God. The promise was supposed to be about loving each other for better or worse, for richer or poorer, and in sickness and health; forsaking all others; and being faithful only unto each other for as long as we both lived. Wedding vows varied in their wording, but to the best of my knowledge, all of them leaned toward a husband and wife being true to each other.

I was not the smartest person in the world, but to my knowledge, no wedding vows incorporated a man, a woman, and his mistresses, or his female friends, as my husband liked to call them. Apparently, he didn't understand that and didn't realize the "Shop Around" song wasn't talking to married people. I loved him so much, but my love wasn't strong or cherished enough by him to motivate him to do whatever it took to keep it. It would have been nice if Yury had declared his love for me and followed through with actions, like the words in Jennifer Holliday's song "You're Gonna Love Me." In a perfect world, he would have been singing that song to me.

While we were dating and early in our marriage, my husband worked for a large American packaging company that had more than one hundred offices in thirty different countries. He had a chemical engineering degree and, at that time, worked as a customer service representative for a large paper corporation that produced paper, corrugated boxes, and specialty chemicals. They had more than ten thousand employees in the United States and many countries throughout the world. Customer satisfaction was his number-one duty. He got paid to wine and dine his clients in fancy restaurants, and if they wanted to be entertained in other ways, such as going to a bar, museum, or ball game, it was my husband's job to keep them happy at the company's expense. One of his customers in Singapore wanted to go to a brothel after dinner. Yury said he went with the businessman but waited in the waiting room until his customer was ready to go.

I squinted, tilted my head, sucked in my lips, and, with a dismayed sound, responded, "Are you sure that's all you did?"

He chuckled. "Baby, you are being silly! Of course that's all I did. Don't get me wrong—those women were beautiful. But I have you. I promise you all I did was sit there and wait for my customer."

Wow, I thought. *I asked him about his trip, and he told me. I would have never known that information if he hadn't shared it with me.* I decided not to push the issue. His job required him to travel from state to state and to other countries on a regular basis. On average, he was away from home anywhere from three days if he was scheduled for any of the thirty offices in the United States to three weeks if he had to visit his clients in one of the seventy offices in other countries, including India, Pakistan, Malaysia, Australia, New Zealand, Indonesia, Thailand, Singapore, and more.

Once, I innocently brushed off a conversation we had during his time home, because I thought he was being honest and opening up to me. Yury mentioned he had seen a black lady in the airport who had a tiny waist and a small, shapely body but the biggest, roundest butt he had ever seen on that size of frame. He said he had followed her for a little while because he was so amazed.

I said, "Huh, and why did you feel like you had to follow her around?"

He said, "I don't know. Her figure was just so unbelievable. Don't worry; all I did was watch her."

I didn't push the subject further, because he didn't have to tell me about it in the first place. I just thought, *OK, my husband is either incredibly honest or really stupid. Don't beat him up for it.*

Weeks passed, and one evening, our home phone rang. We didn't have caller ID at that time. Cell phones were big and bulky and not widely in use then. The technology was still new and wasn't popular yet.

I answered our home phone. The lady on the other end asked for Richard. I told her she had the wrong number. She insisted she didn't. I tried a couple of times to get her off the phone, but she maintained that she had the right number.

"May I speak to Richard?" she asked.

While she spoke, I gasped and then responded cautiously, "Sorry, but you have the wrong number. Please check to make sure you dialed the right number."

She said, "No, no, no. I'm certain I was given the right number."

I said, "Believe me. You have the wrong number."

Then she said, "With all due respect, ma'am, I promise you that I have the right number. Does your Richard have brown hair and wear glasses?"

As a thousand thoughts swam around my brain, I said, "Yes, but you still have the wrong number." I thought, *There is no way in the world my little bookworm could be pursuing other women. He's not like that. That just can't happen, because he is too shy.* I said, "My husband is quiet, shy, and a family man. Trust me. You have the wrong number."

She ended the conversation by saying, "I'm sure I have the right number. I was just calling to warn you that your husband isn't the man you think he is."

I marched into the spare bedroom, where Yury was reading a book, and told him about the phone call. He denied knowing about the lady. Then he added, "Why would I give some lady my phone number, when I'm married and have a new baby?"

He was convincing, so I believed him. His wandering eye was the subject of many of my stormy conversations with him. As a matter of fact, he brought phone numbers written on small pieces of paper home on a regular basis. Each time I asked for the reason behind the phone numbers, he assured me they were work-related. I told him he needed to buy a small phone and address book to keep numbers from work in.

Even though I didn't like his unfaithful eye and hated those small pieces of paper, I didn't think he would do anything more than just look at other women. After all, he was my shy, quiet, country-raised, hardworking bookworm of a husband. I trusted him. He was my diamond in the rough. He cooked breakfast for us before he went to work in the mornings for many years. How many men out there did that? Plus, after work, he was always at home. He didn't smoke, drink alcohol, or use drugs. All he wanted to do was be alone so he could read books. I trained myself to accept him for who he was. I allowed our home to be his castle, as my mother had taught me.

Yury and I had three beautiful, healthy children together: Jillian, Jaren, and Jasper. After I had Jillian, many of my husband's coworkers came to the hospital to visit us, bearing gifts. It was an unexpected and appreciated surprise for me. It was the first time strangers had taken an interest in celebrating an important milestone in my life. We lived in Mount Pleasant, South Carolina, when Jillian was born. My husband was hoping for a boy, so he had me dress our daughter in a baseball outfit when it was time to bring her home from the hospital. I wanted to dress her in a girlie pink outfit I had brought to the hospital, but I decided to put my husband's happiness above my own. I looked at it as a little compromise for one day.

After Jillian turned two months old, one morning, I woke from a dream about my daddy. In the dream, he called me on the phone and said, "You are my daughter. I want you to know you are my daughter. I'll talk to you later. I'm going to Macon, Georgia."

I thought it was just a crazy dream. When I visited my mom's house later that day, she and my sister Wanda were there. I told them about the dream, and we all laughed about it.

Mom said, "Your daddy used to tell me you weren't his child. He used to say you belonged to the insurance man. I never said anything to you before because I didn't want you to have hate in your heart for him."

I thought that was weird since all the insurance men who visited our neighborhood at the time were white. We chalked up the dream to my eating too late at night or not getting enough sleep. Our conversation went in a different direction, when Mom's phone rang. Mom was on the phone for a while. Her joyful voice shifted, and gradually, her tone became serious. She reached for a pen and notebook. Her breathing slowed as she jotted the information down. With our eyes glued to every movement, we anxiously waited for her to hang up to find out what had happened. She placed the phone on the hook.

Almost trembling, she said, "That was a hospital in Florida." Daddy had moved back to his hometown of Alachua, Florida, when I was eleven years old. I was twenty-three years old during the time of the phone call in April 1993. "They called me to let me know that your daddy died today." Mom's voice dragged.

Wanda and I sat there. Our eyes bugged out of our heads, and our mouths dropped wide open. Mom went on to tell us what had happened. I started coming unglued because of the dream I'd had of my dad that morning. That evening, I returned home and checked the mailbox. My knees went wobbly when I saw a letter addressed to me from Daddy. I had written him a letter more than six months before. I'd told him that I had gotten married to Yury and that we were getting ready to have a baby. It was eerie that I received his letter the day he died, and in addition to the dream, it seemed supernatural.

Daddy's funeral was in Jacksonville, Florida. Yury came home from traveling that Friday evening. He planned to drive us to Florida early Saturday morning so we could arrive way before the 4:30 p.m. scheduled start time. Jillian was only two months old. Since Yury was used to traveling to different places, my oldest sister thought it would be good for all of us to have a car caravan. Since all our siblings with families were going to drive their own vehicles to Florida, they wanted everyone to follow behind our vehicle to make sure no one got lost. I thought it was a good idea, but Yury didn't like it because he wanted to leave Charleston at six o'clock in the morning, and he didn't think my family would be ready to go that early.

He was right. I knew he was tired from traveling, which was understandable. I didn't want to stress him out, so I explained the situation to my family. The next morning, we left our house at 6:00 a.m. on the dot. With tight facial muscles and cold eyes, Yury drove our car as if we were the only ones on the road.

I looked over and asked, "Are you OK?"

He sighed. "Fine."

But he continued to drive as if he were either a bat escaping hell or trying to win the grand prize on the Speedway track. I turned my head toward the window and inwardly asked God to help us. To me, it seemed Yury viewed my dad's funeral as an inconvenience. I felt maybe he would have preferred Dad's death and funeral be postponed until his vacation time kicked in. I decided to just get through the negative emotions he was airing in my face. It was better to keep peace so we wouldn't have strife between us during that sad time of mourning for my family.

Even though we left earlier than everyone else, we made a few stops before going to the funeral home, so my family made it there before we did. As we ate lunch on the way, Yury's countenance became more relaxed. I thought he'd behaved as he had because he must have been hungry. However, as soon as we arrived at the funeral home, the stranger I had seen for the first time that morning came back. Not only was his face tense, but his body and movements were too. I asked again if he was OK. He nodded. The church was in the city of Jacksonville and seated around four hundred people. It was more packed than I'd thought it would be.

At first, it was unclear which side of the church was reserved for family. We didn't see anyone we recognized, so we sat on the right side of the church. Moments later, I heard someone calling my name. I looked up and over to the left and saw my sister Tabitha. Then I saw the rest of our family; they were signaling for us to come over. I nudged Yury with my elbow and pointed to where our family was sitting.

With clenched teeth, he said, "I'm not moving."

My family became more animated, continuing to signal us over.

Rising carefully from my seat with Jillian in my arms, I whispered to Yury, "I'm going over there. Come with me."

When I reached the left side, I looked back, and Yury was still sitting on the right side of the church. I shrugged toward my family. They started calling to him, but he sat there as if they were speaking a foreign language he was unfamiliar with or as if suddenly he had cement weighing him down to the chair.

During the service, I noticed that no pastor or anyone else got up to preach Daddy's eulogy. No one said one word. Soft music played as people viewed his body before taking their seats.

The funeral service and burial didn't last long. Later, we shared a meal together at the church and met family members we had only seen a few times. We also met some for the first time. The most bizarre moment of the funeral was when we met one of Daddy's other six children, whom we had known nothing about. Evidently, they knew about us, though; that was why the other five didn't attend the funeral. They were around the same ages as many of my older brothers and sisters. We all were stunned, but we did our best to stay cordial.

Our cheerful, short, and round aunt Virginia on Daddy's side of the family brought a sturdily built, tall, easy-to-look-at gingerbread-colored man dressed in a formal army uniform decorated with many important patches and medals. He was confident, charismatic, articulate, funny, familiar, and warm. I didn't know where Mama was at that time. Maybe she was conversing with other family members out of our view.

Miles took turns shaking the girls' hands and kissing us on our faces, saying in a kind tone, "Look at my beautiful sisters."

We blushed and said, "Thank you."

He gave our brothers a fancy handshake and hug while saying, "It's good to meet you, brothers." He seemed jolly as he asked, "Who is who? What do you do for a living? Are you married? And how many children do you have?"

We went down the birth lineup of my siblings, starting with Barry. "I'm Barry. I am a general manager at a manufacturing company. I have been married to my lovely bride, Cashlyn, for fourteen years, and we have four children: three girls and one boy."

Miles smiled and said, "Nice to meet you, man."

Next, Tabitha spoke. "I'm Tabitha. I'm a paralegal in a lawyer's office. I have been married to Paine for seventeen years, and we have two daughters."

Miles chuckled and said to Tabitha, "I hope he's nothing like his name."

She smiled and sighed without saying a word.

Then Jace spoke with his deep baritone voice. "I'm Jace. I'm a painter. I tried marriage, but that didn't work so well for me, and I have a son."

Miles encouraged him. "Hang in there, brother. Many men feel the same way too."

After Jace, William introduced himself. "I'm William. I'm a musician. I haven't found my bride-to-be yet and don't have any children yet either."

Miles said, "Don't worry, brother. It's coming. Your wife and your children are coming."

The conversation continued the same way and eventually made it to me. I said, "Hi, Miles."

He smiled and said, "Hi. Who are you?"

I said, "I'm Lewisa. I'm a stay-at-home mom. I'm married to Yury and have been for nine months. We have a two-month-old daughter."

He replied, "Wow! You two have an infant. I don't miss those days. Are you getting much sleep?"

I answered, "No. It's rough sometimes."

Miles nodded while laughing and said, "I know. Well, to be honest, my wife knows better than I do. Anyway, I'm a sergeant major in the army. I'm married to Augustina, the love of my life. She couldn't make it today because she is taking care of our three girls, ages nine, seven, and five, and our two sons, ages three and one. She has her hands full, but thank God we have family in California. That's where we live."

Dad's son with the other lady was a high-ranking officer in the military. That was interesting to me. It was an unusual place to find out our papa was a rolling stone, as the Temptations song said. When we first learned of Dad's secret, I thought a trick was being played on us, but no *Candid Camera* crew ever came out of hiding. Even though we were amiable toward our newfound half-brother during the funeral, the shock was overwhelming for both him and us, so we never kept in touch afterward.

Once we got Mama to ourselves, we inquired about our bonus siblings who'd appeared out of nowhere and about the absence of Daddy's eulogy.

Tabitha sat next to Mama, leaned forward, and inquired with a shaky voice, "Mother, why didn't you tell us about Daddy's other children?"

She shrugged and said, "I heard rumors, but I thought they were lies."

Donna moaned and asked, "Why didn't the pastor preach during Daddy's funeral service?"

Mom sighed. "His sisters said the pastor refused to preach your daddy's eulogy because your dad used to interrupt his services. Whenever the pastor got on a topic that hit a nerve or pierced your daddy's heart regarding negative habits and behaviors of the flesh that we need to allow God to clean up, your dad would jump up while the man was preaching and curse him out. Your daddy would tell the pastor, 'I'm tired of you listening to people who know the dirt I've done from my past. That was when I lived in Charleston. You need to stop airing my dirty laundry in front of all these folks.'"

We were speechless. Her response made me wonder if Daddy's funeral was well attended because people had been impacted by his life in a positive way or because they were curious because they knew about Daddy's outbursts in church. I questioned Mama regarding whether they had come hoping to be entertained or to satisfy their curiosity by seeing what the pastor would say during the eulogy.

As the funeral wound down, Yury started thawing out. It didn't dawn on me until much later that Yury wasn't used to being around a lot of black people and was uncomfortable. Since Mama had taught me to be submissive and supportive of my husband, we never had a conversation about it, because I didn't want to embarrass or irritate him. Our home was peaceful, and I wanted it to stay that way. I wanted him to enjoy coming home.

That explained why he'd looked like a detached, out-of-place stranger during our Lamaze class when I was pregnant with Jillian. He'd sat behind me as if he were paired up with a hungry bear, with fear and discomfort painted all over his face. Plus, he hadn't been totally invested in doing the exercises with me. He'd seemed out of place because we were the only interracial couple there. It hadn't helped that we had curious bystanders watching us as if we were a Great Dane married to a kitten. We'd attended only one class because he didn't want to complete the other classes.

Then, years later, during his twentieth high school reunion in Missouri, he didn't want me to go with him. He wanted to hang out with his childhood friend the whole night at the reunion instead. He did manage to pick me up from his parents' house afterward, so I could spend the night in his hotel room with him. Yury had told me when we were still dating that he had seen black people only on TV when he was growing up and had seen them for the first time in person when he went to college.

A year before the funeral, in 1992, when we were married, there still weren't any black people living in Marshfield, Missouri, where Yury was from. The population at that time was just a little more than two thousand people. Well after the year 2000, on one of our trips, I started seeing black people here and there in the small town. It was exciting for me to see. Since I had gotten used to seeing a large variety of groups of people while growing up in Charleston, it was unnerving to visit a city where citizens were not used to seeing or interacting with black people.

Such was the case once when Jillian was still a baby. Yury, his whole family, and I went to church one Sunday in Marshfield. During the entire service, a white lady sitting toward the front of the church sat with her head turned behind her. She stared at me with her face contorted as if I were a three-headed silver rhinoceros with hair curlers and a fuzzy pink bathrobe. She boldly showed she had never seen a black person up close and personal.

It was hard to concentrate on the sermon that Sunday with someone transmitting piercing, unkind eyes at me. I was surprised she didn't change seats with someone so she could really examine me. It was uncomfortable to have someone act as if I were a supersized freaky alien from Jupiter in church. Strangely, no one around her or me seemed aware of the visual hate attack taking place, not even Yury.

SIX

OVER TIME, I got into a daily routine of taking care of our family and growing baby. My husband had two secretaries available to him and those in his department. His boss had a few personal secretaries of his own. One of my husband's secretaries had a chance to see Jillian in the hospital. His other secretary kept begging to see her, so in July 1993, when Jillian was five months old, Yury asked me to bring Jillian to work to finally satisfy the secretary.

Once I pulled into a parking space, my eyes were greeted by a thick, luscious green lawn. The arrangement of bushes, flowers, and trees was vivid, with every imaginable color, and an enormous water fountain sat in the middle of an immaculate pond. The building was grand, with eye-catching coffee-brown bricks dressed with bold, sleek dark-colored glass windows and doors. As I walked the halls, I could see my reflection in the glossy, well-kept marble floors. I paused for a few minutes to take in the massive double wooden doors bearing the company's name. Once I was inside Yury's department, my sight was showered with tastefully done decor. As my eyes swept all around the large space, I was amazed that I didn't see anyone who looked like me. After I greeted my husband, he introduced me to the lady itching to see our baby.

Of average height, with dark hair and hazel eyes, his secretary rushed over to hold Jillian, saying, "Aw, look at those little cheeks. She is such an adorable baby. And aw, what a cute, girlie outfit." She held our baby until I was ready to go.

I met his boss and other coworkers that day too. Some of them gave me short, blank glances and carried on with their work as if it demanded every bit of their attention. Others seemed to stare as if time had stopped, unwillingly displaying dazed, wide eyes with half-frozen smiles while releasing a "Hello" that dragged on in a startled way, all while they attempted to disguise their reaction to the fact that I was ebony in an ivory world. Of course, I still am, to this day, just a little joke.

A couple of weeks later, on August 1, Yury's birthday, his boss and coworkers celebrated his birthday with a birthday cake and presents. Then, shortly after the celebration, Yury's boss called him into his office and told him he was being laid off.

Yury was out of work for eleven months. During that time, I went to work at Spear Technical College as a public safety dispatcher, which was the same as campus police, to help out. Even though Yury had been laid off, he called it being fired. He would say they'd just dressed up the term by saying *laid off*. He took it pretty hard. His job was where he got his value and self-fulfillment. He said that being unemployed made him feel like he wasn't a man, since he was supposed to be the main support for our family.

I did my best to encourage him and let him know we were going to get through it. I told him how grateful I was that he took care of our family, and I assured him God would make a way for him to get another job.

Yury slouched forward on the couch while rocking back and forth and covered his face with his hands. He sighed and said,

"When I'm working, it makes me feel like I'm making a difference in the world."

"It's not the end. You'll find work again," I said to cheer him up.

He looked at me through the opening of his fingers and said, "You don't understand. Working makes me feel like a man. It gives me purpose. I'm the one who is supposed to take care of our family. How can I do that without a job?" He groaned.

Optimistically, I told him, "You are the smartest man I know. You will get another job. Just be patient, and let's trust God to help you."

As I sat beside him on the couch, he placed his head on my lap and moaned, "Why is this happening to me? And when will God help me?"

I stroked his back and shoulder soothingly and said, "I appreciate the way you provided for our family. One day you will be able to do that again."

He responded with a half smile, "I hope so."

"It will happen," I said with a confident nod.

I prayed for him and our family, and both sides of our families joined in that prayer. Before the layoff, our routine consisted of Yury going to work in the morning when he was in town or being gone for three days or up to three weeks whenever he had to visit his customers. If he worked from the local office, when he came home, we would eat dinner together while watching TV or a movie. After that, he would go off into one of the spare bedrooms to read a book. After washing the dishes, I would go into the great room and, later, the family room to watch Christian television, specifically the Linking Christians Incorporated station in 1993.

On Yury's days off, we would watch TV a couple of times together, usually during lunch and dinner.

As per our routine, after I served Yury's food to him as he sat on the couch, sometimes he would smile and say, "Thank you, dear!" which was his pet name for me.

I would reply, "You are welcome," and then we would sit there eating and watching TV.

Then he would go off into the spare bedroom during the other parts of the day to read a book. Depending on what season it was, we went to hockey games or baseball games. On our typical sports outing, I dressed our daughter, Jillian, in something pink, sparkly, or girlie-looking. Sports were Yury's favorite form of entertainment. He concentrated on the game. I went along to keep him company, eat the food, and watch people in the crowd roam around. I enjoyed seeing people of all colors, shapes, and sizes share the same space. It fascinated me. Yury and I didn't show affection toward each other in public because we had never seen it modeled before us by our parents.

Yury also enjoyed nature walks in the deep woods since he had grown up in the country. It was an activity he had partaken in since he was a little boy. I only went with him a few times. I am not fond of nature in the forest. I prefer to stay out of snake and spider territory. I think it's insane to go roaming around for pleasure on the turf of Jason from *Friday the Thirteenth*. Plus, during one of our wilderness adventures, I swore I saw something swimming in a lake we were passing by. It looked as if it could have been a baby alligator. I was scared out of my mind and more than ready to escape mountain-men country. If Grizzly Adams had come walking toward us, it wouldn't have surprised me at all.

Yury did his part to play with and hold Jillian, but there wasn't a lot of verbal communication happening between us.

We visited Yury's parents annually. His sisters and their children would meet us at his parents' house. Early in our marriage, we would stop to visit his brother and his brother's family in Arkansas before going on to Missouri. I loved Yury's family. They accepted me and our children with open arms. Once his dad got over the initial shock before we were married, everything was good. When Yury made a phone call to tell them about me for the first time, it went a little like this:

"Hey, Dad." Yury exhaled.

His dad answered, "Well, hi, Yury! What's going on with you?"

Yury said, "I'm just calling to let you know I'm getting married. And that she is black and pregnant with my baby."

His dad paused. Then he released some spicy, tongue-tingling words. After he regained his composure, he said, "Well, I guess since you're marrying her, you must really love her. Okay, when do we get to meet her?"

After the phone call, Yury told me what his dad had said.

Anyway, Yury was faithful to share the plans with me for our trip to see his parents. During those times, he talked the most. Also, he shared news regarding any changes, such as a pay raise, work-related training dates out of town, or downsizing at work. He never talked to me about the people he worked with in detail. He didn't like to mix his work and home life together.

Then again, for some reason that totally escaped me, he enjoyed ruffling the feathers of some of the women he worked with by saying, "My wife had better have the house cleaned and my dinner ready and on the table when I get home!" As he shared that with me as if it were a joke, he'd cackle hard until his face turned red.

He was amused by the women's disgusted reactions as they lit into him, giving him a piece of their mind.

A short, petite woman wearing her hair in cornrows sucked her teeth and then scolded him. "You'd better get out of here with that foolishness! Your wife is not your slave!" She frowned.

Another lady with tinted glasses and a long, crimpy wig chimed in while shaking her head and index finger from side to side. "Oh,

I know you didn't go there! If I were your wife, I'd tell you to get a broom, a mop, and cleaning products and help clean the house! And make your own dinner and put it on the table! Who do you think you are, talking to your wife like that?"

Yury laughed and said, "My wife stays home all day. I just said that to get you stirred up. Relax. I'm just kidding around."

Some of the women responded with relief. One said more calmly, "Well, if she's home all day, then she should have the house clean and your dinner ready."

The lady with the wig looked Yury up and down and said, "Phew! You almost made me act like a fool up in here."

After work, he would say to me, "I have to talk all day when I'm working. When I come home, all I want to do is relax. Don't expect me to be your girlfriend. If you need someone to do things with and have conversations with, go out and get some girlfriends." He went on to say, "When we were dating, you promised you wouldn't try to change me."

Blinking a few times as I gasped, I said, "Yury, I left my family so you could find work and be fulfilled in that way. I left everyone I love, trust, and did things with for you. I only know you and our children here. I'm cautious when it comes to letting other people into my and our lives. I have to be a guardian for our children while they are young and helpless. I'm not going to make you do anything you don't want to do. Besides, I still talk to my family on the phone. I guess that will do until I meet people I'm comfortable with."

He replied, "Well, good, dear. I have never communicated a lot unless I have to. It's not you. I've always been this way."

I nodded, trying to be understanding, and left the room. Of course, he had his own way to let me know when he wanted attention in the bedroom. He never verbalized that either.

On the other hand, when we visited Yury's family or when his friends came to visit us, he transformed into a new person. In that quick moment, their presence was like magical pixie dust being mysteriously sprinkled on the top of a fairy-tale character's head in a story. Yury became alive. Around them, his eyes leaped for joy like shimmering lights waving and twirling in the distance on a dark moonlit night. He talked more, smiled more, and laughed more too.

There were also quiet times around them as well. Yury had grown up watching his whole family read books and magazines instead of watch a lot of TV. That was how his love of reading and books had developed. When they were through talking, they would sit somewhere and read. However, when Yury was surrounded by those he was closest to, I saw another side of him I didn't know.

There were some conversations I wasn't privy to when he was among his family and friends. For example, after returning to the house from a walk, before entering, I could hear a fully engaged conversation; however, as soon as I entered the house, words were drastically cut off, and everyone sat around as if he or she had just swallowed a canary. I ran into the same situation a number of times, and their behavior was puzzling to me.

Once we were alone, I confronted Yury to find out if he had a problem with me that he was sharing with them. He always denied talking about me or our problems to his family and friends. I was unaware we even had problems that concerned him early in our marriage. I would have believed him if I hadn't gotten displeasing stares from those closest to him. Some people were good at projecting flaming looks of destruction.

I'd thought married life would be slightly different from what I was experiencing. When I saw married life on TV, it seemed much more exciting than what was before me. As time passed, I asked my three married sisters if what I was facing was what being married looked like. When all three of them said yes, I decided to just settle in and do my best to be a good wife. We lived in Mount Pleasant, South Carolina, which was just a hop, skip, and jump from

Charleston. Getting Yury to visit my mom's house every Sunday for dinner, a tradition for many of my older siblings, was like getting a scared child to go to the dentist.

He approached special family events outside our small immediate family with disinterest and scorn. Either I had to drag him, or he flat-out refused to go. He had the same attitude about my sister and her husband visiting our house on a regular basis. He thought they should call before they came and not pop up whenever they wanted. In Mom's house, family was always welcomed. I did what I could to smooth things over.

When it came to my family, he wanted to only spend time with them his way, which meant being tucked away in the living room on the couch, reading a book, until dinnertime. He seemed more at ease about our differences in the presence of only my family and his family. Outside our controlled environment, the tension in his face and body always told on him.

After eleven months of being unemployed, Yury started working for a small chemical corporation. His new job was an hour away from Mount Pleasant. He was thrilled to be able to provide for our family again. We quickly got settled into our new daily routine. Then, one evening, Yury called to say he would be coming home a little late. A coworker's car wouldn't start, and he was giving her a ride home.

I said, "OK."

I was a married woman, so naturally, when my husband mentioned another woman, I wanted to know all the details. When Yury returned, I allowed him to relax for a little while. After dinner and the movie we watched while eating, I asked questions about his coworker. He told me she was black. He had been driving through the parking lot and noticed she couldn't start her car. I asked a lot of probing questions. For example, did they work in the same department?

"No" was his answer for almost every question.

He was just being a Good Samaritan, so I dropped the subject. Time went on.

Yury and I went grocery shopping on Saturday mornings. One Saturday, while at the store, we met the lady he had given a ride home. His mood was melancholy and serious instead of upbeat and happy, as it usually was whenever he saw family or longtime friends. He introduced her to me. We said hello and exchanged some light talk. Then we went our separate ways. I stared at Yury, trying to read his body language.

He looked at me and said, "You don't have anything to worry about."

Still studying him, I answered, "Good."

After that day, Yury didn't want to go grocery shopping together anymore. I didn't question the sudden change; I just brushed it off. Plus, since I hadn't grown up seeing a good marriage from my mom and dad, I treated my husband as if he were an exquisite, mysterious, rare creature. I admired him and didn't want to spook him and have him run away. Since he was smooth and charming and looked me in the eye with a straight face as he spoke, I took his demeanor as a sign of honesty.

Meanwhile, Jillian turned two years old, and she had a healthy vocabulary and knew her ABCs, colors, shapes, and how to count to ten. I read children's books to her every day, often many times a day, starting at six months. I also had her watching children's Christian videos and educational videos regularly. She absorbed information as if her brain were a sponge. It was as if she craved information and couldn't get enough. It paid off once she started school. She was on the honor roll until she was promoted to the eighth grade and decided that socializing was more important than maintaining exceptional grades.

When *The Lion King* came out on VHS in 1994, Jillian probably watched that movie about a thousand times. We bought three copies—one was kept at our house, the second was at my mom's house, and the third was at Donna and Phillip's house—because for the longest time, that was all Jillian wanted to watch. She copied Mufasa's big, powerful roar after watching the movie so often. Whenever she felt uncomfortable around strange people or became upset, she automatically turned into a baby Mufasa. At least she didn't pick up Pumbaa's gas passing. She could speak in plain, understandable English at age two.

She and I went to church every Sunday with my family. I didn't want to be a nagging wife, so I decided to allow Yury to decide when he would join us. Jillian noticed Yury never went with us. She asked him why. He told her he would go soon. One Sunday shortly after their conversation, Yury honored his promise. We all sat in the middle section of the church. We stood for praise and worship and prayer. Yury was as stiff as a board.

"Are you OK?" I asked.

He nodded. Finally, we sat down to hear the preacher's sermon. Yury wore a suit to church. About twenty minutes into the message, I saw him take his jacket off. A moment later, he loosened his tie. Then he took the tie off. After a few seconds, he unbuttoned his dress shirt. Then he took it off. I glanced over and tried not to appear alarmed. I didn't want him to think what he was doing was bizarre. I was trying to look for the positive while his striptease show was going on. He paused for a moment.

I had something to be glad about: at least he still had his undershirt on. Before long, next, he unbuckled his belt, and a few seconds later, he unbuttoned his pants. I didn't know where things were going. It didn't look good. Finally, he took his shoes off. Since I was jolted and embarrassed by his behavior, I didn't look around to see if anyone was watching him perform his striptease act.

When the sermon was over, I was happy and relieved. I wanted to stand up and yell, "Thank you, Jesus!" I'm sure it saved us from having to see Yury sit there in church in his birthday suit. *Thank you, God!* He got redressed, and then we went home. The whole time he was getting undressed, I never looked around to see if everyone around us was astonished by his actions.

Mom, my sisters, and my brothers said later, "I didn't see him taking his clothes off. Maybe God hid that from us."

Once we were home, he told Jillian, "I went to church for you today. I don't know when I'll go back again. When that time comes, I will let you know."

I was grateful he had come that day. He'd kept a promise he made to our daughter, and that made me smile. I figured God was working on him in church. I decided to allow God to do what he knew was best. Even though I was curious why Yury had behaved the way he had, I never brought the subject up, because I didn't want to run him off. The memory of growing up in a black neighborhood and not seeing many black men stick around for long in their wives' or girlfriends' lives was still on my mind. I mostly had seen black women raising their children by themselves. I had a husband, and I wanted to do anything and everything I could to keep him.

When Jillian was three years old, we found out I was pregnant. We were faced with a little scare before Jaren was born, but God brought us through it. *Thank you, Jesus!* After one of my regularly scheduled doctor's appointments while I was pregnant with him, the doctor was concerned Jaren might be born with Edwards syndrome, a birth defect that affected organ development, caused babies' heads to be small, and possibly caused other physical deformities. Most babies born with Edwards syndrome usually only lived for one year. My doctor wanted me to have an amniocentesis to find out for sure if Jaren was at risk for the infirmity. The doctor asked us if we wanted to abort the pregnancy if the results came back positive for the condition.

We said no.

He warned us there was a small chance we could lose the baby due to the amniotic fluid test. A flood of emotions came rushing in. I went to church for prayer and contacted some of the prayer lines at various ministries. I knew God was with me when some of the ladies at church and different ministries prayed with me.

It took almost two weeks to get the results back from the test. When my doctor called to share the results, he told us the test had come back clear. It was the greatest news I had ever heard. I thanked God for showing up and coming through for us. He lifted a heavy burden from my mind.

Meanwhile, Yury had worked for the small chemical company for a little more than a year. He was concerned he had gone as far as he could with the company. He had already reached the highest cap on the pay scale for his position. There was only one more position he could be promoted to, but the person who held that position was just a few years older than Yury, and it didn't look like he was planning to go anywhere anytime soon. Yury became unhappy because there wasn't any room for growth in his job, so we agreed he should look for work somewhere else. His happiness was important to me.

Since Yury was a high-salary worker, he used headhunters to help him find jobs around the United States with corporations that catered to his salary needs. Of course, that meant the possibility of my having to move away from my family should Yury gain employment out of state.

Before we'd started dating, I'd told Yury I had no intention of leaving Charleston or my family. My social relationship with my family was irreplaceable. Losing that connection was not an option. There were a number of people I'd chosen not to go out with because they were in the military. I hadn't wanted to have to make the choice of leaving my family if the relationship became serious and led to marriage. Yury had assured me he was making Charleston his home, and that was one of the reasons I'd continued to see him. As time went on, in December 1995, Yury was offered a job in Macon, Georgia, working for a well-established manufacturing company, because growth wasn't available at the chemical company he was with.

The new company was good to us. They agreed to buy our house in Mount Pleasant, South Carolina, within an agreed-upon time period once it went on the market, so we wouldn't have to be concerned about selling it. But thanks be to God, our house sold quickly. The company paid for packing and moving our belongings to Georgia. Also, they gave Yury a $10,000 bonus to help us get settled in Macon. Something Yury said his boss said to him after he turned in his resignation and finished his shift on his last day of work struck me as a little peculiar.

His boss was angry when Yury was leaving and said to him, "Good riddance to you and your fat wife!"

I scrunched my face and asked, "Why would your boss say something like that to you? I've never met him. How did he know I'm overweight? Did you tell him?"

Yury answered, "No. I don't know. The guy was just being a jerk. But don't worry, baby; I defended your honor by gathering my belongings quickly and dramatically like I was ticked off. Then I stomped out the door." He chuckled.

The incident gnawed at me, so I talked it over with my mom and sisters. They agreed the event sounded fishy.

Mom twisted her lips and said, "If Yury didn't tell his boss about you, then the only logical way for him to have found out about you is through the young lady Yury gave a ride home a while back." She shook her head. "We don't have all of the details here. Something is not right."

During that time, we were more than three years into our marriage. I'd had Jillian, who was three years old, and was pregnant with Jaren. When Yury told me something, since I hadn't caught him telling lies, I made myself believe him. The only things I saw him do around our house were read books, watch TV, play with our daughter, and do minor maintenance and repair to our house and lawn when needed. Around me, he perfectly portrayed the role of a family man. Plus, I didn't see any concrete evidence of infidelity, so I wasn't looking for it.

Moving to Macon, Georgia, in 1995 and giving up my family was a sacrifice demonstrating my true love for Yury and an act of goodwill in which I put his needs before my own. During the grieving process after moving away from my family, to cope with the loss of those relationships I cherished, I turned to Breyers Rocky Road or Heavenly Hash ice cream. I was overweight anyway, so I didn't think it could do anymore harm.

It didn't take long for us to settle into living in a new city and state. Yury enjoyed his new job. He felt satisfied with his new line of work and his salary. There was plenty of room for advancement, so he couldn't have been happier. We moved there two years after the dream in which Daddy had told me he was moving there. Our move seemed divine.

Before long, Yury received various promotions and pay raises. The company paid their employees well. We were living better than we had before, better than I ever had imagined I would. I felt blessed and favored. I thanked God continuously. Everything seemed wonderful. I was going to a fantastic church and met many kindhearted people there. Jaren was born in April 1996. He was a healthy baby boy.

Once Jaren turned two years old and started walking and running around, one day, while playing with Jillian, I realized the little baby boy God had shown me in my dreams when I was brokenhearted over Kent was right in front of my eyes. He was the baby boy I had seen in my closet. I was amazed. God had given me a real glimpse into my future. *God is amazing!*

Around that time, I met Mia and her two-year-old son, Flare, at Rising Hope Church. She was five foot two, with shiny, spiky one-inch black hair. Mia was athletic and could have easily been the next fitness guru if her ambition had driven her there. She looked like a cute life-size baby doll. Mia was a single mother new to Georgia from Las Vegas, Nevada. She'd left her whole family in Nevada for an employment opportunity in Georgia. We hit it off instantly. I was determined to look out for her since neither of us had extended family in Macon, Georgia.

We met one Sunday when she came to pick up her son from the nursery and saw Flare playing with my son, Jaren. They were both two years old. They played as if they knew each other, which made Mia happy she'd left him there. Mia stood in the back corner of the room with her arms folded, showing a peaceful grin on her face.

I noticed her watching the babies play together and asked, "Is he your son?"

Mia smiled wider and answered, "Yes. His name is Flare." She looked at me and said, "Since our babies play so well together, would you like to schedule a playdate for them?"

Watching our children play, I said, "Yes. That would be great. When would you like to start?"

She thought for a minute and said, "Let's exchange phone numbers first. I'll call you soon on my day off, so we can discuss the details together."

I agreed, and our friendship started that day. Flare was the same age as Jaren, and Mia and I had a few things in common. We both came from large families of eleven children. She had seven brothers and three sisters, as I did. Her family was poor like mine, and both our households were filled with love, discipline, and closeness. I was thrilled when she accepted my invitation for dinner at our house.

Before the appointed day, Yury reluctantly welcomed the idea of her coming to our house. Yet he painted on a pleasant face when she arrived at our door.

Once dinner was ready, as we all sat together to partake of the meal, Yury began to warm up. He aimed hundreds of questions Mia's way. I sat and listened in amusement as she answered Yury's inquiries. He grinned, smiled, and laughed from his belly. I was chipper because Yury was being thoroughly entertained by Mia's answers, stories, and personality. I was too.

The evening was lively compared to the quiet setting we normally had when it was just Yury, me, and our children. Sure, Yury and I would be in front of the TV, but that didn't make up for communicating with each other. I only got to see his dynamic temperament once a year around his family and friends. That was the best part of him, but it was reserved for occasions when he was in the presence of those who had known him way back when. Unfortunately, it didn't seem as if I and our life together fell into that category.

Yury wasn't as accepting of Zoe and Nick, an interracial couple from church. Zoe was black, four foot eleven, and slender. Nick was white, five foot six, and muscular. I thought Yury would be happy God had brought a couple into our lives who shared a relationship experience similar to ours. I was. When I invited them to our house months before Mia came into our lives, Yury had an "I just sucked a sour lemon" expression on his face in their presence. Yury's eyes just about bugged out of his head whenever Zoe and Nick talked about their love for God, as if he was convinced they had escaped out of straitjackets and from a psychiatric hospital.

Regarding another person who entered our lives, he flat-out said he didn't like Sage. She was the first neighbor in our neighborhood to reach out to me. Sage got me out of the house regularly to go on girlie excursions with our children before our husbands came home from work, and she didn't take no for an answer. Her two children were the same ages as mine. She was the first white woman I had ever seen discipline her children the way most black women I knew did. If they misbehaved in public, Sage would yank out a small paddle from her pocketbook and strike them while she verbally addressed the unwanted behavior. The first time I witnessed it, I was caught off guard, but I was impressed.

She reminded me of how my mama took care of business. Sage had beautiful, long natural dark red hair and stand-out green eyes. She was tall and had an hourglass figure that made men turn around to watch her walk. Plus, she didn't mind sashaying what her mama had given her. Fashion was her passion, so she purposefully adorned herself as if she were preparing for a close-up photo shoot. Yury thought she behaved as if she wore the pants in her family.

Yury acted as if another acquaintance of mine, Kyra, who was quiet, shy, plain-looking, and a stay-at-home mom like me, didn't exist. He didn't give any of them the time of day. Mia became a regular guest in our house. I began babysitting Flare so she could work a second job for extra money. Everything was going well, or so I thought.

Unbeknownst to me, Mia's friendship was becoming more meaningful and endearing to Yury than I realized. Eventually, whenever she came to our house, she no longer asked for me. She came looking for Yury.

Mia called me on the phone on a Thursday and asked, "Would you mind if I come over for a little while Saturday?"

I said, "That would be great! Come on over." She came over regularly, so it wasn't a big deal.

Saturday came. After Mia rang the doorbell, I opened the door.

She said, "Hi, Lewisa." Then she came in and walked past me with eyes searching side to side in the living room and family room. She asked, "Where is Yury?"

I tilted my head to one side, squinted, twisted my lips, and answered, "He is in the bathroom right now. He'll be out soon."

Mia sat on the couch, but before I could ask her what her visit was all about, Yury walked into the living room.

He smiled at her and said in a cheerful tone, "Well, hi, Mia! What brings you here?"

She stood up, showing all her pearly white teeth, and replied, "I have to talk to you about something. Can we step outside for a few minutes?"

Yury laughed and responded, "Uh-oh! That doesn't sound too good. What's going on?"

She said, "Don't worry. It's not a bad thing. I just want to ask you a question and get a man's perspective."

As he headed out the door that led to the backyard with Mia, I had a blank stare on my face and was speechless. I stood by the door to eavesdrop, but I couldn't hear anything. They were in my view but too far in the center of the one-acre yard for me to hear them. As I saw them talk, I thought to myself, *I trust my husband. I know my husband. He is a good man.* Thinking those thoughts calmed my nerves.

A few minutes later, Yury strolled into the house with a huge beam on his face, acting like a schoolboy in love. Mia drove away in her black Subaru wagon. Yury walked toward our bedroom, and I intersected his path, coming from the foyer, near the living room.

I faced him head-on, saying, "Well, what's the story with Mia? She didn't tell me what's going on."

He looked straight into my eyes and said, "You have nothing to worry about, dear. She only wanted advice on whether she should go out with a man who asked her out or not. She asked me because she wanted a male perspective. Normally, she would ask her brothers, but she was hoping I would say something helpful."

I cleared my throat and then replied, "I wish she had talked to me about wanting to talk to you about her situation first." I shook my head and finger and continued. "If you are new acquaintances or friends with someone, there are certain boundaries you don't cross with each other's significant other."

I waited for a while to make sure I wasn't getting my signals crossed. After a number of visits and after seeing how Yury became overly eager about her visits, I knew I had to take action. I hadn't picked up any signals that something was going on between Yury and Mia, so I hadn't been suspicious beforehand. Now I wondered.

I knew I had to put things on ice after Yury asked me, "How would you feel if I asked Mia to go out to lunch with me?"

Abstaining from violence and profanity, because that was unladylike, I locked my eyes on him and said, "If you even think about asking Mia out to lunch, I will get flaring mad."

Yury quietly left the family room with unease glued to his face. He hibernated for hours in the living room with his face hidden behind a book. I immediately went into cautious mode. I called all hands on deck. It was time to batten down the hatches and sound the alarm. It was time to go to war. Love is a battlefield—like the song. I had to make sure our marriage would survive the strong winds of the storm Yury didn't seem to understand we had just drifted into. I drew back from the friendship with Mia to get our house and our relationship back in order. It took a while, but we were able to put the focus back on our marriage.

I heard teaching from a minister who had done an intimacy challenge with his wife, so I decided to put Yury through the challenge. Yury was excited about it. We agreed we were going to have sex for fifteen consecutive days and nights in a row. To win the challenge, you had to be able to pull it off without backing out from exhaustion. The winner would get a chance to give instruction regarding what the next date night should be like.

During day eight, I planned a surprise romantic candlelit morning. Soft music was playing, strawberries were laid out, and I had on black lingerie. Once Yury entered our house at six thirty in the morning from working the night shift, I waited for him on a blanket spread out on the family room floor. The lights were off, and flames from candles swayed and danced as he made his way closer to his morning treat. Yury's face lit up.

"What's going on here?" he asked with a grin covering his entire face.

I answered, "It's only day eight, so I thought I would spice things up a bit."

Before Yury's eyes adjusted to the dimly lit room, he asked, "Is Mia down there on the floor with you?"

I snapped, "Why would you think I would have Mia on this floor waiting for you? I would not invite Mia to be with me and my husband or just my husband! I am not that kind of person! I didn't think you were that kind of person!"

Yury laughed and said, "You know I'm just playing. I couldn't see in the dark for a little while. I don't know what I was saying. I didn't mean it."

He became Mr. Charming. After a bunch of sweet-talking, we finished the challenge, but we were both exhausted. The challenge ended after that night's session. We both called it a truce. To make up for his thoughtless remark about Mia, Yury showered me with fascinating entertainment excursions, taking me to an array of ballets, concerts, and plays, for more than two years. He orchestrated his apology with perfection that carried our relationship to a deeper place.

Later, we entered our two children into school. Jillian, now age five, was going to kindergarten, and Jaren, at age two, was in preschool. Since I always had wanted to go to college but hadn't gotten a chance to go before marriage, Yury agreed for me to go while the children were out of the house. Despite hearing comments about college being challenging from various people I met in the community, I was able to do better than I'd thought I would, except in algebra, but Yury had a great understanding of math. He ended up tutoring me. However, as time went on, he got stumped on some of my assignments. That was when I reached out for help from Lewton.

He was white and five foot eleven, with a medium build, wavy black hair, steel-blue eyes with lush lashes, and a face that would have attracted Hollywood. Lewton was a bright guy a few years younger than I was. We had some of the same classes. He was enthusiastic about school and helping people. Yury welcomed having a break from my questions. He acted as if Lewton were a gift from God sent to give him some peace. Lewton and I had one face-to-face study session at school. The rest of them were done online through emails.

Out of the blue, Yury said, "Hey, why don't you go out to lunch with Lewton? From what you've told me, he seems like a nice guy."

I folded my arms across my chest, scrunched up my face, and said, "No! I'm married. We are married. Why would I want to eat lunch with another man?"

He cleared his throat. "I know that, but there's nothing wrong with an innocent lunch with someone you enjoy being around."

I narrowed my eyes and said, "I take marriage seriously. I am not going to do that, because that can lead to other things."

Yury said, "It doesn't have to. Doesn't it make you feel good that someone else is giving you attention other than your husband?"

I responded, "No, I'm not looking for attention from other men. I'm not interested in doing anything that's going to make our family fall apart."

Yury sighed and said, "It doesn't have to."

I said, "The answer is no! The Bible clearly says in Proverbs 6:27–28 NIV that if you play with fire, you will be burned, and my mama liked reminding us about that too."

Throwing his hands up in the air, Yury said, "Yeah, yeah, yeah, yeah," as he left the room in frustration.

To make sure temptation wouldn't rear its ugly head in me, I started talking to Lewton about God. I knew that would be one way to make sure no ulterior motives were discovered during our tutoring sessions. It was also a good way to make sure I didn't fall into a trap and disgrace myself and shame my family. He probably thought I was trying to convert him. Lewton was not in favor of hearing about God.

During our tutoring time on the computer, I wrote to Lewton, asking, "Do you know Jesus as your Lord and Savior?"

He emailed back, "Why are you asking me that?"

I responded, "Because God helped me get through some devastating times in my life, including a heartbreak. During that time, I buried myself in reading his Word, the Bible, and God actually reached out to me. He started sharing things with me in dreams."

Lewton wrote, "Hmm."

I wrote, "Would you like to say anything else?"

I didn't get another response. Immediately, he avoided me as if I were a carrier of the bubonic plague. He canceled his email account and steered clear of me at school, even though we had a couple of classes together. I couldn't believe it. I would have understood his reaction a little better if I had shared with him that I was a Satan worshipper who ate babies and drank people's blood. But at least speaking about God or Jesus in the company of a possible unhealthy association certainly was a temptation repellent, which was a good thing.

After I ended my friendship with Mia, she and I, and she and Yury, drifted apart and never communicated again.

SEVEN

THREE MONTHS SLID by faster than a professional baseball player stealing first, second, and third base. Jasper, our third child, was getting close to turning one. It was 1999. All of a sudden, Yury became health conscious. He abandoned his first love of reading books after work. Instead, he was driven to change his appearance. He lifted weights regularly, jogged after work, and added protein products to his diet. His physique was becoming more chiseled, refined, and muscular. His waist shrank. He was in his best shape ever.

I began admiring his ripped body. He looked good. I found myself thinking, *Come on over here, you fine, sexy thing.* That way of thinking was on the wild side according to my strict, ladylike southern upbringing. Then the dreams began and kept invading my sleep.

In the dream, Yury had a rendezvous with a thin, blonde white lady in a bedroom I didn't recognize. They had their fill of lust and did everything imaginable and then some. After waking up from the dream, I was disturbed. It felt real. The dream stirred feelings of anger, disgust, and hysteria in me. The whole morning, I operated out of a cloud of grief. I struggled with how the dream made me feel about Yury versus what I knew about him. I took a few minutes to think about any possible clues I might have missed that would indicate Yury was cheating on me. No clues came to my mind. I had already cut ties with Mia, so I thought we were in the clear. I swept the dream and the way it made me feel to the back of my consciousness.

After tucking the dream away, by nightfall, I was back to my original state of mind. *Don't eat too late. Check. Go to bed at a reasonable time. Most doctors recommend getting at least eight hours of sleep. Check.* I fluffed my pillow and thought, *It's 10:00 p.m., so when the alarm rings at 6:00 a.m., I should have the correct amount of sleep in.* To my disbelief, that night, I had the same dream.

When I woke up, I tried to brush it away again. It was hard to bury it in the back of my mind that time, though. I didn't want to ruffle any feathers, so I thought about the dream but kept it to myself. It was beginning to bother me. I went on with my day as best as I could. I didn't know what to do. My detective radar didn't pick up any abnormal activities. Still, lo and behold, when I went to sleep again, I had the same dream. This time, I couldn't ignore it. When morning came, I allowed Yury to sleep since he was still on the night shift. Once he was awake, I allowed him to go through his daily routine. Once he was ready to relax, I went into the family room, where he was reading a book. I sat on the couch across from the La-Z-Boy chair Yury was in.

I opened the conversation with "We need to talk."

Yury closed his book, placed it in his lap, and looked at me. "What is it?" he asked.

I took a deep breath and said, "Is there anything you need to tell me? I have had the same dream three times in a row that you are cheating on me with a thin, blonde white lady."

Yury laughed. "You should know that's just a dream. You know I like black women."

I shook my head. "No, it was too real. I've never had the same dream three nights in a row before."

He cleared his throat and laughed again. "I don't know what to tell you. Nothing like that is going on."

"Then what is going on?" I asked. "Every now and then, God shows me things in dreams. There was something to that dream."

Dropping his guard, Yury said, "Your dream doesn't apply to me. But since we are talking, what do you think it means if someone—a female—keeps coming around to a man's office to tell him hello?"

I answered, "I would say she has some kind of interest in you."

He was lost in thought and said, "It can't be. She hasn't said she is interested in me. Although she did write the word *yuck* on my tobacco-spit cup that I left on my desk. Why do you think she would do that?"

I said, "If she is coming around your office regularly, telling you hello all the time, and wrote the word *yuck* on your spit cup, I believe she is interested in you. It is a subtle way of flirting. This is my question to you: Did you give her a reason to be interested in you?"

Yury shook his head and said, "No. I mean, I'm nice to her. Every time I see her, I tell her hi too, but I tell everyone I see at work hi."

"You are going to have to be careful with the way you handle this situation. You can't allow her to continue to think there may be something between the two of you. You need to cut things off now. You need to stop going where you usually see her, and whenever she seeks you out, you need to be completely professional. If you don't shut it down now, this could cause problems and threaten our family life," I warned.

"You are reading more into it than is there. I'm sure she is not trying to take me away from you and our family." Yury snickered.

Days turned to nights more times than I remembered. Yury was still keeping up his physical routine and still looking good. Out of the blue, Yury planned a couple of meals he wanted to take for lunch for everyone in his department. The first meal was pizza he ordered for them, and the second order was on a different day. It was a sweet dessert.

Then, during Christmas, he bought a large amount of gift cards to pass out at work. In all of the seven years we had been married, it was the first time he'd wanted to feed and give gifts to everybody he worked with. Before, he always had been concerned about money. Even his family referred to him as a tightwad. My scent-of-a-woman antenna went up when I started seeing Yury smiling all the time. Plus, he was spending money he ordinarily wouldn't have spent. He was happy too—too happy. I only saw him act happy around his family, friends, and Mia. I was suspicious. I knew I needed to confront him for more information about his new person of interest.

"So what's the lady's name at work?" I asked.

He said, "Why do you need to know her name? She didn't do anything to you. You don't need to cause any trouble for her."

My voice went slightly higher. "I have no intention of causing trouble for her. I just want to know her name. You changed the way you look. You want to buy things for people at work now. That's not how you usually act. Something is going on."

Disagreeing, Yury responded, "Trust me. Nothing is going on. You don't need to go drag her into your jealous-wife rant."

"If nothing is going on, then tell me her name. I'm not going to bother her. Since you said I can trust you, tell me her name," I said.

Yury opened his book and put it in front of his eyes, "No, I know you. You want to start something with her," he said.

"I have never started anything with anybody before in my life. I just want to know you are honest enough to share her name with me. I won't contact her," I told him.

He sneered, "No, that's not happening."

I went into full search mode. I looked at every file and folder on the computer. I inspected every printed piece of paper. I examined every handwritten piece of paper. I scoured the clothes he took off after work. I pried through his lunch box. I sifted through his briefcase. I probed his collection of more than three thousand books, which he kept in a wall of bookcases in our formal living room in our 2,500-square-foot house. My investigative effort paid off, because I discovered her name way back in the desk drawer in our living room. It was taped to some papers I had already scanned. Her name was Asha. I felt pleased with myself. It had taken only three hours to find the evidence. I returned to the back of the family room, beaming with joy.

"Would you like to talk a little more about Asha?" I said.

Yury widened his eyes. He spit tobacco into his spit cup and clumsily placed the cup on the table beside him. His hand trembled for a moment, and he said, "I've never heard of that name before. Who is Asa?" He pronounced every syllable slowly.

I corrected him. "Her name is Asha. You do know her. You had her information taped to some important papers in the desk."

He looked down and said, "Do you want to talk? Let's talk. Nothing happened between us. She's married and has children. What I told you already is the only thing that happened. She is not coming around as much anymore. You have nothing to worry about. She is married, and I am married too. Nothing is going to happen between us."

"Yury, you can't play around with things like this. This is how affairs get started. For the sake of our family, you are going to have to let her know you plan to stay faithful to me. You need to make sure she knows she shouldn't visit you anymore," I said.

He raised his voice. "OK, I'll handle it! Don't do a thing to contact her!"

Yury dragged his feet in handling the situation with Asha. More time passed, and he still came home daydreaming; smiling big, goofy grins; and giving 150 percent to his newly chiseled body. One night, as we talked, Yury became overly relaxed. The words passed through his lips before he could stop them.

"I think I love her," he said as he exhaled, lost in his thoughts.

My face contorted, and my stomach soured as my hand held my chest. I said, "We are going to fix this right now! I want to talk to your supervisor at work!"

Yury came back to reality. "Why? You don't need to do that."

"Either we fix it, or I'm leaving with our children!" I said.

With his eyes dropping to the floor, Yury said, "I don't want you to leave. Please, and don't take my children away. I don't want you all to go."

"OK, then that means we are going to ask for a transfer to another department, so our marriage can be saved!" I said.

"Aah! OK!" He left the room, exasperated.

After a bumpy, restless, and rocky night of processing the avalanche that had overtaken my marriage, morning arrived, greeting me with a throbbing headache. I lounged on the sofa as words swarmed my mind in preparation for my phone call with Mrs. Mitchell, Yury's boss. At 9:00 a.m. sharp, Mrs. Mitchell and I discussed the situation at hand. Her voice was warm, friendly, and understanding.

She said, "Yes, I sympathize with your concerns. It's not a problem. I'll have Yury assigned to a new department as soon as he returns to work."

"Thank you so much, Mrs. Mitchell! I truly apologize for bringing our issues to your attention. I'm just trying to save our marriage," I said.

Mrs. Mitchell said in a comforting tone, "Trust me, you don't have to apologize. I'm just glad I could help."

Yury was sound asleep while I was on the phone. He was still on the night shift and had come in that morning at his usual time of six thirty. His alarm clock sounded out at 5:00 p.m. Yury turned it off and headed into the bathroom. Later, he snacked on sliced cheese and peanut butter crackers in front of the computer. Thirty minutes later, he opened the book he was reading in the family room.

I walked in. "Can we talk?"

Yury placed a bookmarker in the book and said, "What did Mrs. Mitchell say?"

"She said she understood what we're going through, and she is going to let you transfer to another department," I said.

Yury grunted with closed eyes and said, "I wish you had just let me take care of it. I wish you had just let me be a man."

I looked into his eyes with disbelief and replied, "Yury, I gave you time to take care of it. You were just poking at the problem instead of cutting it off. I did this to save our marriage and keep our family together."

Approximately a week later, we received a mysterious phone call early in the morning. "Unknown caller" flashed on our caller ID screen. We could tell the incognito caller was a woman using something to muffle her voice. She said, "Don't believe what you have heard. It is not what it seems." Then she hung up.

I told Yury maybe Asha had gotten one of her friends or relatives to make the call for her, but Yury wouldn't entertain that thought, because he didn't think it made sense for her to do that. For the sake of my well-being and to try to heal from it all, I managed to talk Yury into seeing Mrs. Theodore, the marriage counselor at Rising Hope Church. As we entered the glass-walled reception area of the church, a youthful redhead with freckles from face to toes greeted us.

"You must be the DeBlakes, because that's the name I see in our system for a one o'clock appointment." She giggled.

Yury and I said, "Yes."

She continued in a pleasant and friendly tone. "OK, please fill out this form." She handed it to us and said, "Then place it in this basket on the counter. Mrs. Theodore will walk you to her office in a few minutes."

Just as we finished the four-page paperwork, an average-height bronze-colored lady greeted us. "Mr. and Mrs. DeBlake, it's so good to meet you." She shook our hands and said, "I'm Mrs. Theodore. Please follow me to my office."

We did. Her dark hair was pulled back into a bun, and she wore pearl earrings, a one-strand pearl necklace, and a stylish navy-blue skirt suit with comfortable black pumps. In her office, she pointed to a brown leather couch and said, "Please have a seat." She sat in a matching chair in front of us and continued. "How has your morning been?"

"Fine," we both said.

Yury asked, "What about your morning?"

Mrs. Theodore said, "My morning has been uneventful, and I like it like that."

After we exchanged professional pleasantries, Mrs. Theodore inquired about our financial standing. That was when Yury uncovered another bombshell by revealing to our counselor that he brought home twice as much money per month as he'd told me. He raved proudly as he gloated in his bragging rights. I couldn't believe it. The moment affected me like the nerve-racking, irritating sound of scratches on a chalkboard.

My heart sank under the weight of having such an important piece of information hidden from my knowledge by my own husband. I didn't fuss. I didn't let him see that the secret had caught me off guard. I planned to address it at home in a calm, rational manner. Then Mrs. Theodore went straight to business, the reason that had brought us there. I gave a brief run-through of Yury's strong fixation on the lady at his job. As I delivered my spill, an accumulation of emotions erupted from a deep place, but the strongest of them all was anger.

"My dad cheated on my mother. I told Yury when we were dating that I would not stand for him cheating on me," I said with clenched fists, grunts, pauses, long breaths, and slow exhalations.

Mrs. Theodore's response snatched the rug right from under me. She said, "Wait a minute, Mrs. DeBlake. It sounds to me like you haven't dealt with your anger issues that resulted from your father and mother's relationship." Concern flooded her face as she continued. "I want to see you in counseling first, so we can get that matter resolved."

Right then and there, I felt as if my eyes bulged out of my head, my mouth dropped to the floor, and my face drooped out of place. On the other hand, Yury was tickled pink over our counseling session.

Once we were home, he laughed and said, "You thought she was going to fix me, but instead, she wants to fix you." He whistled and danced around our house.

I was confused and tilted my head from side to side. "How is it that she only wants to see me? She was supposed to talk to us about our issue at hand. I'm not going back. And another thing. We have been married for seven years. How is it that I am just finding out today that you make more money than what you told me you did?" I said with tranquil composure.

"You know I'm concerned about our retirement. The other half of my salary goes into both an IRA and a 401(k). It's my job as a husband and father to make sure I plan for our future. I'm not trying to do anything underhanded," Yury said.

"Yury, we are married. We are not supposed to keep secrets from each other. If you want our marriage to work, you can't keep important information from me," I said.

He said, "This is not about keeping secrets. I'm looking out for both you and me."

I'd needed the counselor to address the bombshell that had somehow lodged itself in my brain and destroyed the idea of marriage. Marriage was supposed to be beautiful and sacred, with a husband and wife being faithful and trustworthy toward each other. What had landed in my lap was none of the above.

Our meeting with Mrs. Theodore occurred in May. During our annual summer trip to see Yury's parents, I talked to Yury's daddy about our issues. After dinner, Yury, his mom, and his sisters went outside into the backyard to enjoy the evening breeze. Mr. DeBlake went into the living room to relax on the couch.

I joined him and said, "Yago, I was wondering if I could talk to you about something that happened between Yury and me."

He answered, "Yes?"

After I told Yury's daddy about our sour situation with Asha, his response was an unexpected rude awakening that riddled my emotions. I was waiting for well-thought-out words of wisdom, but that was not what I got.

His daddy nodded and said, "He's a man. That's what men do."

That day tested my claim of being a true southern-bred young lady. Even though the thought of possibly allowing some non–Sunday school words to slip through my lips came to my mind, I resisted and kept my mouth closed. I thought, *It'll be a cold day in hell if Yury and his dad think I'm going to put up with that ridiculous, selfish behavior.*

I could imagine Fred Sandford from the 1972 TV sitcom *Sanford and Son* with his hand on his chest, saying, "Elizabeth, this is the big one. I'm coming home to see you, honey. I'll be the one with a disgusted look plastered on my face."

Meanwhile, still in 1999, as my marriage presented me with challenges and threatened to unravel, my church life took a turn on a slippery, slimy, winding road I never had imagined I would travel. It began when Pastor Audrey Fishner came to visit Rising Hope Church as a guest speaker. She prophesied trouble was coming to the church through a person. It never occurred to me that I would end up being the one she was referring to. It blindsided me.

After we moved to Macon, Georgia, in 1995, Rising Hope was the only church I went to, along with my children. When I started out, I was in a good place spiritually and in good standing with everyone I fellowshipped with. I faithfully volunteered in the children's church. I first was an assistant for the three-year-old toddlers. In December 2000, when I was in my kitchen, singing worship songs to God while washing the dishes, God spoke to my heart and my spirit.

He said, "I have called you to be a great speaker and writer."

It was the first time I had experienced something like that, and I knew without a doubt I had heard from God. It was amazing.

Five years had passed at that church, and I graduated to running the room for eighteen-month-old babies. Then, during year seven in January 2002, Pastor Peggy Zinger approached me to ask if I would be interested in being an assistant to Bunny Marshall, the new nursery coordinator. I was ecstatic that Pastor Zinger had chosen me. I enthusiastically accepted the position and responsibility.

At first, Bunny and I got along splendidly. I had seen Bunny around but had never spoken to her before. She was recently widowed, had heavy eyes and medium-length salt-and-pepper hair, and always moved about as if she were in a hurry. We met briefly in the church's cafeteria.

Before we sat at a table, Bunny extended her hand and said, "Welcome to the team, Lewisa. I'm Bunny Marshall. Please call me Bunny."

I nodded and replied, "OK, I will. Thank you!"

Everything was working wonderfully. We had monthly meetings and brunches and quarterly training for our volunteers. Bunny had two boys named Mike and Mitch. They were the same ages as Jillian and Jaren, nine years old and six years old.

Unfortunately, Mike and Mitch seemed to enjoy making Jillian and Jaren uncomfortable. Sometimes they would take turns pulling Jillian's hair or get close up to Jaren's face as they gave him a hard time in a playful manner. Whenever I saw them in action, I would politely ask them to be a little kinder, and I comforted my children by saying, "They are just playing."

Bunny would just laugh at her children's antics as if they were adorable to her. However, I saw the helpless expressions on my children's faces. They were not amused by what was being dished out to them, and neither was I.

As time went by, the same scenario occurred in different ways. My children started voicing their dislike of the situation to me. It was a sticky case for me because those boys were my boss's children. I chose to handle the situation with kindness and by being polite while praying Bunny would soon intervene. It didn't seem to work as well as I had hoped. Jillian rested her head on my shoulder as we sat on the couch together one day. She was absorbed in watching Jaren and Jasper play a quiet game of tag.

Then she asked, "Mommy, do we have to play with Mike and Mitch?" Her brow furrowed.

"No, you don't have to," I said. "Why did you ask about that?"

She placed her index finger on her lips and thought for a minute. Then she said, "They aren't very nice. To be honest, they act like bullies, because they like to tease us and at times pull my hair."

"Yes, I agree their actions are like what bullies do." I looked down into Jillian's eyes, touched her hair, and said, "I am so proud of you for talking about this subject. In fact, if this or something like it happens again, I want you to use your voice and tell Mike and Mitch to stop in your loudest voice. Then come to me to let me know what they've done. I'll tell them if they can't be kind to you and your brothers, they can't play with you anymore."

Jillian smiled and said, "You are the best mommy in the whole world."

"I try to be." I said and laughed.

On October 31, when the church was having its Hallelujah Night Festival with plenty of large inflated outdoor bouncy toys, rides, games, and food, all free to the public and volunteers, instead of celebrating Halloween, curiosity got the best of Mike and Mitch once they met Yury. They were fascinated by Yury and our relationship with each other. They seemed spellbound by it.

With eyes the size of saucers, the boys gasped. One said, "Wow! Do you live in a big three-story house? Are you rich, Ms. Lewisa?"

"No." I said and shook my head.

"Can we come to see your house one day and play with Jillian and Jaren?" They said and looked at me with great expectations.

Surprised by their questions, I said, "Hmm, let me get back to you on that."

On another occasion, Mitch naively blurted out with the conviction of a genetics philosopher, "Mama said the texture of your children's hair is nothing like Ms. Zoe's son. She said Adan has soft, naturally curly hair, but you are trying really hard to make your children's coarse hair look curly. You have to put all kinds of stuff in your children's hair to get it to look soft, but Adan naturally has better hair." He arrogantly stuck his nose up in the air.

The comment was unexpected. I just stood there watching him with wide eyes and buttoned lips. The questions and the comment came from Mike and Mitch while Bunny was present or within earshot, but their words didn't move her into corrective mother mode. I had been raised in an environment where my mother didn't believe in having children interact with adults as if we were on the same level. She'd taught us children should be quiet unless spoken to by an adult. At that time, the older generation believed children should be seen and not heard.

Mom had expected us to display good manners and proper, positive, and acceptable social behavior in front of her guests and any adult in our presence. If we had asked the same questions of my mother's company, it would have embarrassed her and made her so mad she would have been spitting bricks. She would have said we were smelling our piss and acting too womanish or grown for our age. Then Mom would have squinted and flinched her face, giving us the look of death, as she fumed her disapproval and pulled out her belt, a switch, a shoe, or any other pain-teaching tool she could reach from her pocketbook or around the house to beat us with in front of her company. If we had asked an adult personal questions or anything else she thought was inappropriate, Mom would have made sure we never made that mistake again.

If my mother had been present during that time, she would have told Bunny, "If you don't know how to discipline your children and teach them good manners, I will, because I don't take tea for fever."

I believed the "don't take tea for fever" statement was Mom's way of saying she was tough and didn't put up with foolishness.

Unlike my mother, I hadn't inherited the Dirty Harry "Make my day" gene. Personally, I would have had to be extremely mad and possibly would have required a fifth of whiskey before I could boldly say something like that to someone. I knew many people would have said those questions were innocent. Yes, they probably were, but because of my upbringing, I didn't see it like that.

If my children had said the same things to Bunny, I would have told them they were being impolite and shouldn't ask grown-ups they barely knew questions like that, because it was considered rude, especially if they were asking just to be nosy. Then again, asking someone they were close to could produce the same ramifications. I also would have insisted my children write Bunny an apology letter. I would have had them deliver it to her in person and say they were sorry.

Months later, one day after church, as I was driving through the parking lot to head home, I saw Bunny and her boys walking across the parking lot toward the sidewalk near the street. I slowed down to ask Bunny if she wanted a ride home. She accepted. As it turned out, she didn't live far from the church. Her car had broken down and was in the shop, being repaired. For the next few weeks, I picked them up and dropped them off before and after church and our meetings.

During one of our rides together to her house after church, Bunny said, "You know, we should have the meeting at your house one day, so the atmosphere can be a little more relaxed, and our kids can play together while we make plans for the volunteers."

I said, "Hmm, um, well, we'll see about that."

The request caught me off guard. I didn't know how to respond to it. We already had a lovely environment to meet in at the church. The nursery was large and filled with brand-new baby furniture, toys, linens, and electronics for playing soft music and watching DVDs and VHS tapes. Also, it had lots of space for children to play in. We had a relaxed professional relationship that was still developing despite the little bumps in the road we'd encountered. I didn't want to rush into anything by having Bunny and the boys come to my house. I was still getting to know them, and Mike and Mitch were still annoying Jillian and Jaren. Therefore, I wasn't impressed.

On top of that, I liked it better when I was the initiator inviting people to my house. I considered my house my haven. It was my safe place, my shelter of rest. It was my retreat where I helped to set the atmosphere for my family. I was particular when it came to having people over. Since things weren't going as well as they could have, I wanted more time to get to know Bunny before inviting her over.

Sometime after that conversation, the same topic found its way into our one-on-one time. After having time to search my heart on how to respond to her, I was prepared to tell her the truth.

"I don't invite many people to my house, because I am pretty open. I have to know I can trust whomever I decide to let into the comfort of my home. I like to get to know people before I invite them to my house. I know we are getting to know each other now, but I would like to wait a little while longer before we go that route." The words rolled off my tongue.

I felt lighter after sharing what was on my heart about the matter. I was honest and delivered what was on my mind with care, but from the peeved appearance that took over Bunny's face, it seemed my words had hit her as if I had said she had fat, ugly children with foul breath. She quickly composed herself and flashed a fast, evasive smile. I walked away disappointed because I could see she hadn't heard the sincerity coming from my heart.

Sunday came. I walked past Bunny and her friend Penny Foxx in the lobby of the church.

"Hi, Bunny. Hi, Penny," I called out, looking back at them.

Bunny pushed up her lips as she eyed Penny. "Hi," she said, dragging out the word.

"Uh-huh," Penny said as she rolled her eyes and turned her back to me.

I kept walking but wondered, *What was that all about?*

Soon Penny started picking up Bunny before church and taking her home afterward. They were becoming as tight as peas in a pod. Then, one day, an anonymous donor gave Bunny a twenty-year-old Jeep to get around in since she didn't have the money to buy a new engine for her car in the shop. The Jeep was a faded yellow color, with big patches of rust all over the body of the vehicle. It was free and still running well, so Bunny was grateful for it. I was happy for her too, because it was no picnic to have to rely on other people to take you places. I thought our little storm had passed on between us since Bunny was acting as I remembered in the nursery and during our meetings before we'd hit a bump in the road.

Then Sunday came around again. Once more, as Bunny and Penny conversed, Penny sighed, cut her eyes at me, and turned her head. Her reaction shocked me, but I kept walking. Bunny's face resembled that of the Cheshire Cat from *Alice in Wonderland*. I thought, *Something is wrong.* Since I didn't know Penny well, I figured that meant Bunny had told her something negative about me in order for her to behave the way she was toward me.

A couple of months passed by, and the same scenario played out in both similar and different ways. At that point, I had no doubt ill feelings were lurking behind the scene of Bunny's fake grin and Penny's stealthy attitude. My intuition proved true when we were given an opportunity to visit Pastor Zephyr Reddins's church in Atlanta, Georgia, which was known to be extremely organized and used a church-related curriculum that Rising Hope Church was considering using.

During the morning of the trip, Bunny, Penny, and I were waiting in the church lobby for the rest of the people traveling with us. Before the day of the trip, we'd made plans to carpool together. That worked out well for me since I never had learned how to read a road map and was directionally challenged. I was to ride with Bunny, Penny, and Mona. Mona had offered to use her car and drive. While we waited, Bunny and Penny, who were sitting close together, chatted in soft tones.

Occasionally, one of them would look in my direction and snicker with the other. Then they got up from their seats and walked arm in arm to the ladies' room. At the bend of the corner, Penny glanced back at me and gave me a scornful stare. I felt as if I had been sucked into some kind of catty, nonverbal, bullying high school time warp. Oddly, no one else around us seemed to be aware of the silent, venomous poison being directed toward me.

It was a hot, sunny day. The car ride to Atlanta, Georgia, was pleasant. Mona, Bunny, and Penny filled the car with conversation. I just listened and laughed in the appropriate places. They were absorbed in the topics they were engaged in. We arrived at Christ Life Church just past one o'clock, with a few minutes to spare before our 2:00 p.m. tour and meeting. The exterior of the church was historical red brick with white columns and had large, colorful stained-glass windows with symbols of the cross, Jesus, and Mary. The building seated about two thousand people.

We met with Pastor Gill Tops, Pastor Reddins's associate pastor. All in all, the tour and meeting went well despite a few little sneering looks and giggles from Bunny and Penny. We gathered the information we were seeking in order to improve our church.

On the way back, we passed a heartbreaking scene. Traffic slowed us down to ten miles per hour on a two-way street near a large lake called Lake Jolene. Since the road didn't have shoulders for emergency parking, some cars were sparsely spread out on small patches of land off the road in the dirt and grass. In those areas, some people were walking or standing by their vehicles. Then a few people began running toward the lake. Next, all of a sudden, we heard the bloodcurdling screams of a mother. She had just discovered her child had drowned in the water. She stood on the landside of the lake with both fists pressed against her pain-ridden face. As the mother's legs began to give out, a lady placed her arms around her just as she let out a gut-wrenching sound.

She cried and hollered, "Not my child! Not my son! Lord, no, no, no! Not my child! He's my only child, God!"

My heart ached for her, so I started saying, "Jesus, Jesus, Jesus," over and over again.

Mona, Bunny, and Penny made a few sounds too to express their sympathy for the grieving mother. I was still saying the name of Jesus over and over again. The sound of that mama's cry of agony got to me. All of a sudden, both Bunny and Penny directed hard, unkind gazes at me. I didn't know why they were so put out with me. Maybe they thought I was overdoing it by calling Jesus's name as often as I was. I didn't mean to be irritating; I just truly felt so sorry for that lady. Hearing her pain caused pain in me because of what she was going through.

Mona's eyes stayed on the road, so she missed out on the little fiery sight show Bunny and Penny put on for me. Once we arrived back at Rising Hope Church, we all went our separate ways.

Sunday came back around. This time, when my children and I walked into the church, Bunny and Penny were in the lobby, talking to a group of about ten people. As we passed the small crowd, Bunny's and Penny's chilly eyes followed us. Then the tiny sea of cold eyes joined them. Their faces stretched and crinkled as if they were smelling a putrid odor of cheesy, musty toe jam oozing through my pores. I thought, *They are spreading their hidden offense with subtle, quiet visual hints.*

As time went on, the social temperature began dropping. It went from chilly to cold to freezing.

The following Sunday, there was more of the same thing, but the club of haters grew. My children and I were getting ready to exit the lobby to go outside. As we maneuvered through a thick cloud of hate from the gatherers still in the lobby, a tall, medium-built white man I didn't know, with fury in his eyes, became aggressive toward me for some unknown reason.

I heard some men around him say, "That's her."

"I'll handle this," the medium-built man said as he stood up from a chair. As I walked past, the man charged toward me.

Three other men held him back as he tried to throw a punch at me. I was shaken. My heart was pounding. I looked at him as if he had lost his mind. My children, Jillian, nine; Jaren, six; and Jasper, three, were confused and frightened. I guided them toward the door that led outside.

I didn't know what to think about what had happened, and I was too embarrassed to tell my family or anyone else about it. I did confide in Yury, but he thought everything I said sounded too far out to have happened in a church, so I didn't get any comfort from him. At six o'clock, after I gave Yury his plate of spaghetti and meatballs, I placed dinner on the table for our children. Then I took my plate and sat on the couch beside Yury.

He looked at me and said, "OK, what's wrong? You only have a bird-sized portion of food, and you like spaghetti."

I explained what had happened at church.

He listened intently and said, "That doesn't make any sense. Why would grown men get involved in hearsay involving a group of ladies not getting along?"

I shook my head and breathed out the words. "I don't know. None of what's going on makes any sense."

He thought for a minute and said, "Maybe you unconsciously offended Bunny and Penny. Otherwise, it doesn't make any sense for them to treat you as you've said. You all are church folks. You shouldn't be behaving like you are. It doesn't look good."

"Yury, we are still human beings and not robots," I said.

"Hmm."

After that incident, during one of the Sunday services, Pastor Audrey Fishner was a guest speaker again. She shared with the congregation that Pastor Zinger had told her that her prophecy had come true in the church.

Unfortunately, things got worse. Simultaneously, Yury actually attended a new marriage-improvement class the church started. Nick and Zoe participated too. During one of the sessions, the instructor gave us a sheet of paper to anonymously write down an issue that pertained to our marriages. I told Zoe I was considering asking, "What advice can you give an unsaved husband who surrenders to temptation?" She thought it was a good question and might help other women in the classroom. The following week, it turned out someone else had turned in that same question to be answered by the instructor in front of the class. I was beside myself.

I said out loud, "I wanted to ask that same question! Wow! I was going to ask that!"

I hadn't gotten a chance to turn in my piece of paper. I still had it in my pocketbook. Zoe crooked her head around and looked back at me. She and Nick were sitting in front of Yury and me. She crinkled her nose and opened her mouth. Her face read, *Liar*.

I mouthed, "Really. I didn't do it." I thought about showing them the sheet of paper still in my pocketbook, but I didn't get a chance to.

Zoe didn't look convinced. After the Sunday service, Zoe and Nick were with their group of friends in the lobby. As I was leaving with my family, I saw a few of them pointing at me. There were pouting faces, frowns, teeth sucking, and a combination of hot and icy stares.

The next Sunday, Zoe was a little distant. It seemed she had more important things to tend to instead of attending the marriage class.

The behavior of the people from the previous Sundays was still present. I thought I was safe because I was in the Lord's house. Regrettably, my life began to corkscrew downward. Soon, still in 2002, Yury bought a new black four-door 2002 Dodge Ram truck. I drove it to church from time to time. Doritha, one of Bunny's friends who also took part in the stinging sight war, showed symptoms that she too had some smothered resentment toward me.

The only dealings I had with her were in passing by her from point A to point B and saying hello. She told other people in my presence she had started dating a mechanic. She was excited about him. On a Friday at three o'clock in the morning, out of the still of the night, Yury and I were awakened when we heard Jillian screaming. We both jumped up out of the bed and ran down the hall to her room. On the way, I turned on all the lights on that side of the house. When we reached Jillian's room, she was frantic. Her breathing was heavy. She was sweating and appeared scared.

"What's wrong?" we asked as our hearts drummed.

With a clenched jaw, crazy eyes, and urgency in her voice, she exclaimed, "Some people are after us!"

We had Jillian come out of the bed and sit with me in the living room until she was able to calm down. I turned on all the lights on the other side of the house too. After a while, Jillian returned to bed. Because of the commotion, Yury and I stayed up to regain our composure. He went outside to get the newspaper around six thirty. He looked at his new truck and thought it looked different.

Upon closer inspection, he noticed the tailgate was missing, stolen from the back of the truck. I believed with all my heart that God allowed us to know something was going on by having Jillian scream out. She had never had a nightmare before and never had one after that night. I usually went to bed at one or one thirty in the morning. At that time, I still had some of the lights inside the house turned on near the area where the truck was parked. I had turned them off when I went to bed.

Yury called the police. When they came, they said whoever had stolen the tailgate was a professional, because they hadn't left any scratches or dents. They concluded that at least two or three people must have carried it off, because of the weight and size of it and because the work was meticulous. The theft of such a large and visible part of our new truck was upsetting.

Since the atmosphere at church had become like walking through dry ice, when Sunday came back around, I decided not to tell anyone what had happened. I didn't want them cheering and celebrating behind my back because something negative had happened to my family and me.

Then, at one point, Doritha and I were passing by each other in the children's church. She stopped to talk to me.

"Hi, Lewisa. So how was your weekend?" she said, and she hummed as her smile nearly touched her eyes.

I nodded and said, "It was good. Thanks for asking." I nodded again.

She narrowed her eyes, bared her teeth, and scoffed, "Good? How could your weekend have been good?" Her nose flared with her eyes still narrowed as anger raced throughout her body. Then she scampered away.

I thought, *Who gets agitated because someone told you she had a good weekend?* I did not know what she'd meant, but I didn't like how it had sounded. It seemed as if she knew more than she was saying, and I didn't like it. The feeling I had inside convinced me of her undeniable guilt, but I didn't have any evidence and wasn't sure how to get it. That was when I decided it was time to cut my losses and leave the church.

I wrote my resignation letter and turned it in to Pastor Zinger. She had a meeting with Bunny and me to get a clearer understanding of why I was resigning and what had happened. I wrote down a few of the uncalled-for incidents that had occurred, so I could easily get to the meat of the problem in her presence. As I went over some of them, Pastor Zinger asked for a copy of the incidents.

She said, "I don't think you should leave, because God hasn't released you to go yet."

I didn't understand what that meant but replied, "I can't stay. I'm not safe here."

I never had thought a day would come when unpleasant events caused me to stop going to church, but I found myself there. I felt betrayed by all the wrecking ball events that had demolished my expectation of only goodness occurring in the house of the Lord. At that time, it never dawned on me that all people, even ones who went to church, were flawed. I heard ministers say, "Church is a spiritual hospital for broken, hurt, and sick people to come and be delivered and healed. Don't go there looking for perfect people, because you won't find any." To deal with my rejection, I started writing a book. I continued to spend time with God at home by reading and listening to the Bible, singing praise-and-worship songs to God, and watching Christian television. Four months passed. I began adjusting to my new church-free life.

EIGHT

ONE DAY, UNEXPECTEDLY, I received a phone call from Veronica, the coordinator for the children's church. She was still attending Rising Hope Church. During the time we'd shared together prior to the call, her penetrating pale blues had seemed as if they were stripping away the walls of my soul as her fixed, unreadable face illuminated her mysterious intuition. Her questions—for example, "How does that make you feel? Why do you think he responds that way to you? What do you think the solution is to your concern?"—made me feel as if I'd received a free counseling session after being around her.

Veronica called to invite me to go out to dinner with her on the weekend. It was a welcome surprise since she and I had gone out a number of times in the past and had a pleasant time. On the appointed day, I arrived at the selected restaurant a few minutes early. As was our custom, whoever arrived first held a table. I went ahead and got seated to hold a table for Veronica's arrival. She came five minutes after I was seated, but to my astonishment, DeAnna, her assistant, walked in with her.

Once Veronica and DeAnna arrived, I thought, *This is interesting. This is the first time Veronica has ever invited someone else to come along with her during one of our outings together.* She and DeAnna sat together on the same side of the booth, and I sat on the opposite side. The evening began in an uneventful way. We greeted each other and participated in small talk as we viewed the dinner menu.

However, the evening quickly took on a bizarre twist. Periodically throughout the night, Veronica and DeAnna took turns looking behind them at the exit door. I wondered but didn't ask if they were expecting someone else to join us. Just before our meal was brought out to the table, Veronica and DeAnna took turns going to the ladies' room.

As I sat with one of the ladies as the other walked away from the table, I thought, *What is going on? Either something is up, or these ladies need Depends underwear.* The night continued that way even after our food arrived. Each time the women looked behind them, I wondered if James Bond was going to walk through the door. Were they part of some secret espionage mission, or were we on *Candid Camera*? It was strange. The ladies were jittery, as if they were going through withdrawals from caffeine. I was a bit uncomfortable, but I tried not to show it.

Once our food was before us, the ladies and I partook of our meals. Everything went back to the way the night should have taken place all along before Lucy and Ethel from *I Love Lucy* invaded Veronica's and DeAnna's bodies. Then, just when I was going to pass off the first part of the night as their being famished to the point of being delirious, more looks back and alternating trips to the restroom happened. Unexpectedly, Veronica and DeAnna went to the restroom together.

Once they returned, it was as if they had regained strength. They were filled with courage. Maybe they had their own can of spinach like Popeye. Then it happened. It was the grand finale, the moment of truth. They got to the real reason they'd invited me to dinner.

Veronica spoke. "So, Lewisa, when was the last time you heard from Bunny?"

I cocked my head to the side the way my dog did when she didn't understand something and said, "I haven't heard from or seen Bunny since I left the church."

Wringing her hands while DeAnna twirled her hair, Veronica responded, "So does that mean you don't know what happened to Bunny's Jeep?"

With raised eyebrows, I responded, "No. What happened to Bunny's Jeep?"

Veronica and DeAnna looked at each other. Then Veronica continued. "Bunny parked her Jeep at a gas station because it stopped working. She went back a few days later to have it towed, but it wasn't there."

"Did she call the different towing companies in the area? Maybe one of them towed it at the gas station owner's request," I said.

Veronica nodded and said, "Yes, she has done that already with no luck in finding it."

I shook my head and said, "That's sad. I'm sorry that happened to her, but I don't know what else to tell you."

It seemed they finally believed me, because their interpretation of a good-cop, bad-cop—or perhaps good-cop, silent-cop—interrogation ended. Then we went our separate ways. I couldn't believe they'd had me go out with them under false pretenses just to find out if I had anything to do with Bunny's missing Jeep. Her Jeep was twenty years old and had large rust patches all over it. I thought, *I were a thief, I wouldn't waste my time trying to steal something like that.*

I could have chosen to be insulted by their actions, but it would have put me in a negative state of mind. I didn't want to go there.

Even though it was a rude awakening, I decided to place the incident in God's hands. God was a loving father. He gave me a comforting dream to give me hope and help me know he was going to bring something good out of that messy situation at church.

I dreamed I was standing on the stage with Pastor Peggy Zinger in Rising Hope Church. I had a microphone in my hand. I told everyone present not to blame Bunny and Penny for what had happened between us. God used the incident to get me into what he had called me to do.

I thought after the uncoordinated counterintelligence operation, life would go back to an uneventful normal for me. I was wrong.

I self-published the book *God Sees You: My Story* in May 2003. It is a book that encourages people and lets them know that no matter what difficulties they are going through in their lives, God is with them, and he will get them through to a better tomorrow. In the book, I touched on the incident that had taken place in the restaurant. I didn't go into a lot of detail, because I didn't want to embarrass anyone. In the month of May, I advertised my book with two large magnetic signs on my eggplant-colored Dodge Plymouth van. Yury sold about thirty-five copies to his coworkers on his job. I sold fifteen to family and a few acquaintances.

Then, one sunny day, I was standing outside in our yard, monitoring my three children as they played. The street I lived on was a combination of country and suburbs. It satisfied Yury's need to be in the country and my need to be in a subdivision. More than two hundred acres of cotton, which resembled white snowballs on sturdy, twisted brown twigs as far the eyes could see in every direction, adorned the enormous green field that made way for a palatial, elaborate white Georgian colonial plantation-style mansion with grand columns that demanded attention in the center of the field. Across from the farmlands was a small subdivision of forty-five brick houses with two-car garages, each on one acre of land. All the houses had a matching detached brick building featuring a third garage with an attached storage room.

On the side of the subdivision was an additional hundred-acre cotton field. Yury, our children, and I lived in a house in that subdivision. Our house faced the plantation. There were large, healthy, leafy green pecan trees in our yard and lining the street in the subdivision. For seven years, I was the only coffee-colored person in our area. Traffic was always light since mainly residents or people visiting used the road leading to that area. It was well off the beaten path.

My children were running around, chasing each other as they laughed their best laughs.

Suddenly, I noticed a gray SUV driving slowly past my house. The speed of the vehicle caught my eye and my daughter's too. I was benumbed when it turned out to be Pastor Zinger and her husband. As she drove the speed of molasses, Pastor Zinger shifted her face and body toward the driver's window while her hands held steady on the steering wheel. She was facing me.

Then, as if in slow motion, she laughed an animated laugh similar to that of a jack-in-the-box toy, with her head bobbing back and forth and side to side. Her husband was beside her. He covered his mouth and appeared to be laughing too. I was stunned that she had driven to our neighborhood, was behaving in a manner completely beneath the position of the higher call she answered to, and was mocking me. She was teasing me. I stood there watching the one-vehicle parade, even though it was hard to believe my eyes. I didn't know how to process what was before me.

A few weeks passed, and one morning, I was washing dishes after breakfast while looking out the window over the kitchen sink. The kitchen was off the garage. We had left the garage door open, so I could see the street on the side of the house that faced my neighbors' garage and yard across the street. My eyes caught the image of a man I had never seen before talking to my neighbors in the driveway in front of their garage. The man was white, with a small build, and wearing a suit with sunglasses.

As he talked to our neighbors, he pointed at our house. While our neighbors spoke, they nodded, shook their heads, and pointed at our house too. I was flabbergasted. My eyes and mouth widened. Since I didn't understand what was happening, I didn't want to make more of what I saw without knowing the details. I wasn't close to those particular neighbors. They didn't seem interested in being friendly. So I placed the situation in God's hands.

A few days later, a motorcycle crew of about fifty men, the majority of whom were black, came to our small, quiet subdivision. Oddly, they appeared to be praying as they slowed down in front of my house. They stretched out one hand each and rode by slowly.

In an unexpected turn of events, my neighbors whose garage faced ours started despising us. They stopped their son, Coen, from playing with Jillian and Jaren. However, their withholding their son's friendship as punishment actually turned out to be a blessing in disguise. Not long before that time, Coen had held my children hostage in his backyard. Jillian and Jaren were in Coen's backyard, playing with him and Nolan, another neighborhood child.

It was getting dark, so I went outside to call my children to come home. I could clearly see them, and I knew they could hear me, but they wouldn't come to me. They acted as if their bodies were glued to the fence. I saw Coen saying something to them but couldn't hear what it was. I walked over to Coen's yard to tell my children to come home.

They still hesitated. Their eyes were numbed with horror. Sensing something was wrong, I looked at Coen and Nolan with a piercing glare. Then my children came to me like scared dogs with their tails tucked between their legs. They said Coen had told them if they moved, he was going to hurt them. I forbid my children from playing with him in his yard anymore.

January 2004 came rushing in as quickly as sand in an hourglass flowed from one side to the next. The New Year brought an unexpected change to our lives. There were changes in governmental laws and policies that brought about hefty penalties and fines that affected the profit of the manufacturing company Yury worked for. In order to stay afloat in the midst of losses in revenue, the company decided to cut back on employees.

Yury was one of the many laid off from his well-paying job. That threatened the lifestyle we had gotten used to. He was saved during the first round of layoffs but not the second. He was disappointed, and so was I, but I told him we were going to trust God to bring something good out of that bad situation. Ever since we'd moved to Macon, the children and I had been asking in prayer for God to move us back to Charleston so we could be around family again. I reminded Yury of that fact.

Yury said, "In order for me to consider moving back to Charleston, you need to get a job. If you can find a job making at least twenty thousand dollars a year, we can move back there."

My children and I prayed for God to make a way for me to find a job that paid $20,000 a year. I also had my mom and family members pray for God to make a way for me. In May 2004, my children and I went to Charleston to visit my family for two weeks.

On our first day there, Mom had me call WCCL, a Christian radio station. She told me to ask them to agree in prayer with me for God to make a way for me to find a job that paid what Yury had said I had to make for us to move there. Someone from the radio station prayed with me on the phone. Thirty minutes later, Micah, my youngest brother, who was six foot four, was twenty-eight years old, had an athletic build and kind face, and was away from Mom's house, called her number and asked to speak to me. We usually spoke only briefly in passing when I was in town or whenever I called Mama on the phone.

I came to the phone. "Hello?"

He said, "Hey, Lew, were you serious when you said you wanted a job here?"

"Yes," I responded.

He said, "OK, hold on a minute. I want you to talk to somebody."

A friendly female voice spoke up. "Hello. I'm Vivianna Bailey. I am the vice president at Waterway Tri-County Bank. We need to quickly fill a position, like yesterday, for a data-entry specialist in our operations department. It is an entry-level position, so we will train you if you don't already have experience. Your starting salary will be twenty thousand eight hundred dollars a year. Your work hours will be Monday through Friday from eight thirty to five thirty. Does that sound like something you would be interested in so far?"

"Yes, it does!" I answered with excitement.

Vivianna's voice perked up. "Well, good! Can you come in for an interview tomorrow at one o'clock?"

I grabbed a piece of paper and a pen and said, "Yes." Then I wrote down the pertinent information.

I was excited. Mom, my children, and my brothers and sisters were rejoicing with me because God was working on our prayer. Yury was shocked and skeptical. He reminded me I still had to go through the interview.

I told him, "I have an interview at the bank!" I laughed and said, "Yay! God is working!"

He said, "Wow! That doesn't happen often. Don't get your hopes up too high, but I hope you get the job."

I threw one hand in the air as my lips curled up and allowed my teeth to appear. I replied, "I'm so excited! I believe I'm going to get it."

Hesitating, he said, "OK, whatever you say."

When Micah came back to Mama's house, I asked him how he knew Ms. Bailey.

Micah laughed and replied, "She's a good friend of mine, and by the way, you already got the job."

I narrowed my eyes while smiling and asked, "How do you know that?"

"Trust me." He said and smiled back.

The next day, my interview went well. Ms. Bailey was professional and kind. She was Japanese and tall, with a small build, and wore her blonde-colored hair long, hanging down near her buttocks. Her clothes were stylish, form-fitting, and business sexy. Ms. Bailey's name didn't match the image before me. Once the interview was over, she told me she would get back in touch with me. She had to interview a few more people and thanked me for coming. I went back to Mama's house, puzzled. I questioned Micah about it, thinking he had somehow gotten his communication crossed with her.

He had a big smile on his face. He only said, "Trust me."

Two hours later, Mom's phone rang. "Lewisa, telephone!" Mom called out.

"Hello?" I answered.

"Hello, Mrs. DeBlake. This is Vivianna Bailey. I'm calling to offer you the job as a data-entry specialist with Waterway Tri-County Bank. Are you still interested?"

I said, "Yes! Thank you so much! When would you like me to start?"

"Can you start this Thursday?" she asked.

I responded, "Yes!"

"Great! Welcome aboard! I'll see you Thursday morning at eight thirty. Just ask for me."

I said, "Thank you, and I will!"

My children, my family, and I cheered and thanked God for working out a miracle for me. I called WCCL to give them a praise report. The person I spoke to rejoiced on the phone with me. It was a joyous occasion for us. God had reached back into my past to the disappointment of not being hired during my disastrous bank interview in 1990 after the breakup with Kent. God knew that the unexpected breakup had interfered with my interview that day.

Due to his goodness and ability to turn things in our favor, my heavenly Father decided to compensate me for the injustice surrounding that situation that day. God said, "Ta-da," and gave me my dream job anyway years later. He gave me the desire of my heart. The Lord had the job come to me. I didn't have to go looking for it. He also arranged it so I was able to work in an office upstairs and did not have to deal directly with the public. I felt blessed. *God is wonderful!*

My children jumped around the house, saying, "Yeah! Yeah! Yeah! God answered our prayers!"

Mom waved her hands in the air as she proclaimed, "My God can't fail! God gave you eight hundred dollars more a year than Yury said you had to have. That's just like God. He gave you far above what you asked or thought."

I spoke to Yury, who was still in Georgia, to tell him the good news. He was slightly unenthusiastic and blasé. He sighed and said slowly, "I have to admit I didn't think you were going to find a job making twenty thousand dollars a year since you don't have a college degree. But because I promised you we would move if you were able to meet the requirement, we will move back to Charleston."

I laughed and said, "God did it!"

Yury replied, "No, Micah did it."

I responded, "God arranged for Micah to meet Vivianna because the children and I were praying to move back to Charleston."

"So are you saying you prayed me out of a job?" he asked.

I gasped and said, "No, that thought is ridiculous. Even though we were praying to be around family again, we would never pray for you to lose your job. God knows everything. He knew what was going to happen with the company you worked for, and he knew how to work things out for me to make the amount of money you said I had to have."

God had made a way out of no way for me. I hadn't seen his answer to our prayer coming. We moved back to Charleston. I got my miracle. As it turned out, Micah and Vivianna were dating each other. God was working behind the scenes in order for me to make the money Yury said I had to have so we could move back to Charleston.

Although our children and I were happy that God had heard and answered our prayers, Yury wasn't able to find a job in the Charleston area making anywhere near what he had made in Macon. I knew his interest was in keeping our family in a stable financial environment. Even though Yury was using headhunters to help him find work in the area, only companies offering salaries in the $30,000 range were interested in him, which was less than one-fourth the salary Yury was used to making. After three months of running into the same situation, Yury confided in me.

"As I have told you before, it's important to me to be the breadwinner in our family. I appreciate that you are working at the bank to help contribute toward keeping us going until I find a job. However, I liked how our life was before you started working. I want to be the one working outside the house instead of you. I know you like working at the bank and being around your family again, but would you consider allowing me to look at job opportunities in other states so I can feel like I have worth again?" he asked cautiously.

I sighed and said, "If you are truly unhappy here, then I will give up my family for you again. I honestly don't want to, but your happiness means that much to me."

Yury hugged and kissed me. Then he squealed, "Thanks! I love you, baby!"

"I love you too." I smiled.

My work environment was unique since my new boss was dating my brother. She spent many nonworking hours with my family and me. Sometimes she ate dinner with us at Mom's house and our rented house. Vivianna attended family birthday parties and other special celebrations. Going against professional ethics, she had girlfriends she partied with working for her too. Ms. Bailey was kind and poised in front of my and my family's faces. However, when her girlfriends entered our work area, another side of her emerged. As they gathered, her polished veil gave way to remnants of a perky party girl as the inquisitive chatter began. Ms. Bailey did her best to talk discreetly, but many times, I could hear her dishing information about me to her home-girl clique.

A lady with a heart-shaped face and an in-your-face demeanor blurted out within my earshot in the office, "Hey, Viv, did she actually qualify for this job, or was it a favor because of her brother?"

Vivianna paused for a moment. Then she pursed her lips, squinted, and answered softly, "It was a favor."

The lady said, "Hmm. Then she'd better do her job. She owes you."

I was in a peculiar position, so I did my best not to complain to my family. I did talk to God about it, though. I didn't want any part in coming between my brother and Ms. Bailey in their relationship.

After two weeks of my working at the bank, human resources spoke to Ms. Bailey about a discrepancy on my résumé that concerned them. My brother Conner had talked me into placing information about my book on my résumé. He said it counted as experience for me. I hadn't known how to properly include the fact that I'd self-published a book on my résumé; therefore, I'd included it under work experience and added the publishing company's address along with my information.

As it turned out, that had been an unwise decision, because human resources had interpreted it to mean I'd worked at the publishing company. When they'd called the publishing company to find out about my work experience with them, human resources had been told I never had worked for them. As a result of that conversation, human resources called Ms. Bailey to inform her I had lied on my résumé. They asked her to decide if she wanted to terminate my employment with them or not.

Ms. Bailey said while on the phone, "She lied on her résumé? Well, she's a good worker. I'm going to keep her."

My desk wasn't far from Ms. Bailey's desk. From what I heard, I was able to piece the conversation together. I was stunned because the unforeseen problem had popped up unexpectedly. Also, I was grateful she decided to keep me. However, I thought, *I am going to get Conner for telling me to include my book information on my résumé.* Neither Ms. Bailey nor anyone else ever said anything to me about the issue. However, the bit of information regarding lying on my résumé leaked out and found its way around to everyone working in the bank.

Once again, I faced mean-spirited mean-girl conduct. I encountered looks of disdain and heard conversations among many bystanders contaminated by the venom making its rounds through the pulse of the company. Then my Plymouth Voyager van was mysteriously keyed on the driver's side one day. Amid the gossip and passive-aggressive remarks and tendencies displayed by some people, including Ms. Bailey, I managed to still be kind and quiet unless I was spoken to.

Oddly, during that time, when Ms. Bailey came around my family, she was warm and pleasant to all of us. However, one time, she did something outlandish to Yury in front of everybody. We were all talking in the kitchen. Some people were sitting at the table, and Yury, Mom, Micah, Vivianna, and I were standing. Out of the blue, without any warning, Vivianna placed her arms around Yury's neck and did some kind of move I had seen stripper-pole dancers do on TV.

My family, including Micah, laughed as they asked her what she was doing. I was surprised Mama laughed too at Vivianna's inappropriate behavior. I stood there speechless because it wasn't funny to me, but what was I to say? She was my boss. The expression on Yury's face told me he was aroused by it, but I didn't hold it against him, because he was a guiltless bystander. He hadn't known she was going to do that. None of us had. When Vivianna came back to her senses, she resembled a lost puppy, all cute and innocent. Did I go slap-that-heifer ghetto Jerry Springer on her? No, I didn't. I was having a tunnel-vision experience and felt as if I would faint. Later, when the scene replayed itself in my mind, I wished I had taken some kind of action.

In September 2004, Yury gained employment with a manufacturing company in Pikeville, Kentucky. His salary was well under half of what he was used to making, but the company paid for us to be packed and moved to Kentucky. They also gave Yury a $10,000 bonus to help us get settled in Pikeville.

In addition, our house in Macon sold quickly after being on the market for only nearly a month. God was good to us. The children and I stayed in Charleston until the November school break for Thanksgiving. On my last day at work, I showed a couple of Vivianna's girlfriends my book on Amazon.com and Barnes and Noble's website on the computer. Earlier, they had asked me what I liked doing with my free time, and I'd told them I liked to write. Since no one had given me a chance to explain the juicy rumors about my lying on my résumé, I decided to show them my book online on our work computer.

As my day came to an end at the bank, one of Vivianna's girlfriends said to me, "I have never met anyone like you before. You have inspired me to become a better person."

The children and I moved to Pikeville, Kentucky, to join Yury during Thanksgiving weekend. He had been living there in a motel for two months. Mikell, my niece, who was tall and thin like a model, joined Yury and me on our house search. We chose a house just weeks before the move. It took a while for us to get used to some of the roads in the subdivision we lived in and in other areas too. The terrain was mountainous in comparison to the flat lands I had been used to in Charleston and Macon.

In Pikeville, some of the subdivision roads, including the one we lived on, were narrow two-way roads with a mountain on one side and a cliff with a deep drop on the other. While we were sightseeing in the area, we noticed many of the upscale subdivisions were on flat roads. The population in Pikeville was a little more than six thousand. Charleston, excluding the surrounding areas, had a population of about 136,000, and Macon had a population of about of 153,000.

Because I didn't see other people who looked like me when we were house searching, I asked the real-estate agent if other black people lived in Pikeville. She said the last census taken had confirmed that about 106 African Americans lived there. Also, during our conversation with the agent, she informed us that on average, houses for sale stayed on the market for a year or more before selling. But Pikeville was a swanky-looking small town. Some parts of town had unique, new, contemporary buildings. Other parts of town had historic buildings. The town had one Walmart, which was popular there as it was everywhere else. There were some other stores too, just not like what I was used to. My pet peeve was that there wasn't any place for me to get my hair done.

One day, after months of living there, I saw a black guy working at Applebee's. I asked him, "Do you know where I can go to get my hair done?"

He laughed and said, "There isn't anything like that around here for us. You have to travel to one of the larger cities for something like that. I'm talking three to four hours in whatever direction you choose to go. Or you could practice doing it yourself like my sister does."

I had to do just that. I practiced putting a hair relaxer in my hair. After reading the instructions on the golden plastic jar containing the cream relaxer, I laid out my supplies before tackling the task. I had a towel, a pair of rubber gloves, a comb, basing cream for my scalp, and a timer. The recommended application time for the product was thirteen to sixteen minutes. That was the amount of time allotted for applying the product to new growth from start to finish on a full head of hair. Then I had to allow the product to set and marinade in my hair for fifteen to twenty minutes while smoothing it with a comb. That was done to make sure every strand of hair was covered and relaxed, softened and straight.

Unfortunately, I'd scratched my scalp earlier that day. Chemicals in relaxers burn irritated skin. I accidentally had bought superstrength, and I badly burned my scalp on one side of my head. Thank God it healed after a while and went back to normal. It took close to two months before my scalp completely healed. After that, Yury, our children, and I traveled back to Charleston every two months for my relaxer touch-ups, which was worth the eight-hour trip both going and returning.

In December 2004, Yury had been working with the company for three months. Christmas was coming. He bought thirty ten-dollar gift cards to pass out to the employees he supervised and a few of his coworkers. I was fine with it, especially after he explained he wanted to do something special for them. However, I was concerned when Yury came home with his Christmas gifts. He came back with a well-padded, stylish rust-colored jacket and a high-quality, thick white crewneck sweater.

As I examined his gifts, I said, "Who bought you these expensive clothes?"

Yury shook his head and replied, "Some of the guys bought them for me. They thought I should have heavier clothes for the weather here."

"Men don't buy other men clothes, not men they work with and just met." I shook my head.

"Well, they did," he said with a smile.

I said, "Please tell me you are not up to your old tricks again. I am not going through the same incident you had with Asha on your last job."

Yury responded, "Here. Take the clothes. I just won't wear them, and if they ask me at work why I'm not wearing them, I'll tell them because you don't want me to."

"Don't give them to me. I am just telling you I'm not going through that again," I said.

Yury placed his gifts in his closest, and he didn't wear those clothes. Something didn't feel right down in the deepest part of me regarding that subject, so I was pleased he didn't wear those items. From what I knew about women, they had to have some kind of emotional or physical attraction or connection with someone before they invested time or money into him.

Yury could be sweet when he wanted to be. Every now and then, he still made breakfast in the morning before he left the house for work. He also played with our children and went to all of Jaren's roller hockey lessons and games. Overall, he was a good person with a good heart.

Despite the fact that he liked his alone time, we got along well, except when he chased after other women. I was sure he would have said we got along well when I wasn't telling him God was communicating with me. I didn't talk to him about God on a regular basis. I followed what I'd learned from my mother about not nagging my husband, not pushing God on him, and letting our house be his castle. Howbeit, God allowed our lives to be shaken up. I only told him when God started letting me know a change was coming to our lives. I wanted Yury to get on the same page with me so our marriage would be saved. I didn't see any evidence, but I was hopeful anyway.

NINE

WHILE WE SETTLED into our new house, I started noticing some unusual things going on around us. Yury worked the night shift. One night, I was awakened when I heard someone walking around outside our bedroom window. I got up, went to the window, and carefully looked outside. I was startled when I saw a young lady with short blonde hair standing against our house by the window. I walked softly to the other side of the bedroom to pick up the telephone.

After dialing 911, I told the dispatcher someone was standing outside by my bedroom window. The dispatcher kept me on the phone for a while, but the officer responding was coming from a good distance away. Maybe he came from a different county. It took him close to forty minutes to arrive at our house.

Once he was inside with me, he told me with a grouchy attitude and annoyed expression, "I already checked outside. No one was out there. Did you lock all your windows?"

"Yes, we did," I answered.

He continued in the same tone. "Well, there's nothing more I can do here. Whoever it was is already gone."

I said, "OK, well, thank you."

After he left, I wasn't satisfied with his crusty mood. Maybe he'd had a bad day, such as having an argument with a loved one, or maybe my so-called emergency was keeping him from something he really wanted to do. I thought, *If I'd had a true emergency, it could have possibly turned out crummy.* I was thankful to God that wasn't the case.

In the morning, my neighbor whose house was near our bedroom window came over to talk to me. She said, "I saw the police looking around your house early this morning. I want to apologize for scaring you. The person you saw outside your window was me. I went outside to smoke a cigarette just past one thirty. I don't smoke inside my house. I was just walking around. Please forgive me for making you worry."

"Thank you for telling me that! I'm glad to hear it was only you," I responded. Her confession helped me feel more at ease.

From there, a series of weird things happened. One day a few men showed up at our house to complete some work on its exterior. They said the previous owners had ordered the work before they sold the house to us. That had never happened to us before, and it was the third house we had purchased.

Another day, a man I had never seen before was in our backyard, digging up a sizable rosebush. I didn't go outside to find out why he was in our backyard. I just watched him from the window in unbelief. *What kind of person just goes onto someone else's property and starts digging up a bush without asking first?* I never liked confrontation unless it was absolutely called for. Plus, I didn't know what state of mind the man was in. His action suggested he could have been mentally challenged. Yury was still on the night shift, so he was sleeping and missed out on seeing the ludicrous act.

Another day, I had just returned home from the store. The radio was on. I changed the channel and came across a Christian radio station. I was stunned when the host sounded as if he were talking about my book.

He said as he laughed, "Yeah, so this lady wrote some kind of book about her life. I won't tell you the title of the book. However, in it, she is telling people God sees them. Yeah. It's caused a bit of a stir, and now some ministers are trying to teach her a lesson."

I didn't hear the whole conversation since I just happened to stop on that station after searching through other channels. Just the little bit I did hear sent chills up my spine. Some other things happened that were too complicated to explain. Later, I told Yury about what I had seen and heard.

He said, "That radio host could have been talking about anybody. He didn't say your name, so it's not you. You are not a celebrity, so no one knows who you are. And the man in our yard probably was drunk. He accidentally stumbled into the wrong yard. That's the only logical reason for him to dig up one of our shrubs. Believe me. No one is out to get you, because no one knows you." He placed a hand on my thigh as we sat on the couch together. Then he placed his hands over his eyes with his fingers splayed apart to see me.

I said, "Yury, trust me. You know I love you. We love each other. I wouldn't lie to you!" I raised my voice while holding back tears.

Yury asked, "What is happening to you? You are acting loonier than a Looney Tune!"

"No, Yury! I'm sure of what I heard. I'm sure of what I have seen too. I don't have any doubts these things are all connected."

He closed his eyes, rubbed his forehead with his hand, and grunted, "That's it! I don't want to hear another word!" He inched away from me.

I told him, "Maybe someone from Rising Hope Church somehow got in touch with them. I am sure the little bit I heard on the radio sounded like they were talking about me."

"You are crazy! You are completely mad! Nobody is out to get you. Why would anybody be talking about your book? Nobody knows you." He slammed his fist on the coffee table. "You are going to have to get yourself together, or I'm going to divorce you." He got up from the couch and left the living room.

Our argument left me depleted and downhearted. I had no words. It was the first time he'd threatened to divorce me. I was dumbfounded and discouraged. I didn't understand why God was allowing me to go through this ordeal.

I recalled watching a Warner Bros. cartoon of a dancing and singing frog many years before. In the cartoon, a man who was down on his luck found a box with a frog inside. At first, the frog looked like an ordinary frog. Then the frog sang the song "Hello, My Baby" and danced with a top hat and cane. The man thought he'd found treasure and means to a better future. Unfortunately, the frog concealed his talents when in front of an audience. He camouflaged himself as just an ordinary frog, which infuriated the crowd and dashed the man's dreams.

Many of the things I was experiencing put me in the mind of that man and frog. There were things happening that only I was privy to. I was experiencing a private spiritual battle. Whenever I tried to show or explain what I was going through to Yury, my family, or my church family, they didn't see or hear anything. It was upsetting. I felt as if I were on the verge of going insane, but I held on to God. He kept my mind safe.

One morning, I woke up from a dream. In the dream, I saw a large drinking glass surrounded by darkness. However, somehow, there was light coming from the center, and from inside the center of the glass, I heard the voice of the Lord say, "Joseph, Joseph, you were chosen."

On the outside of the glass, I heard many preachers' voices saying in unison, "Die to yourself. Die to yourself. Die to yourself."

God's voice was friendly and warm. It sounded as if he were smiling as he talked to me. His voice was familiar, as if I had heard it before. As he spoke, I found myself thinking, *What are you so happy about? Don't you see what's going on and happening in my life? Don't you see who is against me?*

Another time, God showed me a dream in which I was in a gorgeous house. It was spacious, grandiose, and furnished and decorated to my liking. I saw myself in my huge closet. There were clothes, shoes, pocketbooks, and jewelry already in place. As I was admiring everything, I named what I was going to give to my sisters.

When Jillian turned twelve, Yury reluctantly kept his word from when she was three and got her a dog. I was impressed with him because he honored his word, even though he didn't want to. Our home life was quiet and simple. My husband was a dedicated hard worker.

Once he entered our house, he would play with the children for a little while before hiding in his quiet place. He continued to relax after work by reading a book in another room for hours at a time. He didn't talk often, except to ask what was for dinner. We would watch TV together at eight o'clock. Then he would go to bed at ten. Of course, he would let me know in little ways when he wanted special attention from me. That was our life.

Life in Pikeville, Kentucky, was far from what I was used to. Since we rarely saw black people there, the children and I found ourselves becoming amazed and excited anytime we saw one or more. Like the popular line in the movie *The Sixth Sense*, when the little boy said, "I see dead people," my children and I were telling my side of the family, "We saw black people."

Growing up among a variety of people and then being reduced to being around one race and being the only minority made for a strange experience. Plus, it was difficult for me to get adjusted to being surrounded by mountains—gray mountains. That and the complicated spiritual situation I found myself in made me depressed. I didn't go around with my head down, have problems engaging in family activities, or want to sleep all day, but I was in a blue funk.

Therefore, in April 2006, Yury accepted a new job in Greensboro, North Carolina. God was involved in the process of selling our house in Pikeville. Instead of being on the market for a year or more before selling, as the real estate agent predicted, our house sold for the full asking price in less than a month. A pastor and his wife bought our house. I had heard ministers say God had a sense of humor. I didn't see that coming. *God is amazing!*

We rented a house in Greensboro for a year. In the rental, I had a dream. I dreamed Yury and I were sleeping in our bed. I was awakened by a bright light. As I turned my head to Yury, I could tell he felt the heat from the light, but he couldn't hear the voice of God when God started talking to me. I knew that because even though Yury was still asleep, his body was squirming in discomfort, as if he were hot. By then, I was standing up.

Then I heard God say, "I'm about to release you to the public. But first, I want you to look me in my eyes and promise you are going to keep my ways and my commands."

I looked around our bedroom and said, "OK, but how am I supposed to do that?"

God said, "Look up at the ceiling."

When I did, I saw two blue eyeballs looking down at me through the ceiling. It was kind of a funny sight to me. As I looked at the eyes, I said, "I promise to keep your ways and your commands."

After that night, I often wondered why God showed me blue eyeballs coming from the ceiling, especially after I heard teachings that Jesus was Jewish. Then I remembered when I was growing up, all the pictures on our wall depicted Jesus with blond hair and blue eyes.

Since that dream was significant, I told Yury about it. He was not impressed, not that I was trying to impress him. I believed that couples were supposed to talk and make decisions together, especially when they were married.

He said, "I told you if you don't stop talking like that, I'm going to divorce you."

I was sad. I had been praying for Yury to come back to God ever since we got married. Early in our marriage, I'd discovered he wasn't interested in serving God with me or helping me raise our children in the ways of God. Still, I never pushed him, because of what my mom had taught me.

At that point, I wanted to tell him I'd lost my shape after having three babies with him, and in our vows, we'd promised we were going to be with each other until death. I wanted to say, "God is calling me, and you are saying no, so which way would you like to go?" But I didn't want our life to turn into a crazy Lifetime movie or end up being a story on *Snapped* on TV. Besides, God, the law of the land, and the police community frowned on things like that. Honestly, I wanted to drop down on the floor and have a massive temper tantrum. During my meltdown, I wanted to lie on my back, flail my arms and legs in the air, and scream in the highest decibel possible. However, I couldn't, because Mama had taught us that a mother was supposed to be her children's rock. My children were watching me to see how I handled things.

As time went on, God miraculously turned my problematic, hard-to-explain private spiritual battle in my favor. My awesome, caring Father God changed the hearts of people connected to my private spiritual conflict. God marked me as his own child, his daughter. My Savior and the lover of my soul made it so that those who once had viewed me as questionable now brushed me off in a state of restoration and encouraged me.

While watching Linking Christians Inc., I heard ministers, including Bishop Wiseman, say things like "If people want to leave your life, don't force them to stay. If God intended for them to stay in your life, then there is nothing you could say or do to make them leave."

Then an energetic tan young man with a booming voice looked at the camera, pointed his finger, and said, "Since you are losing your husband because God is calling you, God said to stop crying. He has already chosen another one for you. And don't worry. This one already spends time with him and loves him."

After hearing those words, I was encouraged, knowing God knew and saw what happened in my life. Around that time, I dreamed Pastor Ash Strong was visiting my mother's house. She was sitting at the table, talking and laughing with Mom, my siblings, and me. She was wearing a rare hand chain bracelet that covered her whole hand, and she noticed Donna was wearing one similar to hers. Pastor Strong reached over for Donna's hand to get a closer look. She began admiring it. Then the dream ended. I didn't know what the dream meant, but I was sure it meant something. After looking online, I saw Pastor Strong was scheduled to speak in Charleston. Since I was expecting something to happen there, I talked Yury into taking me to her meeting.

I told Yury, "All I know is God is showing me different things in dreams. Maybe he chose her for me to learn from."

Reluctantly, Yury took me there. Her meeting was packed. There wasn't an empty seat anywhere.

Toward the end of Pastor Strong's meeting, she said with emphasis, "Once we're done here, I'm going straight home without making any pit stops."

Yury looked at me and said, "See? She is not going to your mother's house. You are not hearing from God. The devil is tricking you. You need to stop this now."

I didn't understand what was going on. I felt let down by God, but I knew better than to turn my back on him. Yury was not happy with me. I didn't know he had put up a mental protective wall between us.

Soon I had a number of dreams showing me in different churches with Bishop Adam Wiseman and his wife, Joy. They pastored a church of about five thousand people in Dallas, Texas. He and his adorable wife operated their church with a spirit of excellence. I watched them on Linking Christians Inc.

The large church building was adorned in a combination of brick on the lower level and stucco on the upper level, with cathedral windows and a tall steeple. It sat in the middle of a five-acre spread of land. Bishop Wiseman clearly spent a lot of time in the presence of the Lord, because he exuded buckets of wisdom. A black cowboy hat and western boots were his signature dress. Later, God allowed him to help guide me prophetically in the direction of God's plan for my life. By that time, I was going to Pastor Stonefish's church, Heavenly Dimension Church, in Greensboro, North Carolina.

Then God showed me a number of dreams in which I was walking alone on the property of Bishop Wiseman's church in Dallas. During their sermons, God spoke to me through the voice of Bishop Wiseman and Pastor Stonefish to walk by faith to fulfill my destiny in Dallas. Again, I told Yury what God was showing me. I begged him to go with me so our family could stay together. As usual, he didn't believe it and didn't want to hear about it.

I said, "Let's make an appointment with Pastor Stonefish to talk about it."

"God doesn't get involved with people's lives. I'll go on one condition. If Pastor Stonefish tells you God is not sending you to Dallas, I don't want to hear anything more about moving to Texas," Yury said.

Nodding, I said, "Yes, you have a deal."

I was sure God was going to show up in Pastor Stonefish's office, since Mama and some of the women at church had told me God didn't break up families in order for us to fulfill our destiny. After hearing that, I expected Pastor Stonefish to confirm to Yury what God was showing me. Unfortunately, that didn't happen. After Yury and I explained our situation to Pastor Stonefish, I waited with great expectation for his words of wisdom.

He said, "God doesn't separate families."

If I had been dramatic, I would have slid out of my chair and fainted on the floor. Yury stared at the pastor and then at me before looking down at the floor. I wished I could snap my fingers and vanish out of the room. The moment made me relate on a deep personal level with the character Evan Baxter in the movie *Evan Almighty*. In the movie, Evan Baxter won a seat in Congress. At first, his new life appeared bright. Then God threw a monkey wrench into his life and the lives of his family when he chose Evan to be a modern-day Noah and told him to build an ark.

The heavenly assignment caused havoc in both Evan's political life and his home life. Evan's new zany behavior placed stress on his family relationships too, which resulted in them leaving him. Eventually, God paid a visit to Evan's wife and sons in a restaurant when they stopped to eat along the way to her parents' house in another state. God approached her in a nonintrusive way and helped her see the situation from a different angle. Shazam—her eyes were opened, and she found understanding. She returned home with their sons to stand by her husband throughout the rest of his mission.

That was what I'd hoped for that day in Pastor Stonefish's office. As Yury and I left the office together, I walked out on legs with the strength of Jell-O. Yury lowered his head, darted past me, grunted through his teeth, and said, "You need help! Go talk to a head doctor!"

Seconds turned to minutes. Minutes turned to hours. Hours turned to days. Days turned to weeks. Weeks turned to months. Months turned to another year. Many of the same things were happening. Yury and I were cordial toward each other. Our life looked as it always had on the surface. I learned to stay away from the taboo subject in order to keep peace in our home. However, God was making it clear that he was calling me. I was hearing all kinds of encouraging, prophetic words.

In 2007, year fifteen of our marriage, since our landlords' grandchildren were moving in with them, they decided to move back into their house. Consequently, we had to find another place to live, so we bought a house in Greensboro. Shortly after we got settled into our new house, I had a dream. In the dream, I saw Yury standing beside a petite, small-built black lady. The top part of her hair from the root halfway down was colored an orangie red, while the bottom portion of her shoulder-length hair remained black. Also, in the dream, Yury never said it, but I somehow knew she worked at the same place he did.

Yury said, "I'm leaving."

I said, "You mean to tell me that you have been sleeping with her during the same time you were sleeping with me?"

He responded, "You can keep the house."

I answered in shock, "I can't pay for this house. I'm only working part-time."

Yury said, "That's your problem."

I woke up from the dream shaking in my boots. Based on experience from my past, I knew God was showing me something. This was serious. Strangely, I was still a housewife when I had the dream; I was not working outside our house yet. We lived far from family, and Yury and I didn't want strangers taking care of our children.

The dream drove me to break the silence regarding talking to Yury about God-related material. Our marriage was on the line, and it was my duty to try to save it. When I talked to Yury, he shut me down about the dream. He wanted me to get out of my fairy-tale dreams, because he was done with them.

Simultaneously, I was being led to step out on faith and go to Dallas. I didn't have a plan. I didn't have any answers. I was walking by faith. I heard a minister say, "Walking by faith is walking by what we hear God saying to us." Even though I was scared, I knew I had to obey what I was hearing. God was using ministers I watched on TV and Pastor Stonefish to prophetically tell me I only had a small window of time to be obedient.

I would forever remember the look on Yury's face when I told him I was going to Dallas. The hurt I saw on his face caused me pain. During my children's nightly Bible story reading time and prayers, I informed them whenever God revealed something to me. I omitted telling them the juicy part of the dream, out of respect for Yury. I told them God was telling me to go to Dallas. At that time, I believed the dream I'd had about the lady standing by Yury meant if I didn't go to Dallas that was going to happen in our lives. It scared me badly. Jillian was fourteen, Jaren was eleven, and Jasper was eight years old. I was clueless about what to pray, but I trusted God.

My children said, "If God is warning you, you'd better listen."

Shaken up by the whole ordeal, I went to Dallas for a few days. I knew I could not tell my family, or they would try to talk me out of it. I knew in order to obey God, I would have to tell my family everything after I moved to Dallas, so they couldn't stop me. Shortly after we moved into the house we bought in Greensboro, Yury and I discussed my going to Dallas to visit the church and talk to someone there about what I was experiencing. Yury and I just talked about it, but no action was taken on my part. I wanted him to go with me, but he wasn't interested. The dream of him with the lady put heat under my bottom, so to speak. I rushed to Dallas on a Friday evening without telling Yury I was going. I already knew he didn't understand what I was going through. He must have been stressed out by what I was going through, believed, and told him.

However, he didn't verbalize it to me. Then again, many times, he rubbed the sides of his temples as the warmth faded from his jasper-green eyes. They started to appear cold and distant. I knew leaving town without telling Yury might have seemed juvenile, but God had my attention, and time was of the essence. I'd heard many preachers say God knew how to get people's attention.

Yury was ticked off by my actions. Since he did not understand what was going on with me, he had every right to feel that way. In Dallas, I didn't know what I was supposed to do. Once I settled into my hotel room, I called Yury at our house to let him know I had landed safely and was in my room.

He asked in a rough tone, "What are your plans?"

The inflection in his voice made my stomach turn. I told him, "I'm going to church Sunday, and I'll make an appointment to talk to one of the pastors here."

"Well, let me know how it goes," he said, sounding more relaxed and hopeful.

I said, "OK, I will."

I took an airplane to Dallas and a taxicab to church. The church looked the same in person as it did on TV. The building was adorned in red brick on the bottom and tan stucco on the top portion. It had cathedral windows and a tall steeple. Greeters stood in front of the ten entrance doors and inside the church, so everyone was acknowledged.

Everyone was friendly, and the atmosphere was electric. The praise-and-worship portion of service was like attending a concert. The singers and musicians were better than many well-known professionals. During the church service, I was nervous because I didn't know what to expect. However, God met me there. In his sermon, Bishop Wiseman seemed to be talking directly to me.

He said, "It's no accident that you are here in this room this morning. God is waiting on you. He knows you are here. God has a plan for your life."

Those words went right through me. After church, I still didn't know what I was supposed to do. I was beginning to panic, so I called Linking Christians Inc. Before a prayer counselor picked up, through their phone service, I heard a recording of Bishop Wiseman's voice say, "God is with you. Trust him. He won't fail you."

I looked at the phone with my mouth wide open. Then a prayer counselor answered the phone. She prayed with me for God's direction and guidance.

Monday morning, I made an appointment to talk to Pastor Tarren, one of the ministers at Bishop Wiseman's church. During the appointment, I spoke as best as I could about why I had come to Dallas and why I needed to talk to someone with spiritual experience. Pastor Tarren, with his mocha skin, lined-up low-cut hair, and Versace glasses, looked as if he'd just stepped out of *GQ* magazine. He greeted me warmly. His smile covered his face.

He extended his hand to shake mine and said, "Well, hi there, Mrs. DeBlake." The pitch of his voice sounded as if he were singing.

I said, "Hi, Pastor Tarren."

"It's good to meet you."

"Thank you! It's good to meet you too."

We walked down a long corridor to his office. A dark gray accent wall was before us once the door opened. A large abstract painting of different hues of grays and blues hung on the wall above his mahogany desk.

"Please have a seat," he said as he sat. "How did you end up here?"

I cleared my throat and started slowly. "God has been showing me different things in my dreams. Also, I have been getting prophetic words confirming what I saw in my dreams. The thing is, my family thinks I need to visit the funny farm because of it. My husband doesn't want to come to Dallas, and he won't let me bring our children. This is the place God told me to come, so I'm here."

He said, "I know what you're going through. God told me to come to Dallas too. He didn't give me any details either. That's what walking by faith is all about. You have to listen to what God tells you and obey, not knowing what to do or how to do it. It was rough for us when we first came. Nothing was working. My family and I went back to our hometown to regroup. A year later, God told us to try again. The second time around, it was still hard, but eventually, God turned things around in our favor. If you are going to be in Dallas, you will need a vehicle to get around in. This city is big and spread out, and public transportation doesn't go everywhere."

I asked, "Does this church have a place for people to stay who come to Dallas by faith?"

"No, you will need to make your own way for your housing or go to a shelter until God makes a way for you," he said, shaking his head.

I called Yury after the meeting and told him what the pastor had said.

He released air from his mouth that sounded like puffs of bubbles and sputtered, "So what does that mean to you?"

I told him, "I'm coming back, because I am not prepared to be here right now. Also, I'll look for a job to pay off my travel expenses that I placed on our credit card."

Yury paused in silence for a minute and then said, "OK, we'll talk some more when you get back. When are you coming back?"

I said, "Tomorrow. Hey, my suitcase hasn't arrived here yet, so I had to buy another outfit, underwear, and toiletries so I could attend church yesterday morning. A person with the airline said someone will deliver my suitcase to me later today."

Yury said, "See? That means God doesn't want you to be there, because if he did, everything would have worked out well for you."

I answered, "No, I don't think so."

I had traveled by airplane to Dallas, and I stayed four nights in a hotel because I didn't have a place to stay. I was clueless. Therefore, I went back to Greensboro. I used our credit card to fund my miniexcursion. Yury wasn't happy. I told him I would pay it back. The only problem was, I didn't have a job, but that was about to change.

TEN

UPON MY RETURN to our home, Yury started sitting on the opposite side of the couch instead of near me like he used to. He stopped looking at me and faced me only if I talked directly to him and faced him straight on. Kindness had been erased from his face and replaced with animosity. The evidence was clear each time he narrowed his eyes, clenched his teeth, or frowned.

Heavenly Dimension Church, the church Pastor Stonefish pastored, was having a large community outreach with plenty of free food, games, and activities to let the community know they were there for them. The church's staff printed invitations for the congregation to pass out to the public. With a handful in tow, I walked around my neighborhood, passing the invitations out to neighbors I knew and didn't know. Then I started passing them out to employees at various businesses. I enjoyed eating Chick-fil-A's food. While I was there waiting for my food order, I gave one of the community outreach invitations to one of the employees.

She smiled and said, "Thank you so much! Hey, we are hiring. Would you like an application?"

I nodded and said, "Yes."

I learned through ministers that with God, there weren't any coincidences. She walked behind the counter and toward the kitchen. Moments later, she came back with a man with bowlegs, a heavy French accent, and a herculean beach bod. He was the owner of that Chick-fil-A franchise. He approached me with an employment application in his hand.

He said, "Hello," and he shook my hand and introduced himself as Mr. Xavier.

I smiled and responded, "Hi. I'm Lewisa. Nice to meet you."

He said, "Lana gave me your church's invitation and told me you are interested in employment here."

"Yes, we are having a community outreach festival with free food, games, and activities. And yes, I am interested in employment here," I said.

Mr. Xavier asked, "Do you have time to fill out an application right now?"

"Well, would it be OK if I take it home, fill it out, and bring it back today? I mainly came here today to pass out the invitations and pick up food," I said.

He said, "Yes, if you can come back with your application at four o'clock, I can interview you. Make sure you bring your Social Security card and driver's license with you."

I replied, "OK, thank you! I will."

I went back at four o'clock with my application, SS card, and driver's license. The interview went well, and Mr. Xavier said, "I'll get back to you soon. I don't normally hire people on the spot."

I said, "I understand. Thank you again!"

At five thirty, I received a phone call from Mr. Xavier. He said, "Lewisa, I'm impressed that you were out inviting people to attend your church's outreach. I would like you to join our team. Are you still interested?"

I answered, "Yes."

Landing a part-time job two weeks after returning to Greensboro allowed me to pay off the debt I'd accumulated when I stepped out on faith and went to Dallas. The icicles that chilled Yury's and my home life began to thaw out. Even though he was not a big fan of chicken, he chose to visit me at work a few times. The fact that Yury began smiling again and looked relaxed instead of stressed gave me hope.

However, the dream I'd had in 2007 of Yury telling me he was leaving me was on my mind too. In the dream, I'd told Yury I was only working part-time. Now I was working part-time. The whole thing seemed astounding.

A few months passed. Then God showed me another dream. I was in a large church. The dream had three different settings. First, Bishop Adam Wiseman was preaching. His wife was behind him on the stage with a large group of other people. I was in the back of the church.

Then the dream shifted. Second, I was in a classroom, helping a teacher move tables, chairs, and other things around.

Then the dream shifted again. Third, I was in the hallway of a school, and Luca, the Christian guitarist, was standing in front of me. He didn't say anything. He just stood there staring at me. Then the dream ended.

I called my mother on the phone the next day to tell her about the dream and to ask her what she thought it meant. She didn't know the meaning.

She said to me, "I don't know why you are dreaming about those people."

I wasn't trying to dream about them. I couldn't force myself to dream about anything or anyone. I wondered what the dream meant. Then, one day, I was watching Linking Christians Inc., Pastor Yadar was preaching. All of a sudden, he stopped talking for a moment. Then he watched the camera closely, as if he were talking directly to me. He said, "The dream means he"—Luca—"is your husband."

Afterward, he went back to preaching where he'd left off. I just stood there with my eyes wide as I viewed the TV. I knew those prophetic words were for me. I was amazed, puzzled, and excited at the same time. It didn't make any sense, but that was not unusual. *Many times, when God communicates with people, it doesn't make sense. It takes faith to do or have whatever he said,* I thought.

I told my children about the dream and the prophetic words. I was sure they didn't understand it, but they were excited. I told them Luca had served God for twenty-five years. I was sure once God let him know he'd chosen me for him, Luca probably would kick his dog or cat and ask God, "Why me?" He would say, "But, God, she's black! You know how much it's going to cost to feed her? I'll probably have to call Nutrisystem, Jenny Craig, and Weight Watchers to get her body to an acceptable size. Her first gift is going to be a treadmill." I told the kids he was probably praying for someone fit like Halle Berry, but instead, God was sending him Monique. I thought Monique was beautiful too, but a lot of men seemed to want the perfect-sized lady as a trophy wife. I thought, *Some men act like if a woman's body is not tight, then she just ain't right. Many of them are shallow and don't want a woman with a pure heart if she isn't wrapped in a good-looking package.*

I told Yury about the dream and what Pastor Yadar had said, and I said, "If you don't go with me so I can do what God wants me to do, he is going to give me a different husband instead of you."

He frowned. "That's insane! God doesn't do things like that! You know what the women at work are saying about our situation? They are saying that an idle mind is the devil's playground. You don't have anything constructive to do, so the devil is just having a field day with your mind."

"That's not true," I said. "God spoke to many people in the Bible through dreams and by prophets. There is even a scripture in the Bible where God took the wives of men and gave them to other men: 'Therefore I will give their wives to other men and their field to other owners. From the least to the greatest, all are greedy for gain; prophets and priest alike, all practice deceit' (Jeremiah 8:10 NIV). I don't worship the devil. I am a believer. I spend time with God. I'm always singing to him. He loves it when we sing to him."

Yury said, "I don't want to hear any more about this! You are not hearing from God!" He raised his voice as he bared a clenched jaw and a red face.

I never understood how Yury thought it was OK to tell his coworkers, especially the women, about what went on in our personal lives. At the same time, he would tell me he didn't mix his home life and work life together. I talked to my mom, hoping to get a better response from her about our spiritual dilemma, but that wasn't the case.

Mama disapproved. "No, no, no! Oh no! God doesn't do things like that. He is not going to give you a different husband when you already have a husband. Maybe God was showing you he is going to make Yury a new person. You got that wrong. There is no way in the world God is going to have Luca become your husband. That's the devil. God doesn't do things like that."

As days gave way to nights, time ran its course, and a few years passed. Yury's and my marriage looked basically the same as it always had—to me, that was. We went to work and to baseball or hockey games, according to the season. We attended our children's school's PTA meetings, programs, and awards. Sometimes, on Yury's days off, we quietly ate breakfast or lunch in diners and restaurants and occasionally went out for dinner as a family, all with little eye contact.

Occasionally, we would see a ballet, concert, symphony orchestra, or play. From time to time, we still went walking together outside for exercise. Our walks were in silence, but even though I felt a disconnect in my spirit, we still walked. Also, we played Monopoly, other board games, and many card games as a family too. It was our life, and I was used to it. I still didn't try to change Yury, complain, or nag, as per Mom's training I'd grown up with. I started eating my dinner with him on the couch, which was near the dinner table, instead of at the dinner table, where I had trained our children to eat with me. The only time Yury joined us at the table was for a Thanksgiving or Christmas meal, but that was not always guaranteed.

We watched a movie every night after dinner, but there wasn't a whole lot of communicating going on between us. And yes, we still danced under the sheets whenever the mood hit him. In addition, in the midst of my being blind to what was developing beneath the surface of our lives, miraculously, God continued to guide and encourage me through Bishop Wiseman, the church I used to belong to, and many other ministers on TV to embrace and go after the plan he had for my life.

I had no idea that my longtime dream of Yury's and my marriage standing the test of time and leading us to one day be an old, frail-looking couple normally seen at the mall was going to be impossible. When I saw those couples, the old man usually stood in the middle of the mall, looking lost, as he held the pocketbook of his wife of fifty years while she sightsees in a store. Couples like that are beautiful to me.

Everything we were going through was interfering with my personal desire for us to have a stay-together fight song. I'd chosen for us Shania Twain's "You're Still the One." Since there had been so much opposition regarding our coming together, I thought it was the perfect song for us. I also liked the Rascal Flats song "I Will Stand by You," which made me sob uncontrollably.

Just as the blades of a fan twirled quickly in motion, generating a breeze that cooled the stuffy, stale air, the year 2009 blew in. God was still leading me to go back to Dallas by dreams and prophetic words through Bishop Wiseman, Pastor Stonefish, and many TV ministers.

Then, one Sunday in April, I heard Pastor Stonefish say, "You need to decide if you are going to follow God or not. You have to decide if you are going after your destiny. You only have a small window of time to make a move."

My mouth dropped open. I knew those words were for me, and I had to tell Yury about it, which I dreaded. I decided to talk to Yury that same day after lunch and after he had a chance to relax for a little while. First, I asked God to help me. Then it was time to face my fears.

I went to Yury and said, "I need to tell you that God has been letting me know he wants me to go back to Dallas."

He rolled his eyes and shouted, "Ugh! I don't want to hear that again! You promised me when we went to see Pastor Stonefish two years ago that if he said you weren't hearing from God, you would drop all this foolishness! You are wearing me out! I can't take this anymore!"

"Yury, I am sure I am hearing from God. I want you and our family to be together. You could look for a job there. Then we can all still be together," I said, trying to convince him.

"I don't want to move to Texas. My home—our home—is right here in Greensboro. I'm not looking for another job and giving up the one I have to go down a rabbit hole into la-la land with you. As my wife, you are supposed to stay where I am—where I have my job!" Yury snarled.

I said, "So are you telling me you are staying here, and only our children and I are going to Texas?"

He snapped, "You are not taking our children with you! You don't even know where you are going to live or how you are going to make money. I am not going to let you disrupt our children's lives because you decided you are starstruck over a man with a big church. You know, people are saying you have lost it, and it's not worth it. Even your own mother disagrees with you about your claim of hearing from God. That should tell you something right there!"

"Yury, do you remember what I told you Pastor Tarren said when I went to visit him in Dallas? He said his story is similar to mine, and he knew what I was going through. The only thing different is his whole family was with him," I said.

Shaking his head, he said, "Please don't tell me that nonsense. I don't believe that for one minute. No true man would leave everything and move his family cross-country without knowing how he is going to provide for them. That's ridiculous! I think he was just trying to make you feel better. There's no way in the world responsible people would do something like that. God doesn't tell people to go here or there. He doesn't get involved in our lives like that. He gives us free will. Those TV preachers are nothing but a bunch of charlatans. They are just after money. The bottom line is, you are going to Texas just because you want to go to Texas. When are you planning to leave?"

"After school closes, so maybe in July, when you all go to visit your family. I don't want the children to see me moving my things out of the house," I answered.

He said, "Have you told the children?"

"I have been talking to them about what God has been telling me, but I wanted to talk to you first about going back to Dallas," I said.

He pounded his fist on the desk. "I hate God! And leaving your children is pathetic! I hope you know I'm not going to wait for you to find out what's going to happen. As soon as you leave, I'm going on with my life. Have you told your mom yet?"

I shook my head and said, "No."

He walked away and said, "Well, good luck with that."

Right then and there, it seemed as if an invisible box covered me and shielded the yearning I had to be accepted and understood by Yury, my mother, and my siblings. He couldn't see my heart was crushed and crying out, *Why can't you just love me wholeheartedly as if I'm more precious and valuable than rare gold to you? Why can't you just love me the way I need you to love me right now? I would do it, and already have done it, for you.*

My conversation that night with Mom went just as I had pictured it playing out in my mind. She was downright mad. I was sure if she could have teleported herself from Charleston, South Carolina, to Greensboro, North Carolina, at that moment, she would have.

Her voice fluctuated with emotion, which started with yelling. "No! I already told you God didn't tell you any such thing! So you are turning out to be just like Donna, huh?" Donna had had a similar but different experience about seventeen or eighteen years before my ordeal began. "When I left your daddy, I left because I had no other choice! I took my children with me! A mother stays with her children! When God does something, he works everything out for your good. That should tell you that you are hearing from the devil! If God were talking to you, he would let Yury know he is talking to you, so Yury could get on board too."

Mom's pitch softened a bit, but it was still penetrating as she continued. "God is not the author of confusion. He does not tear families apart. You are not hearing from God. Your heart is pure, so the devil has crept into your life and deceived you. I serve the God of Abraham, Isaac, and Jacob. I don't know what God you are serving, but it's not the same one I serve. You need to get on your knees and ask God to forgive you. Then you need to give your life to the one and only true God. I'm talking about the God of Abraham, Isaac, and Jacob. When you talk to him, you need to say that, so the devil can leave you alone. There is no way in the world God is going to have you leave your children behind to go after him. Your children need you. I am totally disappointed in you. I never thought the day would come when you would stoop so low and abandon your children because you let the devil trick your mind."

As Mom spoke, I sat in silence as tears trickled down my face. Later, Mama told my brothers and sisters about our conversation. Many of them called me, and our conversations were similar to my talk with Mom but not as harsh. Mom was so unsettled and worried about us and what I believed that she had my oldest brother, Barry in Durham, North Carolina, pay a special visit to our house to talk to me. Barry had played tennis way before it became popular for blacks, was highly intelligent and articulate, read a lot, and had the gift of gab. He could talk for hours and never run out of things to say.

That day, we went for a walk in my neighborhood. His voice was silvery and had the sound of a caring father, which was a relief for me. If he had come off in anger or with any negativity, I didn't think I could have handled it. Of course, he was also in favor of my staying in North Carolina with my family.

He began by saying, "I'm sure you've figured out why I'm here, so why don't you tell me in your own words what's going on with you?"

I inhaled and exhaled and then said, "God called me and is leading me to go to Dallas, but Yury doesn't want to go. He doesn't think I heard from God, because he doesn't think God tells people to go here or there. Mom is going ballistic since Yury is not on board, so she is telling me the devil is talking to me."

Barry looked down at the ground as I spoke. Then he looked at my face with care and said, "I can't tell you what you heard. I'm not going to say it's the devil either, but from the little bit I've learned from going to church, God usually sends families out to do things for him together. God created family, so I don't think it's wise to separate yourself from the people who love you in order to do God's work. Take some time to pray about it and think about it. If God truly has something for you to do, he knows how to move on Yury's heart so that you and your beautiful family can do his will together."

I nodded and said in agreement, "Yes, he knows how to do that. I promise I will pray and think about what you've said."

Barry gave me a side hug as we walked, and he smiled and said, "That's all I ask of you."

Unlike Roberta Flack's song "Killing Me Softly with His Song," my family were killing me softly with their words. The sting of their words hurt a lot, especially the ones that rolled off Yury's tongue. After Barry left to go back home, Mom called me instead of waiting for my nightly phone call.

Mom started by saying, "I'm calling to find out if Barry was able to talk some sense into your head, so was he?"

"Mom, I am sure of what I told you, and I don't serve the devil. I only serve the God you introduced me to a long time ago. He is the God of Abraham, Isaac, and Jacob," I answered.

Mom interrupted before I could say more. "Listen here. My God would never do what you told me he told you to do."

I said, "I asked Yury to go to Texas with me so our whole family could be together. He said no. I told him I wanted to take the children with me, but he said no. I didn't want to fight with him about it, and I don't want the children to see us arguing." Jillian was sixteen, Jaren was thirteen, and Jasper was ten. "I'm all about family, just like you taught us, Mom, but sometimes God does things we don't understand."

Mom sounded strident. "I don't blame Yury for saying no! You are supposed to follow him! He is not supposed to follow you! He has been the one out there working to give you and your children a good life. He's been taking care of y'all like a good man should. He's right not to go! You don't know if he will be able to find a good-paying job in Texas. Why mess up something if it's working? If you keep this mess up, you are going to drive Yury to go after other women. Then you'll have nothing to say, because it will be your fault! Those poor children! That's all I've got to say! I'll wait for your phone call tonight." She hung up, still sounding hot.

If that moment had been a movie scene, the camera would have moved in close to focus on the emotional state painted on my face as images of my family members twirled around me like a tornado while shouting different objections in anger and dismay regarding what I'd told them.

I recalled the words God had spoken to me in my dreams in 2005, "Joseph, Joseph, you were chosen," and the many different ministers' voices echoing in the dream, "Die to yourself. Die to yourself. Die to yourself." I imagined the camera zooming in on my face as my hands clamped down on my flyaway hair, red veins protruded from my stressed eyes, and my lips spread apart, exposing my tightly clenched teeth.

For many years, I had heard people talk about taking a Valium whenever they faced tumultuous situations. I could have used one. Then I would have asked God to wake me up once the storm in my life was over, but unfortunately, things didn't work like that. Just like my family, I did not understand why God had chosen Dallas for me.

There had been a couple of times when I thought about visiting Dallas. First, when I was a child, the TV show *Dallas* was popular. I was hooked on it, especially when everyone was trying to figure out who'd shot J. R. Ewing. Most of America were on the edge of our seats then. Second, when my family and I heard Bishop Wiseman preach on TV, I wanted to visit his church with my family. I never had longed to live in Dallas. I had been watching Clive Stern in

California on TV ever since I was eight years old and Pastor Reddins in Atlanta since he first came on TV in the late 1980s. If I had been doing my own choosing, I would have chosen a person or church closer to home.

Since I was facing a life-altering decision, I went to my Sunday school teacher to ask him if he could connect me with an older, more seasoned woman in God to help guide me. I was introduced to Mama Ginger. She was in her late seventies, appeared twenty years younger than her age, and had a bubbly personality. I'd met her at a women's meeting a few months prior to my request.

The night before the women's meeting, Jillian and I were talking in her bedroom after we read the Bible, which had been our custom since she was a toddler. We talked about the kind of man she wanted God to send into her life when she got older. We'd heard a minister say it was important to be specific, so when God sent the right person, you would know it was him or her. Jillian was going to think about it first before telling God what she wanted.

During the women's meeting the next day, the ladies running it ended up talking about relationships. They asked a few women to share their testimony about God sending their spouses into their lives.

Mama Ginger said, "I was praying for another husband after my first husband died. I specifically asked God to have the man he chose for me sit in the seat next to me in church. Maybe a month later, a nice man started coming to church and sat next to me. We started talking to get to know each other. He was a widower, just like I was a widow. Six months later, we got married."

As she spoke, Jillian and I looked at each other with our eyes and mouths wide open. We were amazed and knew God had allowed us to see he'd heard our prayers. The expression on Jillian's face was priceless to me. I would never forget it. God allowed her to witness him getting involved in our lives.

After we left the church and arrived home, Jillian said, "God heard our prayers."

When Mama Ginger and I met the second time, we decided to go for coffee at Starbucks to talk about my issue. I gave her a brief run-through of what God was leading me to do.

She watched me with care and responded, "Oh, sweetie, I can tell you genuinely want to please our Father God. However, it's always a good idea to check God's Word for guidance whenever you're faced with an important decision, and to be totally honest with you, honey, there is nothing in the Bible that supports what you are saying God is telling you to do. God doesn't break marriages apart. I'm going to give you homework. I want you to watch the movie *Fireproof*, which Kirk Cameron stars in."

I lowered my head and said, "OK, thank you for your time."

"Let me know how everything turns out," she added.

What about Joseph? I thought after our meeting. I was basically a woman of few words. Plus, since I had been taught to always be polite and treat others the way I wanted to be treated, per my nature, I preferred to listen and observe more than I spoke. I knew that in the Bible, God allowed life's circumstances and situations to separate a few families because of the plan he had for their lives. Some of those separations were tragic, such as the loss of Job's ten children and all his possessions (Job 1:13–22 NIV). God had Abraham and Sarah move away from his family to go by faith to a place God would tell them about later (Genesis 12:1 NIV). Joseph was separated from his father, mother, and brothers by their own hands; from everyone else he knew; and from his homeland (Genesis 37:24–28 NIV).

I watched *Fireproof*. It was a great movie. I didn't do the love-dare challenge, because I was already serving Yury by waiting on him hand and foot and being kind to him even when he was distant, looked as if he'd sucked on a lemon, grunted, rolled his eyes, and said he didn't want to hear me talk about my God situation. I was grateful for Mama Ginger's time, but I was still sure I heard from God. I was 100 percent certain regarding where God wanted me to go. I had heard about how important it was to obey God's leading. That was what I wanted to do: obey God. Even though the way God was leading me felt like a cruel punishment, I'd heard ministers refer to what Job said in the Bible: "Though He [God] slay me, I will trust Him" (Job 13:15–18 NIV). I wanted to be that faithful to God, even though following God made my whole family misunderstand me and despise my actions.

Soon we went from winter's sleepy branches to spring's invigorating, waving leaves in varying shades of green to summer's brilliant rays so warm and hot that they both caressed and baked uncovered skin. Acting out of character for me, based on what I was hearing with my spiritual ears and in dreams, I decided to move to Dallas in July 2009. I was going totally by faith with no preparation, only based on what God was showing and telling me. He showed me in a dream and told me prophetically that he had a house and job for me there. Yury insisted our children stay with him, and I didn't want to create extra chaos amid the sting they were already feeling. Even though they never showed or talked to me about their feelings regarding our situation, I trusted God would work it out.

ELEVEN

BEFORE I KNEW it, the month of July was before me. It was time to go to Dallas. A few weeks before I left, God confirmed the school I was supposed to go to work at. Morning Glory Christian School was advertised for the first time on Linking Christians Inc. I knew the moment was not a coincidence; God was leading me. It reminded me of what I had seen in my dreams a few years earlier. That confirmation helped calm my skittish feelings over walking into the unknown.

In the face of my children, I appeared brave and sure of the move, because I didn't want them to worry about me. Their lives were comfortable with their daddy. Since I didn't have any evidence regarding what I was believing God for, I didn't want to force my children to give up what they were used to. I trusted God to make a way for them to be in my life again. I thought of a scripture from the Bible that talked about the same subject: "And everyone who has left houses or brothers or sisters or father or mother or wife or children or fields for my sake will receive a hundred times as much and will inherit eternal life" (Matthew 19:29 NIV).

I was grateful God already knew I was suppressing my fears. The day he let me know which school to go to, I felt his love for me and knew he was truly leading me. It boosted my confidence. Once I decided to go after what God was calling me to do, unbeknownst to me, my husband changed. Again, he thought I was crazy and was hearing from the devil. He wanted nothing to do with God. He even told me to tell God no and not follow him.

As I prepared myself mentally to leave, for the fourth time, Yury said if I didn't stop talking to him about what God was showing me, he was going to divorce me. He was disappointed and secretly harbored resentment toward me. I guess it was hard to be in a meaningful relationship with someone he believed was going through a midlife crisis or had lost her mind.

With only weeks left before the huge change in our lives, without my knowledge, he turned his heart away from me. In fact, he had a long time ago. I had no idea he was on the prowl for other women, until the secrets started coming out. Before I shared with Yury what God was calling me to do, he seemed satisfied with our life together. He used to rest his head on my lap and sleep on me. Sometimes he would give me a hug just because, and he would feed me whenever he cooked something new. In order to survive the fact that the man I had planned to spend the rest of my life with refused to stay with me through good and bad times, I worshipped God. That played a huge part in why I was walking through my nightmare of a life in a daze but hoping, trusting, and looking to God to bring about the promises he'd promised me many years ago.

While on my journey, I stumbled many times in trying to break free from the confusion, disappointment, heaviness, and hurt. Consequently, Yury and I decided to file for a separation through the court system. I still didn't want to fight, so our children wouldn't be dragged into the middle of a legal battle. Therefore, Yury and I wrote our own separation agreement together. I basically gave in to what Yury wanted, to my detriment, because he said he had to think about the children's future.

On a positive note, after we separated, Yury helped me choose an apartment not far from the church, and he drove my vehicle to Texas for me at a reduced price compared to what the moving company wanted to charge me. He returned by airplane a few days later. On July 15, 2009, in year seventeen of our marriage, at six o'clock in the morning, Yury and our children went to visit his family in Missouri. The movers came at nine o'clock to help me pack and move my belongings out of our house.

Before that day came, I prayed for God to show up, tap Yury on his shoulder, and say something like "Behold, it is I who is leading your wife to go to Dallas. Join her, or the life you once knew with her will be over."

But those prayers were never answered. Some of our snooping neighbors came to the door to find out why we were moving.

I told them, "I'm the only one moving. It's a faith move for me. I'm following the calling of God on my life."

A few of them asked, "So does that mean Yury and the children are staying here?"

"Yes, until God makes a way for them to be a regular part of my life again," I answered.

With arched eyebrows and empty stares, many of them said, "Oh. Well, I wish you well. I hope it works out."

I flew to Dallas on Friday, July 17, 2009, and took a taxicab to my one-bedroom apartment on the southwest side of Dallas. Before that day, the only other time I ever had lived in an apartment had been when Yury was first hired in Macon, Georgia. His employer provided their new transplants with temporary apartments until they got their own places. We'd bought our house a month later. A temporary apartment was a perk for those in supervisory positions.

My new apartment was small, plain, old, and blah compared to our house. The house I walked away from in order to be obedient to God's calling was approximately 2,500 square feet and had four spacious bedrooms, three bathrooms, a playroom, a living room, a dining room, a family room, a sizable eat-in kitchen, a laundry room the size of a bedroom, and huge usable attic space large enough to add two additional rooms to our brick house.

If Yury and I hadn't moved four different times to four different states, I would have been terrified at the idea of making such a move. I still had fear, but I didn't allow myself to think about it. I didn't necessarily travel to Texas in the spirit of *OK, God, let's get this done.* My family was my prize possession. I felt as if God had stripped me of everyone I loved, which made me feel like the black sheep of his family. I was not an adventurous person, so I felt as if God had led me into the wilderness. I was isolated from everyone I knew and far away from my familiar surroundings.

To help learn my way around, I took a taxicab where I needed to go and wrote down the directions on how to get there and back. I had a GPS, but I didn't trust it. Whenever I listened to Amy—that was the name I gave my artificial intelligence navigation voice—I pictured a lady who'd graduated from Harvard University and lived in a $50 million penthouse apartment in New York City. She had a personal fashion stylist, a maid, and a dog named Sasha that had pink-painted claws. She spent her downtime getting massages and facials. Amy was authorized to give directions to and from cities, states, and countries all over the world to billions of people, all from the comfort of her apartment. Her voice was too calm, docile, and relaxed for me.

I needed a GPS that had the voice of Maxine. Maxine would have the voice of my mother. Her voice would be feisty, loud, and strong. I pictured Maxine as the highest-ranked female in the military. She had a palatial $3 million ranch-style vacation home with a horse ranch on thirty acres of land somewhere in Texas. She talked to the same number of people, but she worked from the Pentagon, and her main residence was a town house worth about the same amount in Washington, DC. She was used to handling high-pressure situations and commanding thousands of people. During her downtime, she jogged five miles every weekend. Maxine was the person I would have preferred to lead me through uncharted waters.

During my nightly phone call with Mama, after I told her I'd moved to Dallas, our conversation went the same way it had when I told her about what God had revealed to me about Luca. She yelled, screamed, cussed, and called on God—the God of Abraham, Isaac, and Jacob, not the one I'd gotten duped into serving. She convinced my brothers and sisters to call me often to help me come back to my senses too. Mama even called Yury to apologize for my actions on behalf of the family.

Mom told me she'd talked to Yury and said, "Yury, I'm just calling you to tell you I had no idea that foolish daughter of mine was going to leave you and the children behind to allegedly go after God. She has shocked me. I didn't know she was going to do something so disgusting. I didn't raise her like that. I am not happy with her actions at all. Don't you worry. We are praying to the real God I serve.

"He knows how to defeat that devil that has Lewisa's head twisted all around. Don't let what Lewisa did keep you and the children from coming to visit us. We are still your family. Don't you worry, because God still sits on his throne, and he is not pleased that Lewisa allowed the devil to trick her. Y'all's children need both you and her. I'm mad! I never thought she would do something as low and selfish as this. I told all my children that it's disgraceful for a mother to leave her children. I'm going to keep in touch with you and those children until we can talk some sense back into Lewisa. I'm so sorry, and I'll talk to you soon."

Yury mainly nodded while Mama talked. However, he did say hello when he answered the phone and goodbye when the call ended.

Tabitha's conversation with me was more probing than hostile. She said, "Sister dear, Mom said you are in Texas now."

I answered, "Yes."

"Would you care to tell me how you ended up in Texas? I'm just curious," she said.

I went through the short version of why I had moved to Texas.

She said, "But, Lewisa, you are a woman. I don't think God would send a woman far away from her family and people she knows. I don't think God would tell you to leave the cushy life you had. God is love, and that doesn't sound like love to me. And remember, Mom always told us the Bible says to honor your father and mother so your days on earth will be long—Exodus 20:12 NIV. Well, Mom doesn't feel like you are honoring her."

I said, "I understand that what I've been telling you all doesn't make sense. I get that, but I'm one hundred percent certain I heard from God. The Bible tells us that his ways are not like our ways, and his thoughts are higher than our thoughts—Isaiah 55:8–9 NIV."

She responded, "I'm not going to pretend I understand what you're going through, because I don't know. My main concern is regarding your family. I can't wrap my head around you leaving your husband and children. That's not like you. I've seen the way you interact with your children and how well you get along with Yury. You love them. You love your husband. But my call is not to gang up on you. It's to lend a listening ear if you ever need to talk to someone. Just know I love you and your family, and if there is anything I can do for you and them, just let me know."

I said, "Thank you! I appreciate that!"

Even though Yury had given me an unfair separation settlement, I had enough money to pay for my apartment for a year in advance. I also had a few thousand dollars to use for food and other essential expenses. I managed to go around the area closest to my apartment to get everything done when settling into a new city and state. I had to get car insurance; renter's insurance for my apartment; a Texas driver's license, vehicle registration, and license plate; and more. I went by taxicab to get it all done.

The first time I went to Great Is the Lord Church, which Bishop Wiseman presided over, I took a taxicab that day too. After that, I drove myself to every church service. During the church service, again, God made it known that he knew I was there. He spoke through Bishop Wiseman regarding what had led me to Dallas. God knew I'd left my family behind in order to follow his will for my life. Hearing that gave me great comfort. That day, the church announced they were raffling off a house. I knew God was reminding me he had not forgotten about the house he'd promised me. I wrote down the pertinent information and later contacted the real estate agent. She took my contact information. I had come completely by faith, so I was not working anywhere. I never heard from her again.

Being in that foreign large city with its massive population had my insides quivering. Then encountering God in ways I wasn't used to had me tilting my head to one side the way dogs did when they didn't understand something. Once school opened in August, I went to the school I had seen advertised on TV. I filled out an application and was told there weren't any openings at that moment. Then, three months later, they called and asked me to interview for a substitute teacher position for third, fourth, and fifth grade.

The day of the interview, I knew God was at work, because at that time, I only had eleven college credit hours. The interview went well. I was amazed the principal didn't seem fazed by my lack of education or experience. At the end of the interview, he said they would get back in touch with me soon. I was happy because God was working things out on my behalf. I went back to my apartment filled with hope and expectation.

When I talked to my family on the phone, they were excited for me. They even said that if I got hired, they would know God was working. Hearing their merriment, though it was mixed with some skepticism, made me elated. Yury was unconvinced God was at work, but Jillian, Jaren, and Jasper were excited because they believed what I told them.

One week went by with no update on the substitute teacher position. Then two weeks went by with no word still. Week three came along, and I started getting restless. I began asking different family members what they thought was going on. I asked their opinion on what I should do next and got into doubt instead of going to God, the one who'd sent me there in the first place.

Then Friday of week three came. I received a phone call stating they had decided to go with someone else. Deep down in my spirit, I knew that phone call happened the way it did because I wasn't operating in total faith. I had turned to the opinions of people instead of talking to God about my concerns, even though I knew ultimately, he was working out things on my behalf in order to fulfil what he'd shown me in my dreams.

I knew some would have said, "No, child, you didn't get the job simply because you weren't qualified." However, that was not true, because my limited college credit hours were on the application before I was called in for an interview for the substitute teacher position. The school was a Christian-affiliated school, and the principal didn't look at me as if I were absurd during the interview. I believed God was going to make a way for me to go to school and work at the same time. Receiving the bad news was discouraging and depressing to me. Then, just when I thought things could not get any worse, they did when I shared the news with my mom.

She thundered, "Aha! I knew God didn't send you out there! There ain't no way in the world God would have you walk away from your marriage and your children to come after him! That's nothing but the devil!" She paused for a minute and then yelled, "Satan! I command you to come out of my daughter and go back to hell, where you belong, in Jesus's name! And I'm not talking about the God she is serving! I'm talking about the God of Abraham, Isaac, and Jacob—the one and only God! I'm going to put a stop to this nonsense! I'm personally calling Bishop Wiseman, so he can tell you to go back home to your family."

In my mind, that day, Mom's actions took her off my Mother of the Year list. I wondered how many people had ever had their mother or father try to cast the devil out of them. Mom made that phone call and left a message.

The next day, I made an appointment to talk to Pastor Tarren, whom I had talked to the first time I came to Dallas. He saw me a few days later. To help ease Mom's mind, I told her about the consultation. Mom demanded to be part of the meeting via the telephone.

I agreed. I was not crazy.

During the appointment, I updated Pastor Tarren on how God had led me to Dallas again. I explained how my endeavor had greatly affected my mother, which in turn had made her insist on being included during our meeting. Pastor Tarren, who was joined by his wife, Sheila, was understanding and complied. His wife was understanding too. On the phone, Mom's voice was thick with emotion, sounding both firm and palpitating.

Mom asked, "Who am I speaking to?"

Pastor Tarren answered, "I'm Pastor Tarren. What would you like me to call you?"

"Call me Mrs. True," Mom said.

Pastor Tarren said, "Hello. I like your name, Mrs. True."

She said, "Thank you."

"You are welcome. Mrs. True, how can I help you today?"

Mom's voice became breathy and brittle. "My daughter Lewisa left her husband and children to move to Dallas because the devil tricked her and made her believe God wants her out there. I need y'all to talk to her and let her know God wouldn't break up her home."

Pastor Tarren said, "Mrs. True, I can hear the suffering you are going through in your voice. I promise you we will counsel and pray for Lewisa. We are going to trust God for his solution because he does all things well. Do you believe that, Mrs. True?"

"Oh yes, I do," Mom said in a matter-of-fact tone.

Pastor Tarren listened to Mom as he delicately agreed with her concerns. His wife did too. Mom agreed to allow the pastor to pray for us.

He said, "Father God, who art in heaven, thank you for being our Lord and Savior! We, your children, ask you to come into the midst of this precious family's situation. Master, we trust you to work everything out according to your will and purpose in Jesus's name. We call it done in the mighty name of Jesus Christ. Amen!"

After the phone call, Pastor Tarren shared that since Mom was in such an exasperated state, it was best that he tread lightly. His approach was one of compassion laced with meekness. His goal was to allow her to be heard and acknowledge the validity of her burden.

Pastor Tarren told me, "Keep praying, believing, and trusting God, but also, make sure you continue to keep in touch with your children. Whenever you are able to spend time with them, do so. Your situation is not too hard for God. He will bring you through."

Many probably would have wondered where our faith was or thought my experience of walking on the water, so to speak, was too far out. When I was growing up, none of the churches my family and I were affiliated with ever taught us to follow God the way God was leading me to follow him.

One of my earliest memories of going to church was when I was four or five years old. It was Easter Sunday. Mom bought a beautiful pastel-blue dress for me. She topped my attire off with frilly, girlie white socks and shiny patent-leather shoes. I felt like a million bucks. I didn't remember what Donna and Wanda wore, but I imagined it was something similar to what I had on. During that time, most black people believed it was fitting to dress well when entering the house of the Lord. Our best clothes were set apart exclusively for Sunday.

The church we went to that day was Holy Holy Trinity Church. Every time I heard the name, it made something inside me want to get quiet and pay reverence to God.

The church had close to one hundred people. Someone played a pipe organ. The sound was heavy, serious, and majestic. When I heard it, my body automatically stiffened. The sound made my steps a little less playful. Before we left the house, Mom explained we were going to church and into the presence of God. In his presence, we were supposed to show respect and keep quiet. She also showed us the strap she'd placed in her pocketbook in case we were tempted by the devil to start showing off in front of everybody. We knew better than to try her, because she believed in giving whippings in public.

The atmosphere was tranquil. Actually, it was too serene. I thought once the preacher started his sermon, the service would awaken from its comatose feeling and get better, but it did not. The congregation was a mixture of people in their thirties through their eighties and older, plus a few young children and babies, but no teenagers. After the announcements, Reverend Nick stood behind the podium. He was in his fifties or sixties, had brown skin, was five foot two, and had a bald head. Back then, it was not fashionable yet for men to sport a bald head. Montel Williams, who later made taking pride in a bald head a cool thing, wasn't on television yet.

Once Reverend Nick started talking, a second hush came over the church. I didn't know how it was possible for a second hush to fall on an already quiet place, but it did. It sounded as if the sound system were malfunctioning, because at points, his voice was strong, and other times, it seemed as if he were preaching from many miles away. Halfway through his sermon, half the congregation had fallen asleep. I didn't blame them, because the atmosphere was peaceful. Mom didn't allow us to join the action of the crowd.

Periodically, the people responded with a half-hearted courtesy clap. They did so every time Reverend Nick preached himself into a jolly-good frenzy, but still, most people didn't have a clue what he said. There were a few times during the service, when the microphone was working its best, when Mama said, "Amen!" When that word left her lips, some of the people who were awake zoned in on her with various expressions of shock, as if she had broken the sacred oath of silence. It even woke some of the people who had drifted off to sleep. I guessed it was the crowd's way of quietly reprimanding her for disturbing the muted stillness in the air.

We only went back to that church a few more times for essential holidays. Finally, Mom decided it was not the right fit for us because it was too dead. She didn't believe we served a sleeping God. About three or four years later, when I was eight years old, Mom first got cable television. It was the best thing that had ever happened to us, because we were introduced to Christian television. It changed my life. I found myself giving up after-school cartoons and comedies to watch the GTG channel. I gave my heart to God one night afterward. I found rest in knowing I could talk to God in prayer regarding everything that concerned me. During that time, my concerns were school-related issues.

I witnessed miracles, and a few people left the church I attended because they believed they were called by God other places, but I didn't remember any teachings about the mechanics of how that worked exactly. They did not use the word *destiny*, but they did talk about embracing God's plan for your life. Pastor Stonefish encouraged us to follow God's will for our lives. Many television ministers did the same, but I didn't have a clear understanding of what that meant. The concept of going after my destiny was completely over my head. I learned through repetition and hands-on education. It helped if I saw an example of how things should be done and was not just thrown in and forced to figure it out. In essence, to a small degree, I suffered from test anxiety.

According to Google, there were two groups of outward symptoms of test anxiety: a severe group and a moderate group. People who fell into the severe group encountered manifestations of perspiration, convulsion, a fast heartbeat, a dehydrated mouth, passing out, and vomiting. People in the moderate group experienced twitchiness in their abdomens.

When the test was an actual school test in the subject of history, biology, or sociology, for example, I fit into the moderate test anxiety group. However, my encounter with tests on my spiritual journey pushed me over into the severe test anxiety group. Since I didn't get the job God promised me, I didn't see the point of staying in Dallas, because he hadn't shown me I wasn't getting the job. Also, he didn't give me an update on what to do next when I didn't get the job. That great disappointment occurred in October.

In order to function in Dallas in the first place, I had to repress the searing and agonizing pain I felt at having to leave my family behind in Greensboro. I never dealt with it. I never allowed myself to shed a tear, because I thought it would interfere with completing my mission. I was operating in robotic mode so I wouldn't fall apart.

After the setback, I was still being encouraged through prophetic words, but I had no clue what my next step should be. I waited around until December came, and after a total of five months of living in Dallas, I decided to go back to North Carolina to be with my family. Yury and I talked from time to time on the phone. He had signed up on many online dating sites and had many dates with many women, but he didn't have a girlfriend.

He told me, "You are not welcome back in our house to live, but you can come visit the children and eat dinner with us periodically."

Therefore, I got an apartment in Greensboro. I hired the same moving company to move me back and into my apartment, but my furniture and vehicle were delivered a week past my arrival back in Greensboro. While I waited, Yury allowed me to stay with them and with him in our bedroom. At first, he was despondent around me. His face was tense and displayed a frown and lifeless eyes. Once I began reaching over to touch his face, shoulders, and hands, his icy heart slowly melted away.

I told Yury, "You know I love you. I wanted you and our children with me. Remember, I asked you to go with me." Then I hugged him.

I felt his body go limp as he collapsed into my embrace. I could tell he was happy I was home again. His body shuddered in my arms, and he groaned, "You left me! You just up and left me!"

I interrupted him. "Baby, I'm sorry. I wanted you to go with me."

He snapped loudly, "Don't *baby* me!"

"I wanted you and our family to stay together. You know it's true," I said.

I knew he loved me. I loved him too. When my furniture arrived at my apartment, the movers moved it inside, but I never moved in with it. After a few weeks, we gave up my apartment, and I moved back into our house permanently.

When I told Mom I was back home, she proclaimed, "Uh-huh! I'm not surprised. God heard my prayers. I'm talking about the real God, the God of Abraham, Isaac, and Jacob. He may not come right when you want him to, but he is always right on time. God knows my family served him faithfully all their lives on earth, so the devil didn't have any choice but to let you go. Now you need to go back to being the woman Yury fell in love with, so you can honor God with your marriage and keep your family together."

Many of my prying neighbors stopped me in our neighborhood to inquire why I had come back. I gave them the short version of my voyage. Some of them listened as their dead eyes gave them away by informing me they didn't have a clue what I was talking about. I went back to Chick-fil-A, which welcomed me back with open arms. Going back helped me pay off the cost of the move and other debt I'd obtained by walking by faith and placed on my credit card. Being back with my family was pure jubilation. It satisfied me to know that God had called me to do a hard thing and that I had done it. I hadn't known what to do and had messed it up, but I had been obedient.

TWELVE

MY FIRST SUNDAY back in church, Pastor Stonefish prophetically said, "God is saying there is someone here today who is in the wrong place."

I gasped and thought, *Oh my goodness, God knows I'm back in Greensboro. He told on me.* There wasn't any doubt in my mind those words Pastor Stonefish spoke from God were for me. I was nervous and thought, *Oh, Jesus, what's next?* Because of the unique and foreign nature of my departure from the church, I hadn't told the congregation I was leaving to step out on faith.

It took a month before Yury decided he would give us and our marriage another try because he said our children were happier since I had come back. Still, he was dealing with hurt and struggled with the abandonment and rejection he'd felt when I left him. Pain took up residence in his eyes. It replaced the evidence of love and care that used to stare back at me. At times, he was openly standoffish, as if I were a stranger. I knew it was going to take a while to rebuild trust again, so I didn't try to rush it. I continued being kind, positive, and supportive. I was affectionate. I hugged him and said I loved him a lot.

On mornings, evenings, and nights when he required sexual healing, the Yury I had known before our split somehow found his way back to me. Since we were back together, he promised me he'd deleted his dating profile. He made me promise I would stop watching television ministers. I did my best to honor that request. I kept the promise for three months. While Yury was at work, I checked the family computer and saw he still had a private sign-in and password.

I called him at work and asked, "Yury, are you still using dating websites?"

He whispered, "I'm not active right now."

I said, "Aren't we back together?"

He paused and then said, "Yes, I'll delete it."

"You promise?" I asked.

Yury answered quickly, "Lewisa, yes, I promise, but you need to promise me that you will stop looking at TV preachers."

I said, "I promise."

However, I broke my promise because Yury was still reading all the time, and he and I went back to living in separate parts of the house again.

Since I was accustomed to watching Christian television and God was ingrained in me, I missed it. Yury didn't verbalize his grievance to me. I could tell he disapproved by the heavy expression in his eyes. I thought my action pounded another nail into our marital coffin.

One day, after trying to guess his password by putting in every name, place, or word I thought was meaningful to Yury, I typed in, "Harry Truman," and I saw that he had not deleted his dating profile. I started deleting his love-connection notices for him. *People say all is fair in love and war,* I thought. Plus, I was fighting for our marriage. That morning, before going to work, Yury had responded to a note from careerwomb150,000.

She had written, "Hi, Yury. I came across you profile several times. You effuse a quiet strength. I have a hunch you are someone worth knowing. If you're interested in me, write back. It could be fun."

Yury had responded, "Thank you, careerwomb150,000, for contacting me! I'll respond about myself in detail once I get home from work this evening. Your inquiry has given me something to look forward to."

As I read their writing, my hand covered my mouth. The weight of what was happening made me sit down. Then I texted Yury: "Have you deleted your dating profile yet?"

Yury replied, "Yes, I did it this morning before leaving for work. Why?"

"Oh, I was just wondering because you agreed to give us another chance. If we are back together, that means starting another relationship is not an option."

"Dear, I know that already. It's already taken care of."

"OK, I'm trusting you to do the right thing."

"Trust me. I am."

I knew he was lying to me. I didn't like it. I decided not to get angry or confront him. *There are many ways to achieve a goal, right?* I just started deleting every message from his love connections, and I kept checking with him to make sure he wasn't still looking to make a love connection, since he'd agreed we were back together. During a later date, when I checked the dating site again, I saw he had truly deleted his profile. I was happy.

We got through Christmas, and the New Year, 2010, came in. One day early in the year, Yury called me from work to invite me to have lunch in a community hall inside a church with him and his coworkers. He said they had plenty of food to choose from on their buffet spread, and the food tasted great. The last time he'd invited me out with his coworkers had been when Jillian was a baby.

I met him at work. A medium-height man possibly in his thirties was standing beside Yury. A short black woman with medium-length, curly hair and a fit body was standing in front of them when I parked in the parking lot. The plan was to carpool in the man's car.

As we all walked to his vehicle, the man said to me, "So you are really religious, hmm?"

I answered slowly because his question was unexpected. "I wouldn't use the word *religious*, but I am a Christian." I glanced over at Yury, who strolled with his eyes focused on the ground.

The lady said, "Hey, man, you'd better be careful about what you're saying to her before she does some kind of Christian voodoo kung fu ritual on you, and you end up with your eyes attached to your bottom."

I didn't say anything. I just looked again at Yury, who was silent and still looking down at the ground with a smug grin on his face. Normally, in our relationship in the past, if something like that had happened, I would have waited until we got home and told him I didn't appreciate his getting his coworkers all in our business. I would have handled it in a calm way, but I would have addressed it because I didn't believe in holding things in if there was a problem. I liked to talk about things so he knew where I stood on issues that could possibly turn heated or be blown out of proportion. I didn't believe it was healthy for relationship partners to just hold stuff in and pretend like nothing was wrong.

However, since our relationship was still on shaky ground, I let it go and just talked to God. The church I was a member of offered a recovery class for people who had gone through a divorce. At that time, we weren't divorced yet. We were only legally separated on paper. Still, both Yury and I were hurting in different ways. Yury more than likely felt betrayed, disappointed, disrespected, rejected, short-changed, undervalued, and unloved.

Since he thought I was deranged and had refused to go with me, I was fighting with those same emotions. I was also hurting because I knew he had lost confidence in me and respect for me. It was a hard pill to swallow. Therefore, I was delighted when Yury agreed to take the class with me. It gave me a sense of hope because he was willing.

The day of the class, there were more people in attendance than we expected. Everyone was given the chance to explain how he or she had ended up taking the divorce recovery class. Those who spoke before Yury and me were already divorced.

When it was Yury's turn to talk, he cleared his throat and said in a controlled but slightly wounded tone, "Lewisa was a good wife to me, and she was a good mother to our children. Our marriage was torn apart because when she gets an idea into her head, no one can talk her out of it. Plus, on top of that, she left me. She just up and left me." His voice cracked a little.

I said, "Yury, I asked you to go with me so our family could stay together."

He shook his head and said, "That doesn't make sense."

The group counselor asked us, "Were you two once married?"

"We are still married. We were separated for five months," I said.

The next day, the group counselor called our house to inform us the class was for people who were already divorced. Since we didn't fit into that category, she suggested we consider going to a marriage counselor. Yury decided he wanted to think first before going the marriage-counseling route. We were trapped in a *Men Are from Mars, Women Are from Venus* standoff and could not find our way out of it. I wanted to do whatever it took to save the marriage and please God, but Yury was hesitant and unsure if the process was worth it. We were worlds away from being on the same page or seeing eye to eye.

As time marched forward, before I even realized it, Yury reverted back to bringing pieces of paper home with phone numbers on them, as he used to early in our marriage. One day he brought home an address. When I inquired about the mysterious information, he always said, "It's work-related."

Not long after that, Yury told me, "I have to go out of town for four days to attend a class for work. I'm carpooling with a lady who is also a supervisor in my department."

I stared him down.

He said, "Don't worry. Her name is Tanya, and she is married. We are going together to help each other drive since we have to go to the same place anyway. We are not attracted to each other. This is strictly work-related. I wouldn't tell you about her if there was something between us."

I relaxed and said, "Well, that must be true. You wouldn't mention her if you were up to no good."

I learned from him the day before the trip that Tanya was the lady I'd met in the parking lot the day Yury had called me to come eat lunch with him and his coworkers. She'd made the comment about me doing a Christian voodoo kung fu ritual. I didn't like the fact that Yury was carpooling with her, but I knew his company sent him to take classes other places sometimes, so I didn't fuss.

I didn't see any deceit in his eyes, and I was practicing trust with him. When he returned home, I was just happy he'd made it back safely.

On top of that trip, Yury started exercising every day again. Even though I was concerned when Yury's fitness pattern emerged again, I didn't have evidence that something was going on.

One day he told me, "There's a lady from work who is selling an elliptical machine I'm interested in buying. I told her I would come by her house around eight o'clock tonight to pick it up."

I asked, "Who is this lady?"

"It's Tanya. I'm just going to her house to pick up the machine. Then I'll be right back," he said.

I said, "Well, if you are going, I am going with you."

"Oh no, you are not!" Yury said.

I asked, "Why can't I go? You said you are only picking up the exercise machine from her house, and she is only a lady from work. So what difference does it make?"

"Well, dear, she may not want you in her house," he said, sounding concerned and unsettled.

I said again, "If you are going this time of night, I am going."

Yury picked up his cell phone to call Tanya. He told her, "My wife is insisting on coming with me. You're going to call your mother to ask her to come over? OK, I'm really sorry about this. I didn't know she was going to respond like this. I'm really sorry." He hung up and then said to me, "I hope you're happy with yourself. Now she is calling her mother to have her come to her house in case you start something."

I said, "Yury, that doesn't make any sense. If you are only going to pick up an exercise machine from her and if you two are only coworkers, then why would she mind me coming to her house with you to pick up the machine? And if you two are only coworkers, why is she calling her mother to come over to her house after you told her I was coming with you? Why would I need to start something with her?"

He shrugged and said, "Maybe she just doesn't want you in her house. And you know what? You are not going with me! I am just going to get something I need from her for a reduced price, for goodness sake! Why do you always have to make things so hard just because a lady is involved? You are not going with me!"

I shook my head and replied, "You are not going either then. You wouldn't be carrying on like this if something weren't going on. If she is truly only just a lady you work with, then this wouldn't be a big deal. You can take Jaren and Jasper with you. Then I will stay home, but you are not going by yourself."

I had Jaren and Jasper go with him. Once they returned, Jaren told me Tanya's mother had been waiting at her house with her for Yury's arrival. Tanya was not married, as Yury had told me during the trip they took together for the work-related class. From that point on, I did my best to be more observant. After that incident, on the surface, everything seemed to be back in order. I wasn't hearing any more about Tanya.

Just as the waves in the ocean billowed, rolled, swelled, and tossed, the many changes of the season brought in the year 2012, year twenty of our marriage. By that time, I had worked enough part-time hours at Chick-fil-A to earn one of their $1,000 scholarships for school. I had started volunteering as a teacher's assistant at my son's elementary school after I returned from Dallas. I had been there for two years by then, but I learned I still had to go to school, so I did part-time. I only took a couple of classes at a time.

Back in 2006, when we'd first moved to Greensboro, North Carolina, I'd filled out an application with one of the school systems there. I never heard anything from them. I checked on the status of my application every now and then, but there wasn't any feedback. Then, one day, the supervisor of the after-school program at my son's former elementary school came into Chick-fil-A. I served her. I asked her whom I should talk to about my application on file with the school system.

She made a phone call for me, and I basically got hired that same day. I still had to go to orientation and so on, but her phone call did it. I knew God was at work through her, because my application had been on file since 2006. God had led her to me. Two weeks later, I left Chick-fil-A and started working in an elementary school with their after-school program. I thought, *OK, I'm not in Dallas, but I am working in a school, so maybe God will be satisfied with what's happening here.*

Also, 2012 was the year I met Bonita at a family fun day celebration sponsored by Yury's job. He was friendly toward her in my presence. He used his extra kind, cheerful, honeyed voice as he talked to her. It was the same sound he'd used on me when he first started coming to the bookstore before we began dating. I had to introduce myself to her as his wife. She was black and had a small build and orangie-red hair from her root halfway down her medium-length black hair.

I wasn't thinking of the dream I'd had of such a lady in 2007, which had made me hop on a plane to go to Dallas without telling Yury. At the time, I didn't realize it was her. I didn't realize it until years later. She was twenty years younger than Yury. I was only seven years younger than he was.

During the family day festivities, the attention my husband was giving her irritated me, but I waited until we got home to discuss the matter. Our children were with us at the family event. I didn't like to cause a scene in public or private.

After settling in at home following the family day, I told Yury, "The way you were acting around Bonita really bothered me because that's the same way you used to act around me before we started dating. Plus, you didn't introduce me to her. I had to do it myself."

He said, "Nah, I was just being nice to her because she just started working for the company. I was just trying to make her feel welcome, and I wasn't thinking—that's all."

I took his words at face value and dropped the case. Over time, I made many attempts to invite Yury to various couples' and marriage-building classes and even a couples' retreat the church was offering to try to restore and strengthen our broken relationship, but he declined. I could tell there was some kind of invisible barrier between us.

Whenever I would talk to him about it, he would tell me that we were fine and that I didn't have anything to worry about. I believed

Yury because I had been brought up by a mother who taught us our word was our bond. I longed for our relationship to work. *Cinderella never divorced Prince Charming, right? Snow White and her prince never went for counseling, and look at Barbie and Ken. They have been together since the 1960s and never had one argument. Just joking!*

The bottom line was, I didn't want to have to start over. I continued working at the elementary school, taking classes, and studying while doing an awkward job of balancing it all along with my family life. We all survived. On the surface, our life appeared comfy and relaxed, as if we had conquered our marital storm. Yury had partially taken down the disguised wall he had privately barricaded his emotions behind. At the same time, the large blinking lights inside me were signaling me to take a closer look.

Unfortunately, I couldn't put my finger on what was happening, so I ignored it. I wasn't aware of what to look for. I was in denial. Yury started using his cell phone more than he ever had before. He was talking and texting more. After a while, he kept his cell phone by his side at all times instead of leaving it in the family room like he used to. He started going to work more on his days off, going in two or three hours earlier, and staying later than he used to. He started secluding himself in parts of the house he never had used before. A few times, he took more food to work than normal—double portions—and he began chewing gum for the first time and buying wine coolers, when he never had drunk alcohol before.

Movies with historical ethnic conflicts suddenly became interesting to him, when I never had been able to get him to watch those kinds of movies with me before. He also started watching a TV series geared toward the interests of a younger audience. He started taking more cash from our account than he used to. He stopped me from washing his clothes and took over doing it himself. Also, he changed the kind of clothes he wore and grew his hair longer than he normally did. In addition, he continued to exercise every day.

Plus, he was buying gifts for other women and giving them money too. I found that out later.

Occasionally, he became argumentative, critical, impatient, and sarcastic at that time too—characteristics he never had displayed in the beginning or middle parts of our marriage. Since I hoped we would eventually head toward a better place in our relationship, I allowed him to travel at least a few times a month to different cities and states to go see bluegrass country music concerts. Going with him was out of the question. I tried a few times, but bluegrass was not my cup of tea—no offense to all the blue grass aficionados. Furthermore, during our intimate time, something didn't feel the same, but I couldn't figure it out. Maybe I felt that our time together wasn't just our time anymore. His heart and soul weren't in it the way they used to be. It seemed he didn't have only me on his mind anymore.

My women's intuition was saying, *Ding, ding, ding*, but we were speaking two different languages. I missed it. I didn't see the signs. There wasn't any proof, only a feeling. I was working, going to school, and working on being a good wife and mother. Like lightning flashing and zipping across the sky, we found ourselves a little further along in our lives. We drifted into the year 2015, year twenty-three of our marriage. God was still speaking to me prophetically through many people, including Pastor Stonefish. Then, one day, I was passing by the TV in the family room en route to the laundry room, and I heard the words "Your husband is cheating on you."

I didn't know who said it. It was a woman's voice. After those words came out of her mouth, she continued preaching, and I knew the message was for me. I didn't know what to do, because I hadn't seen any proof. I thought, *God, help me, please.*

Then God started leading me to go where Luca was performing to start my new life with him. He reminded me of the dream I'd had of Luca in 2007. Then God guided me by having me hear prophetically that it was time to walk by faith and trust what God showed me. That kind of thing didn't happen every day, so I was under extreme pressure. It felt similar to the TV show *Married at First Sight*, but those people didn't normally show up having just stepped out of a chaotic marital situation at home.

While I was watching Linking Christians Inc., Bishop Wiseman looked at the TV camera and said, "God has already told you who he chose for you. Walking by faith is not for the faint of heart. Listen up. God said once you go where he is sending you, someone is going to point you out. This is your confirmation. God has already been dealing with you. God said, 'My sheep hear my voice.' Listen to his voice."

I was told prophetically that someone was going to point me out. I couldn't explain it, but I knew that message was for me. I wasn't sure what that was going to look like in my life, so I was nervous. I didn't know what to do or what to say.

One of my coworkers went with me to Gaffney, South Carolina. I was not adventurous, and Yury had plans that weekend. When we got there, we were told the concert had been moved from the church where it was originally scheduled to a school next door instead. Hearing about that change in plans, I knew God was working, because in my dreams in 2007, I had seen Luca in a school in Dallas.

Then, in 2008, I'd dreamed I was sitting on our couch with a good-looking man. He was holding my hand. Then he looked at me and said he loved me. I looked at him, admiring his looks, even though I couldn't really see him clearly. It was as if his face were concealed some kind of way, but I could still see beauty there. I knew that dream was from God and that he was telling me he was going to give me a new husband if my husband didn't follow God with me.

But that evening, I was shaking on the inside because I didn't know what to do or what to say.

During his concert in 2015, Luca, who had jet-black hair, medium olive skin, and the picturesque, symmetrical features of a heartthrob and was five foot eleven, handsome, and of Latin descent, looked at me. I was sitting in the second row, and he said, "Welcome to your open door." He looked directly at me from the stage.

Then he continued playing his guitar. I could have pinched myself. It was really happening and not a dream. I stood there wondering, *What does that mean exactly? How am I supposed to respond to an open door? God, what am I supposed to do?*

After the concert ended, a few people were given the opportunity to meet Luca. I was among those people. I heard a few people behind me ask loudly to speak to Luca, and they were allowed to go in the back with the band to do so. I waited with the few who were allowed to shake his hand.

Once face-to-face with Luca, I had no idea what I was supposed to do or say. My heart was pounding in my chest. Luca was friendly. His assistant told us we only had a minute with him. I didn't say anything except "Hi." Then my time was up. I walked away feeling like a failure. I'd thought God would give me a little more information, as he had some of the people in the Bible. There were a few people who'd gotten specific instructions from God.

I thought of Acts 9:10–17 NIV in the Bible:

> In Damascus there was a disciple named Ananias. The Lord called him in a vision, "Ananias!"
>
> "Yes, Lord," he answered.
>
> The Lord told him, "Go to the house of Judas on Straight Street and ask for a man from Tarsus named Saul, for he is praying. In a vision he has seen a man named Ananias come and place his hands on him to restore his sight."
>
> "Lord," Ananias answered, "I have heard many reports about this man and all the harm he has done

to your holy people in Jerusalem. And he has come here with authority from the chief priests to arrest all who call on your name."

But the Lord said to Ananias, "Go! This man is my chosen instrument to proclaim my name to the Gentiles and their kings and to the people of Israel. I will show him how much he must suffer for my name."

Then Ananias went to the house and entered it. Placing his hands on Saul, he said, "Brother Saul, the Lord—Jesus, who appeared to you on the road as you were coming here—has sent me so that you may see again and be filled with the Holy Spirit."

If God had given me a script or set of things to say, I would have practiced what to tell Luca that night. God knew I felt lousy for failing to step into what he promised me that night. Days after that, I heard prophetic words of comfort regarding my failure. God used Bishop Wiseman prophetically to let me know God had already told Luca about me. I was being beckoned to step into my new life. I decided to do that. *Everything God tells you to do has to be done by faith.*

Since the end of the school year was approaching and I was stepping out on faith again, I turned in my resignation. After telling Yury what I was hearing from God, he took a deep breath, pressed his lips together, and closed his eyes for a few long minutes. I reminded him that we could pray to God together, and maybe God would change his mind and allow us to do what he wanted me to do. Yury still didn't want any part of it.

Many months later, on July 4, Yury's and my movie-watching time was disrupted when he received a text message saying, "Happy Fourth."

I asked, "Who sent you that message?"

Yury smiled and said, "I don't know. Maybe it's just a random text message." He let me see the message and added, "It could be one of the guys I work with."

I said, "No, a man wouldn't send another man a message like that."

Still smiling, he responded, "I don't know who this could be. I don't recognize the number."

As my stomach churned and my face muscles tightened, I glowered at him with penetrating x-ray vision, but he used his kryptonite ability to weaken my prowess to recognize the truth. His body language was calm, cool, and collected, so I didn't press the issue any more. However, my insides were signaling that something wasn't right.

A few months later, Yury was talking on his cell phone in our bedroom. I took a break from doing homework and walked in there. He told me he was talking to one of his sisters.

He asked me, "Would you like to say hello?"

I nodded and said into the phone, "Hello. How are you and everyone else?"

"Hello. I'm fine, and we are good," said the female voice on the other end, which sounded different from Yury's sisters' voices. I ignored it because I had more homework to do.

Yury had assured me I could trust him, so I didn't think to question the woman further. He said things like "No other woman wants me, because I'm a handful to put up with," "I'm too old to cheat," "Nobody is trying to take me from you," and the clincher, "Since I can't perform like I used to, you have nothing to worry about." I thought our marriage was getting back to a better place. Some might have thought, *Really? Duh! Go back and look at what things looked like throughout the course of your marriage. And, girl, you should know that being led to step out on faith to see Luca didn't help your case.*

It all seemed complicated. My insides were telling me something was wrong. Some might have thought I shouldn't blame Yury for his actions and might have had a hard time with my story and wondered why God would lead a wife one way while he knew her husband was hell-bent on not complying with it. It was simple: we had two different sets of values. I wanted to please God, even though my walk was leading me into isolation, rejection, loss of family, and being misunderstood. Since Yury wasn't in tune with God, he concentrated on what he could see and understand with his eyes and mind only: his carnal senses.

Therefore, he turned to and leaned on others, particularly women, to help him cope, which ultimately led to secret indiscretions. God led me to go see Luca again in July 2015 in Atlanta, Georgia. I had heard ministers, mainly on TV, tell people that our speech should line up with the Word of God. If you expected God to do something in your life, you couldn't speak against what you were hoping for.

A few days before the trip, I went to my hairdresser. Normally, our conversation was pretty simple. I was not someone who liked to share everything about myself. I didn't mind sharing some things, but for the most part, I was mostly private. However, if I felt I could trust someone, then it was a different story. My life was in a peculiar place, with all kinds of complications due to God's wanting to use my life. It also had plenty of pain, hard-to-explain situations, and confusion running through it.

I wasn't going on a vacation trip with my whole family to enjoy our time together. It was the opposite. This trip was about stepping into my new life based on what I heard God telling me. I was in the process of losing my marriage and being distant from my children. *Happy occasion? I don't think so.* I had no intention of telling her or anyone else I had a trip coming up during which I had to walk by faith in order to obey God and step into what he said was mine. Things like that were hard to talk about, especially when I didn't have a clue about what to expect or what to do. I didn't have any details. That was what walking by faith was all about: no answers. That day in the salon, I planned to just sit there quietly and get my hair done.

My hairdresser asked me, "Do you have any plans this weekend?" She never had asked me that before.

I said, "No." I felt as if I might cry if I had to talk about what was happening in my life. I didn't want to cry in the salon.

After leaving the salon, before my trip, I heard prophetically, meaning words inspired by God given to ministers and people in a relationship with him for someone else, "You can't be ashamed of the things of God and still think you're going to step into his promises."

I could tell by the look on Yury's face that he was hurt because I was leaving. He looked as if he were losing his best friend. His head hung down. His eyes looked puffy, and his face appeared tight, but he didn't try to stop me. He didn't say a word. Although I heard the prophetic word hinting that something was wrong and was able to read between the lines, I still went to Atlanta, because I had already bought my airplane ticket and reserved a hotel room.

I arrived the night before the concert, and the next day, I found out Luca's concert had been canceled just minutes after I got to the church. I sat in the taxicab stunned with my mouth dropped open to the floor. I somehow knew in my spirit that my telling my hairdresser no when she asked if I had any plans that weekend had something to do with what was happening.

Then I thought, *No, wait.* The cancellation coincided with the prophetic word. Because I was 100 percent sure God was leading me through dreams and confirming his plan through ministers' prophetic words, the cancelling of the concert wasn't a sign to me that I was on the wrong path. It made my mind go back to what Bishop Wiseman had said: "You can't be ashamed of the things of God and still think you're going to step into his promises."

I went back home with shame attached to my face. I believed my leaving for the concert and the purpose behind my going to the event, especially since it didn't happen, nailed the second nail in our marital coffin. For the next five months, we carried on our daily routine together. I noticed Yury kept his cell phone with him all the time now. He said it was because he was on call after work and on some weekends.

THIRTEEN

ONE NIGHT IN January 2016, while we were watching a movie, Yury got another text message.

I asked, "Who is that, and what does it say?"

Yury read it out loud: "Having fun in the snow?" He said, "But I don't know who it's from. I don't recognize the number."

I said, "Let me see the number."

He jumped up from the couch and exclaimed, "No!" as he deleted the message.

I said, "If nothing is wrong and you don't have anything to hide, you wouldn't be deleting the message."

I called Yury's mother on the phone to tell her what had happened, but it was a waste of my time.

She said, "I don't know what to tell you. Maybe he's behaving that way because you left him a few years ago to go to Dallas."

I said, "No, we had similar issues way before God called me to go there."

"Well, I don't know what to tell you."

"Ok, thank you!" I said and hung up.

Once I got off the phone, I told Yury, "You are sleeping upstairs until you can be honest about what's going on."

He said, "No, I'm not!"

I placed my hands on my hips, looked him square in his eyes, and said with defiance, "Yes, you are!"

That night, he slept upstairs. However, after a while, it seemed he was enjoying himself up there. He walked around the house whistling with a smile on his face. He had pep in his step and acted as if he didn't have a care in the world. Week after week passed, yet Yury failed to come clean and tell me the truth. Instead, he was snug as a bug occupying Jillian's bedroom. Jillian had moved out of our house by then to live with roommates. She wanted her independence because she thought her mama was too strict. (In my opinion, I was a walk in the park compared to how strict Mama had been on me and the rest of her children.)

Before I knew it, a month had passed by, and still, it seemed Yury had no intention of giving in and telling the truth. He had settled in and was quite comfortable sleeping in Jillian's old bed. It didn't look as if he had any remorse over covering up his actions from me. Another month passed with the same scenario. Then, lo and behold, in March 2016, while Yury was mowing the lawn, he slipped up and left his cell phone unattended.

If that had never happened, I would have remained in the dark. I searched through his cell phone. First, I searched his text messages, but he had deleted all of them. Then I searched the pictures in his phone, and I found a picture of a black lady I didn't know. She had sent him a selfie. It was a headshot only. She was smiling. As I studied it, my stomach got queasy. My heart started pounding harder, and I became upset. After I took a picture of her with my cell phone for evidence, I put his cell phone back where he had left it. Then I waited until after he had finished mowing the lawn, taken a shower, and relaxed for thirty minutes.

I went to him upstairs and told him, "We need to talk." To be honest, I wanted to storm up those stairs, kick the door down, toss things around, turn them upside down, and proceed like Rambo, but ever since I was a little girl, Mama had said, "Carry yourself like a lady."

Yury's eyes widened as he responded, "Talk about what?"

I squinted and asked, "Who is that black lady in your phone? And why do you have her picture?"

He scratched his head, pursed his lips, and said, "Her name is Bonita. You met her a few years ago at the company family day. Do you remember?"

I shook my head and said, "She doesn't look like the lady I met that day, and why do you have her picture?"

Yury said, "Yes, she is the same lady. She changed her hair from the last time you saw her. I have her picture because she wanted me to see her new hairstyle."

I said, "Yury, that doesn't make any sense. That's not a good reason to have her picture. Are you sleeping with her? And how long have you been talking to her on your phone?"

He cleared his throat and proceeded. "No, I'm not sleeping with her. She's married. We are just friends. We just talk to each other about issues we both are going through in our marriages. I have been talking to her for a little over a year now."

I sat there and just stared at Yury in disbelief. Then I said calmly, "I want you to call her so I can talk to her."

He resisted. "I don't know her number, and I don't think that's a good idea."

I restated what I'd said and added, "You were caught with her picture. Plus, if you tell me the truth, I'll let you come back into our bedroom."

Yury dialed the number, told her what had happened, and said I wanted to talk to her. Then he handed me his phone.

I said in a pleasant tone, "Hi, Bonita. Like Yury said, I found your picture in his phone. Why are you talking to my husband?"

She said, "I'm sorry. Yury and I are only friends. We just talk to each other about different things we are going through. I'm married. I have a husband."

"How did you two start talking to each other? Did you go after him, or did he seek you out?" I asked.

She said, "No, ma'am, he's the one who kept coming after me. He kept asking me to go out to lunch with him, but I kept telling him no."

I asked, "Do you think your husband would be okay if he found out you're talking on the phone with my husband or that you sent him your picture?"

She said, "No, he wouldn't be happy about that. I want to apologize to you for talking to your husband. I promise I will stop talking to him, and if he reaches out to me, I will let you know."

I accepted her apology. "OK. Well, I would appreciate that." We hung up.

I focused my attention on Yury.

Yury slouched in his chair and said, "There wasn't anything going on between us. We are just friends."

I told him, "If you have to hide it, then that means you know it's wrong to be talking to her, accepting pictures, and doing whatever else is going on."

He shook his head, saying, "I don't think anything is wrong with having a female friend."

I said, "As your wife, I think something is very wrong with your having female friends like that, especially when things are done in secret."

He said, "We'll have to agree to disagree."

I believed that a lady refrained from violence unless it was absolutely necessary, so I did.

Mind-bogglingly, Bonita turned out to be the woman God had shown me in my dreams in 2007. She started working for the company in 2012, and she ended up being the first woman I found out Yury was having inappropriate dealings with in 2015. I was amazed God had shown me what was going to happen eight years before it actually happened. A few weeks later, after I found out about Bonita, just when I thought things couldn't get any worse, they did.

Around the same time I found out about Bonita, I accidentally came across a secret file Yury hadn't intended for me to find. However, I believe God wanted me to see it. It contained a year and six months' worth of conversations he'd had with a lady named Sophie. They worked at the same place too, and she was black and married too.

Yury and Sophie also talked about problems they were both having in their marriages. According to their conversation, they met sometimes for breakfast and lunch. They even spent time strolling in the park together, hugging each other, and calling each other's house when their spouses weren't home. I couldn't believe it. Yury even had her call our house when I was working and called her *dear*—my pet name. My conservative-spending husband promised to wine and dine her at Ruth's Chris Steak House, an expensive restaurant he never offered to wine and dine me in.

They didn't get a chance to go, but I had him take me there after I found out about his chicanery. He also asked her for sex, but she wasn't ready. She broke off their relationship when her husband got into some kind of serious accident. What disturbed me the most about both women was that they both went to church on a regular basis and called themselves Christians. Learning that bit of information took my breath away.

I wondered, *How could two women who profess to be Christians do something like this, when they have husbands and children of their own?* However, I'd heard preachers warn about the downfall of sin and temptation, and I could see how that could happen if people gave into temptation and sin. Also, many preachers said, "Going to church doesn't make someone a Christian, just like standing in a barn doesn't make him or her a cow. Being a Christian is all about having a personal relationship with God, living life as he instructed, and following his will for our lives."

As I read the conversations Yury had with Sophie, I was appalled. I hadn't even known he could talk like that. He never had tried to get to know me the way he was getting to know her through conversation. I never had known that side of him. Around me, he only ever wanted to either read books or watch movies.

When I confronted Yury, he said, "I'll admit I was out of line. I went a little too far, but we were only friends."

I asked, "Do you think there's anything wrong with your actions?"

He exhaled and said, "Well, I think I went too far by spending time with her, but nothing happened. We were only friends, and that's it. I don't think it's wrong to have female friends."

I said, "So are you saying you feel like it's OK to be married and have female friends you talk secretly with, take out to lunch, and spend private time with?"

Yury nodded and said, "Yes, I don't see anything wrong with that."

I said, "Well, I do." Then I implemented the silent treatment.

After having those humongous bombshells dropped into the middle of our already fragile relationship, I felt a whirlwind of crippling emotions. I ended up calling Mama to tell her about my plight. When I was a child, Mama and many other people had said, "Sometimes you have to laugh to keep from crying," or, in other words, "You have to use laughter to help you cope with pain or problems."

In the same way, the Bible said in Proverbs 17:22 NIV, "A joyful heart is good medicine, but a crushed spirit dries up the bones."

When I told Mom, that was exactly what she did: she laughed. I didn't understand what was going on at that time. *Could it be pseudobulbar affect?* In my mind, I knew she wasn't an insensitive person, but I couldn't figure out why she was reacting that way. I was looking for the strong, feisty, fighting Mama I knew she could be. However, while Mom laughed, I could hear pain and sadness mixed in with her laughter.

Then she said, "Yury had better mind. Your marriage means you two are in a covenant with God. Yury is going to have to answer to God for his actions. Lewisa, you leave Yury in God's hands. Don't try to fight back or get even. No, God wouldn't be pleased with that. You leave it to God because the battle belongs to him."

I felt as if my world were reeling out of control. Yury was still trying to make good with Bonita. She contacted me to let me know, and at the same time, God was letting me know it was time to get ready to go see Luca again through the ministers God was using to help guide me. I wanted to lie down in the fetal position with my thumb in my mouth and have someone rock me until sunny days returned to my life. For the first time in my life, I understood the opening quote from *A Tale of Two Cities* by Charles Dickens: "It was the best of times, it was the worst of times."

The next date to walk by faith to see Luca was in April, and the city was Anderson, South Carolina. Yury drove me there because again, I was not adventurous and didn't trust Amy, my GPS lady. Yury knew why I was going. He took me to the concert and waited in our hotel room, reading a book and bathing in buried emotions, until it was over. He was a good and kind person. If my husband had chosen to walk by faith with me, I would have been the happiest person in the world. Good people could still make unwise choices. Plus, with God leading me to go various places, Yury thought I was a few fries short of a Happy Meal.

At the concert, I knew God was working from what I heard. Luca said, "Someone here tonight is experiencing something unfortunate, like a loss or a broken relationship. I want to let you know that tonight starts your new beginning. Your second chance, your part two, starts tonight."

I had much fear operating in me because I didn't know what I was supposed to do or say. I felt light-headed and as if I were going to throw up.

After the concert was over, when it was my turn to meet him, I heard him say, "Now, you are Lewisa, right?"

I was nervous, but I said, "Yes."

Then I did the dumbest thing: I turned my back on him to face his assistant. Then my time with him was up. Since there was a large group of people around us, I couldn't concentrate. My belly had all kinds of quivers going on inside. I walked away feeling angry with myself and asking God, *Why would you put me in a situation like this, when you already know I don't know what I'm doing? God, I'm a private person. Wouldn't it be better to have me meet him in a private setting?* I walked away feeling like a failure.

Then God allowed me to know through many means prophetically that he knew I had blown it, but he hadn't given up on my yet. I started hearing minsters on Linking Christians Inc. talk about their failures while learning how to walk by faith. One man's whole family disowned him for becoming a Christian. Another man talked about how nervous he had been when God called him to preach. He said his voice would tremble, making it hard for others to understand him. A lady said she had a stuttering problem, but the more she preached, the better she could speak. They all encouraged me to follow God anyway because he would help me get to what he promised me.

At home, things didn't get better. Yury was still carrying on his hidden agenda. On the sly, he was still looking for another woman.

I could tell he had already mentally checked out of our marriage, because periodically, he asked me how I wanted to do things if we got a divorce and if I would marry again if we got a divorce.

On the morning of July 11, 2016, our twenty-fourth wedding anniversary, Yury texted me, "Happy anniversary." I texted him back the same words. Then, a few minutes later, Bonita texted me to let me know Yury had just texted her. I confronted him at work through a text about it, but he denied doing it.

I wrote, "When was the last time you texted Bonita?"

Yury replied, "It's been about two weeks since I last communicated with her. Why are you asking?"

"We'll talk when you get home."

Once he got home from work, he quietly eased into the house through the back door leading from the garage into the kitchen. He stepped lightly. I was sitting on the couch in the family room, in view of the kitchen door. Acting caught off guard, he mouthed, "Oh no," without words.

I looked at him with a blank stare and said, "We need to talk."

He rolled his eyes, put his belongings down, sat by me, and said, "Oh no. Here it goes."

I said, "So when did you say you last texted Bonita?"

He placed his index finger over his lips to think and said, "I don't know now, but it's been a while."

I told him, "Take a look at this." I showed him Bonita's screen shot she'd forwarded to my phone. It read, "Did you have a good holiday?"

He said, "Crap! I only see her as a friend."

I told him, "I want a divorce."

"I only married you because you were pregnant," he said. "I knew you were going to leave again anyway. Furthermore, I know it appears like Bonita is some kind of saint because she told you I contacted her, but I bet she didn't tell you she was sending naked pictures of herself to me."

My eyes grew big, and I slowly shook my head and said, "No, she didn't. Why are you telling me about that now?"

He said, "You're divorcing me, so secrets are unnecessary."

He didn't fall apart. He didn't look sad. I believed he'd been hoping for it for a long time. I thought, *After I found out I was pregnant, I asked you if you were only marrying me because I was pregnant. You said you loved me, so I married you.*

A few months earlier, he'd told me, "You believe what you believe about God wanting to use your life, and I believe you didn't hear from him. Neither one of us is going to change our mind, so there's no need to hold on to the marriage."

On the other hand, for me, divorce was a monumental, earth-shattering decision. I loved my husband. My dream of having only one husband was over. Sinking into the abyss of our tattered marriage, I desperately pursued the truth. I'd heard many stories of women and a few men in movies and on TV who dealt with the feelings of panic, anger, and helplessness that came along with being sucked into the lies of an unfaithful spouse or mate. Knowing I was headed for a divorce shifted my mind and emotions into a rip-roaring roller-coaster ride displaying deep dips, swift speeds, towering turns, and tilting twists. In a last attempt to save our marriage, I made an appointment with Mrs. Carrie Wilson, a private marriage counselor. Since both Yury and I were still hurting, he agreed to go with me.

I called two Christian marriage-counseling offices and decided whoever returned my call first was the counselor I would choose. Mrs. Wilson called first. I thought Mrs. Wilson, who reminded me of Blanche on *The Golden Girls*, except with cinnamon-colored skin, was going to start our session out with a Bible scripture or prayer to invite God into the atmosphere of our situation, but she didn't.

Once we finished our paperwork with our financial information, Mrs. Wilson dived straight into business. She started with me. She asked what brought us to her office. I told her about finding out about Bonita by finding her picture in Yury's phone and about finding out about Sophie. I showed her Bonita's picture. I even mentioned the incident with Tanya. Then I told her that the call of God on my life had been like the stake that killed Dracula in our marriage.

Mrs. Wilson asked Yury, "Why did you have Bonita's picture in your phone? And why are you communicating with so many women when you are already married?"

After hearing Mrs. Wilson address Yury's behavior the way she did, I began feeling hopeful that something good could come from our meeting with her. I was pleased with Mrs. Wilson's strong sense of right and wrong. I was also praying God would use her to help open Yury's eyes regarding morality.

Yury cleared his throat and answered, "First, the picture of Bonita is totally innocent. If you take a closer look, you will see her children in the backseat. She was just showing me her children. And I talk to women on my job as friends, but my wife doesn't understand that. She likes to make more out of it than it actually is."

I shook my head and said, "No, that's not true. Both Yury and Bonita told me she was showing him her new hairstyle. No children are in the picture, and it's not true that he's been only talking to women. He has been buying them gifts, giving them money, taking them out to breakfast and lunch, going for walks in the park, hugging one that I know of, asking for sex, and talking to them on the phone and at work about our and their marital issues. That's not just being friends."

Mrs. Wilson nodded and said, "I agree with your wife, Mr. DeBlake. It's inappropriate for a married man to behave like that with other women. What is the reason for your actions?"

He tugged on his shirt collar and said, "Well, my wife's actions have damaged our marriage. She believes God wants to use her, and she has been on a goose hunt, going everywhere, because she thinks God is telling her to travel to all of these far-out places. She even believes God told her she's going to marry Luca. He is a Christian entertainer who plays the guitar. Her pastor and family have already tried talking her out of it, but she won't listen. I am at my wits' end. I can't take it anymore."

She locked eyes on me and spoke slowly. "Mrs. DeBlake, in your opinion, is what he said true?"

"Some of what he said is true. Yes, we talked to my pastor about God showing and telling me to go to Texas. At that time, there was no talk of Luca during our meeting. Yes, also, my family don't understand what's going on with me. It's hard to explain," I told her.

Mrs. Wilson clear her throat and said, "So how exactly did God let you know you are supposed to marry—what's his name?"

Yury interjected. "Luca."

I answered, "First through a dream. Then through words of confirmation called prophetic words through many different ministers."

Mrs. Wilson widened her eyes, adjusted her glasses, and said, "Hmm, I see." She wrote something in her notebook.

Yury started laughing and said, "See what I mean? Who ever heard of such a thing? You know, she only chose you because you're black."

Caught off guard, I flashed a glare at Yury and said, "That's not true! She was the first person who called me back. That's the reason I chose her."

"Hmm, Mr. DeBlake, what was your parents' marriage like?" Seeming undaunted, she hunted for the answer.

Yury thought for a minute and said, "I guess their marriage was like any other marriage. They raised four children. They taught us how to work. Money was tight, but we always had a place to live and food on the table."

Mrs. Wilson said, "I see. So would you say your mother and father encountered infidelity in their marriage?"

Yury shook his head while saying, "No. No, they did not." He sat up straight.

I gasped and let out a short laugh and said, "That's not true! When we were dating, Yury told me his father used to run around on his mother. I can't believe he's lying. He has told me so many lies. I believed him because he seemed so sincere. I didn't know he was a liar."

"I never told you any such thing," he snapped.

I sat there amazed, wondering, *Who is this man?*

Mrs. Wilson looked at her clock and said, "Well, it looks like our time is up for today. Let's make another appointment separately first. Then I'll bring you two back together so we can have another session like this one."

We agreed and made an appointment with her receptionist. However, once we got home, Yury said, "I don't want to go back. I don't see the point in going back."

I told him, "Maybe it will help us. We already made another appointment. Let's just see where it goes."

Yury said, "Let me think about it."

Days later, Yury had me cancel our appointment. Then, the next day, he asked me to contact Mrs. Wilson to reinstate our appointment. I texted her to let her know what had been happening and to request another appointment.

I wrote, "Hi, Mrs. Wilson. Since our marriage situation seems difficult, Yury has been having second thoughts about continuing with counseling, but he decided to give it another try. Is our previous appointment still available?"

Mrs. Wilson replied, "Sorry, but your original appointment time has been taken. I have a 3:30 p.m. opening on the same day if that works for you."

I said, "Yes, we will take the 3:30 p.m. appointment. Also, is there a way you can help bring the truth out of my husband? He keeps lying to me. He hid the file that had Sophie's information and keeps denying things I know I read in it. Do you believe you can help us get to the truth?"

Mrs. Wilson said, "I don't think I'm the right fit for your and your husband's concern, so I think it would be best if you found help elsewhere. I would like to recommend the Institute for the Mentally Impaired, Day Springs Mental Care, or Happy Hollows Mental Health Services. I hope one of these facilities will be able to better serve you. Best regards."

"OK, thank you!"

Her response caught me off guard and left me dazed and shocked. I never had thought she would become impatient, overwhelmed, or insulted because I asked her to help me get the truth from my husband. Many couples ended up on a counselor's couch because of infidelity, so my call for help wasn't an act of going berserk, being delirious, or acting like a lunatic. I'd had no idea my request would make her think I was insane and have her swiftly turn against me, deny me her service, and suggest I get a mental evaluation. I had the feeling our counseling session was the first of its kind she had dealt with, which obviously had made her feel it was too complicated for her to handle.

Once I ended the text conversation, Yury asked, "What did she say?"

I read Mrs. Wilson's response to him.

"Ha! Whew! Ha ha! See? I told you, dear. Even the marriage counselor thinks you're crazy. You have had all kinds of professional people tell you that you are on the wrong track. And you still won't listen. Ha! Whew!" He patted his knee as his body rocked forward and back with each laugh.

I just left the room.

A few months passed. During that downward-spiraling time in our lives, God led me to go see Luca in September 2016 in Kingstree, South Carolina. Again, Yury took me there. Beforehand, I made up my mind to face Luca head-on. I decided to push down my fears of not knowing what to say or what to do. I took a little note to give him. I handed it to his assistant. This time, I actually faced him.

Again, on this trip, after I told Luca, "Hi," I turned to his assistant. Yes, again.

His assistant asked me, "Do you have anything else to say to Luca?"

Since I had already prepared a note for him, I said, "No."

His assistant asked me, "Are you sure?"

I answered, "Yes." I was still nervous.

Yury and I made an agreement that he would stay at our house and move out after Jasper's high school graduation on June 11, 2017. Mistrust was running high between us. Our opposite agendas drove a razor-sharp wedge straight into the heart of our marriage. Yury continued displaying suspicious behavior and started guarding his cell phone again.

I was led to step out on faith again for the last time and went to Woodfield, South Carolina, two months later in November 2016 to see Luca again. I bombed again. I couldn't get myself together. I couldn't relax in that atmosphere. A horrible image was in my head. I was afraid that somehow, thousands of women were going to be so angry with me for marrying Luca that they would start burning Bibles and rioting in church parking lots everywhere. After the concert that night, things didn't go well either. No surprise there. I told God through my frustration that I wasn't going to any more of Luca's concerts.

At home, Yury and I were cordial toward each other and did our best to work as a family. I didn't want negativity in our house, because our children didn't deserve that. Of course, because Yury was still tampering with some veiled activities, I went into full detective mode with a hunger to decipher the encrypted code. We had already decided on a divorce, but we were still living together and operating as a family. I needed to know the truth. Lies could do permanent damage to a marriage or relationship, especially when it was already in jeopardy.

The final nail in our marital coffin was a text message that appeared on Yury's cell phone on December 25, 2016, Christmas morning. It read, "Merry Christmas to you too, sweetie!"

When I saw it, it upset me. I still loved my husband and was in shock about the direction our lives were going in.

I pointed it out to Yury and asked, "Who is she?"

He looked at the number and said, "I don't know who that is."

I had heard him say that many times before, so I wasn't buying his statement. I called the number to find out who had written the message. I got a hold of a lady.

"Hello?" she answered.

I said, "Hello. My name is Lewisa DeBlake. I'm calling because I found your text message on my husband's cell phone, and I want to know who you are."

Her voice was soft and halting as she said, "What? What does the text message say? And also, who is your husband? I'm happily married."

I read the text message to her and said, "My husband's name is Yury DeBlake."

She responded, sounding disoriented, "I don't know any Yury DeBlake. Where do you live? Where is he from?"

"We live in Greensboro, North Carolina, and he is from Marshfield, Missouri," I told her.

Still puzzled, she asked, "What did you say your last name is again?"

I said, "DeBlake."

She replied, more energized, "Hey, is he related to Dazmar DeBlake?"

I said, "Yes, she is his sister."

She said, "I know his sister Dazmar. I sent that text message to her and some other friends of ours, but I promise you I did not send that message to your husband. I don't even know your husband."

I said, "Oh, I'm sorry! I wonder how your text message ended up on his phone. I'm going to call Dazmar to ask her about it. Again, I am so sorry!"

She said, sounding relieved and understanding, "It's okay. No harm was done."

I called Dazmar and told her what had happened with the text message from her friend appearing on Yury's cell phone.

I said, "How did your friend's text message end up on Yury's phone? She said she doesn't know him, and Yury said he doesn't know her."

"Hmm, I think somehow Yury was added to our group text," she said.

I asked, "Well, how did that happen, since your friend said she doesn't know Yury?"

Dazmar cautiously replied, "I really don't know. I'm thinking at this point it was some kind of accidental inclusion."

I exhaled and said, "OK, I don't understand that, but at least Yury wasn't lying. Thank you! Sorry if I ruined your Christmas."

She said in a zesty way, "No, not a problem."

Prior to that December 2016 conversation, back in March 2016, I'd had a conversation with Yury's younger sister Dazmar the day I found out about Bonita.

On that day, I'd told her, "I have had it with Yury. He always lies about other women, and I am sick of it. I'm done with the marriage."

After talking to the mysterious lady and Dazmar, I went back to Yury to share the information I'd found out with him. Then I apologized for getting upset about the text and not believing him. Yury didn't want any part of my apology. He was ticked off. It was the straw that broke the camel's back. For him, the second shoe had dropped.

He exploded, "That's it! I'm leaving! I'm moving out!"

I gasped. "What about the house?"

He blurted out, "That's your problem!"

Then he grabbed some of his belongings and went out for a few hours. Interestingly, our conversation was similar to the conversation Yury and I had had in my dreams in 2007 when God first showed me Bonita. Yury moved out on January 14, 2017.

During that time, God flooded me with all kinds of encouraging words, messages, and prophetic words through many people. He was saying through them, "I've got you." One minister on TV told about his divorce and said he'd thought his life was over, but God had brought the love of his life to him. They had been happily married for twenty years. Another one looked at the camera and said, "Dry your eyes. After your divorce, God is going to bring someone amazing into your life."

FOURTEEN

ON JANUARY 30, 2017, while I was watching Linking Christians Inc., an apostle of the gospel had a word from God for me. He said, "God is speaking to me about a Lewisa. You have been trusting God for a good husband. God says that husband cometh February 14. Get ready for what I'm about to do. This is your season, and, Lewisa, God is saying there is a relocation coming for you and your family. Get ready; your wealthy season is now."

When I heard those words, I rejoiced. I was happy God wanted me to know he knew what had just happened in my marriage. I told my children. Jillian was working, Jaren was serving our country, and Jasper was in school. I texted Jillian and Jaren the exact prophetic words the minister had spoken pertaining to me.

Jillian wrote back, "Wow! That's good news, Mom! He actually said your name?"

I said, "Yes. Thank you!"

"Does Dad know?"

"No. I don't think it's a good idea to tell him."

"Yes, that's right. Tell me how it turns out."

"OK, I will."

When I told Jaren, he replied, "Mom, the man said your name?"

I said, "Yes, he did. That made my day."

"I'm glad to hear that! I want you to be happy, so I'm pleased that God has the answer for your problem."

"Thank you! I am too."

"All right, Mom. Let me know how it goes."

"OK, I will."

When I told Jasper, he just said, "Cool, Mom!"

I bought a new outfit. I bought Luca a gift, and as that day approached, I cleaned up my house.

Yury called me on February 12 to inform me he had to come by our house on February 13 to pay our lawn man. I agreed he could come to the house to do that. On that day, before Yury came over, two black men I didn't know pulled up in our driveway and parked in front of our garage.

One stayed in the vehicle while the other came through the garage to the door leading to the kitchen. He rang the doorbell. I was a little surprised because most of our guests and strangers usually used our front door. Every once in a while, our neighbors and family would come through the garage to the kitchen door. The top part of the kitchen door was a glass windowpane. We never covered it with curtains or blinds.

At first, I thought Jasper had left his house key at home, because he had done that before. Instead, it was one of the men. I opened the door. He was holding a large bottle of Fabuloso All-Purpose Cleaner, which could be purchased at most grocery stores.

His demeanor was friendly. He asked, "Who does the cleaning in your house?"

I answered carefully, "I do," thinking, *This is weird.*

He said, "Does your husband ever help you out?"

I said, "Sometimes."

He asked, "Is your husband home?"

I spoke slowly. "No, not right now."

He said, "Do you know when your husband will be home? Because I don't believe in stepping into another man's house when he's not home."

In my mind, I thought, *God, what is going on?* I wasn't going to tell him my husband and I were separated, so I answered, "Oh, around five or five thirty."

He said, "OK, I'll come back."

I said, "OK."

Then he said, "I'm thirsty. Would you mind if I have something cold to drink with ice in it? It's really hot out here." That day, the temperature was 59 degrees Fahrenheit.

I told him, "We don't have any sodas," thinking *Lord, what is going on here?*

He said, "That's OK. Just something cold to drink with ice, please."

I got a cup and went to the freezer for ice. Then I opened the refrigerator, poured him a cup of cold Arnold Palmer Half and Half lemonade and iced tea in a large plastic cup, and gave it to him. Then he turned and walked away with my cup. He made friendly small talk for a few minutes with Jasper, who had come home from school. Then he left with the other guy still sitting in the vehicle.

The man's request for a cold drink with ice reminded me of the Bible story in Genesis 24:12–14 NIV, Genesis 24:12–14, when Abraham sent his servant to find a wife for his son, Isaac. Abraham's servant prayed to God for help, asking God to allow the woman God chose as Isaac's wife to give him a drink of water and give water to his camels too. That act would serve as confirmation that she was the woman God had chosen. I had a feeling that was happening to me too.

When Yury stopped by later, I told him what had happened. He thought it was weird too, and so did Jasper. Then Yury informed me that the lawn guy had decided he needed cash to pay for some kind of lawn inventory he needed to pick up.

Yury said, "I'll have to come back by tomorrow after work on Valentine's Day because I only brought my checkbook today. Since the lawn man wants cash, I'll have to bring it back tomorrow. Is that all right with you, Lewisa?"

I hesitated. "Um." I thought, *The lawn guy never required cash before.* He had been taking care of our lawn for more than a year.

Yury widened his eyes as if he were thinking, *Really?* and he said, "Huh?"

I didn't want to tell him about my prophecy. I didn't want him to mess it up. So I told him, "Well, if you are only coming to pay the guy, okay."

The two men never came back. On Valentine's Day, I didn't know what time Luca was supposed to come, so I started waiting for him at ten o'clock in the morning. Yury showed up at our house, the one he'd moved out of, at five o'clock that evening. There still wasn't any sign of Luca. Yury opened the front door and just stood there as if he were expecting someone.

He said, "Since I'm already here, do you mind me eating dinner with you all?"

I hesitated and said, "Um, I guess that works for right now."

Dinner was ready a little after six o'clock. Luca still hadn't come. Yury and I ate dinner on the couch, as we had before he moved out. We watched the news and a movie. Time kept ticking on, and finally, ten o'clock came.

Yury said, "Well, it's getting late. I'm going home now."

I asked, "Are you planning to come back tomorrow too?" My insides were telling me his reason for coming was disguised. In my spirit, I knew he knew more than he told me. During that time, I was in survival mode, so missing him wasn't part of the equation. I didn't recognize my life anymore, so there wasn't any time for that.

He shook his head and answered, "No."

I was disappointed and perplexed because Luca never came. I started thinking a lot about the two mysterious men who'd shown up at my door the day before my prophecy was supposed to be fulfilled. Yury never came back to eat at our house again after February 14. He didn't come back again to hang out with us like that either. I thought Yury's actions were shady and weird. Why had he chosen the day of my prophecy to come spend time with us until ten o'clock that night? Then, suddenly, afterward, he became disinterested in coming back to our house to spend time with us again.

The next evening, I heard a minister with a short Santa Claus beard, mustache, and radio-personality voice on Linking Christians Inc. mention prophetically that Luca hadn't shown up because he'd had a flashback of a traumatic experience that had happened in his life many years ago. It caused him debilitating emotional distress.

He explained, "It's possible for someone who has been walking with God for a long time to go through a setback. The reason he didn't show up was because he had a flashback of a traumatic experience from years ago. That loss caused him to go through debilitating emotional distress, and it resurfaced on the appointed day."

I was still discouraged that he hadn't shown up, but I could understand being traumatized. The predicament I found my life—our lives—in had me traveling down that same road. Then I thought about what could have possibly happened if Luca had come, since Yury had been hell-bent on snooping around that evening.

We put our house up for sale in early March 2017 and got an offer a week later. It was the second offer. The first one was presented the second day the house was on the market, but our agent thought it was ridiculous. She told us about it but had already told the interested party she wasn't going to present his lowball offer to us. Then we started the process of divorcing.

Again, Yury and I wrote out our own separation agreement together. Again, I went along with what he wanted, because I wanted the process to be a smooth transaction and transition because of our children. I had seen how a few messy divorces played out on TV, and I didn't want arguments, fights, and hate rearing their ugly head and making things more complicated for our family.

The day of my appointment at Stein, Hanes, and Sims law firm, I parked in front of a six-story gray-and-black building with sleek tiles and dark windows. The reception area was decorated with rich dark cherry wainscoting on the walls and the same color desk, coffee tables, and side tables. The couch and six wingback chairs were covered with an elegant gray-and-black-striped material.

The receptionist looked like a twenty-year-old Lady Gaga wannabe, with straight bleached-blonde hair flowing down to her bottom. Her clothes were boutique glamour couture. Her white blouse was sleeveless on the left side and had a long, puffy sleeve on the right that was draped with an oversized white bow on top of her right shoulder. Her high-waisted black pants had loose-fitting legs with slits on the side seams and tapered bottom hems. She topped off the outfit with six-inch red-bottomed shoes. Her outfit must have cost more than my whole wardrobe. She walked me to a conference room that had walls of glass and wood trim with double glass doors. The room featured a large, handcrafted cherry table with twenty-two chairs decorated in the same elegant gray-and-black-striped material as the chairs in the waiting room.

She handed me a packet of papers and said, "Please fill these out, and Mr. Hanes will be in shortly."

I said, "OK."

When Mr. Hanes came into the room, he walked over to me and said with a smile, "Well, hello, Mrs. DeBlake." He shook my hand.

I said, "Hello."

He said, "I'll let you finish your paperwork. I'll come back in a few minutes, and we'll get started."

I said, "OK, sounds good."

Kevin Hanes took my case. He was a sharp dresser, wearing a custom, tailored navy suit. His fingernails were manicured, his skin had a pampered glow, and every strand of his neatly cropped black hair was in place. He had a persona that indicated he had been born into the good life, but he wasn't conceited. He just looked like money, and he wore it well. However, my passivity irked my lawyer.

After viewing Yury's and my separation agreement, he shook his head and said, "This agreement benefits your husband more than it does you. Did you hire me because you want me to fight for you? Because I can help you become more financially comfortable than what you agreed to here. The alimony he's offering you is a start, but I can help you get more. You told me you asked your husband to go to Texas with you, but he said no. Therefore, he's choosing to walk away from the marriage. For that reason, he needs to make sure your lifestyle stays comfortable."

I said, "No, I don't want to fight Yury. That will only cause our children to experience more sadness and stress than they're already feeling."

"Mrs. DeBlake, I can tell you are a very kind lady, but you are basically paying me two hundred seventy-five dollars an hour to tie my own hands behind my back. I've been in law for a while now, and believe me when I tell you I can help your financial state only if you let me fight for you. Look at it this way. Once your divorce proceeding is over, I don't want you to think back and say to yourself, 'I wish I had …' As your lawyer, if you end up in that state of mind, I will feel like I didn't do all I could have done for you. With all due respect, Mrs. DeBlake, you gave your husband over twenty-four years of your life. I can help you get what you deserve." His eyes showed concern.

I nodded, saying, "I believe you can, Mr. Hanes, but keeping peace in our lives means more to me than the extra money you can get me."

Mr. Hanes sighed and said, "OK, I'll just help guide you through the process. I won't fight for you unless you change your mind."

I told him, "I'm sure. I don't want to fight."

I was still getting prophetic encouragement to go after what God had for me. However, I felt stumped. I didn't know what I was supposed to do next since the prophecy I'd gotten in January hadn't worked out well on February 14. There had been all kinds of glitches. I felt swindled. I also was still hurting because my marriage had slipped through my fingers, and no matter what I did to try to save it, it didn't work. I was frustrated too because I had really been counting on Luca to show up.

Around that time, our children and I spent time at Yury's new residence before and after our house was being updated and before and after we placed it on the market. We did the same thing before our house showings and sometimes for family meals and movie watching because Yury and I wanted the divorce to be easy on our children.

During one of our evening house showings, as we'd agreed, Yury allowed me to stay at his house. Jillian, who still lived with her roommates, was working. Jaren was still away in the military, and Jasper worked the evening shift. As I waited, I watched movies on Netflix. Around four thirty, Yury came home with food from Chick-fil-A. I was a happy camper. While eating our food, we watched *The Quiet Man* starring John Wayne and Maureen O'Hara. Just before seven o'clock, the movie ended. Yury and I got up to put the trash from the food into the garbage can. While standing there, he reached over to hug me for what seemed like forever.

Then he moaned, "Ooh!" His voice sounded small and croaky, as if it were coming from deep within him.

I hugged him tighter, pressed my body into his, and said, "What does that mean? Why don't you try to tell me how you feel instead of keeping it bottled up inside?"

Then Yury kissed me and led me to his bedroom, where we engaged in physical calisthenics. After our workout was over, Yury sat on the edge of the bed, leaning over with his head resting in his hands.

I asked, "Are you all right? Do you want to talk?"

He shook his head and said, "I'm fine, and no, I don't want to talk."

I massaged his shoulders and then got dressed. He'd put the moves on me, and I had fallen for it. I knew he once had loved me, and I missed the part of him that was sweet, kind, good, and sincere, or so I'd thought. I didn't know he was proficient at turning on and off his sugary-sweet emotions. He could turn on charm the way a world-renowned actor could evoke a magnitude of emotions from one scene to another without missing a beat. I'd heard that some scholars had said, "Many years ago, actors used to be called hypocrites." I was unaware Yury had his doctorate in manipulating people and situations to maneuver things in his favor.

I didn't know I was being worked over by a slippery-tongued expert. He cleverly hid the truth that he acted one way in front of my face and the opposite way around others behind my back. It was a scary thing to be trapped in a sticky web of lies and know the one you loved was the spider. Mama used to say, "When you tell a lie, it's always hard to keep the facts straight. Then again, you'll always remember the truth, even if the best prosecuting attorney tries to trip you up. Also, what you do in the dark will come to the light. Your sin will find you out." She combined Bible scriptures Luke 12:2–3 NIV and Numbers 32:23 NIV, Numbers 32:23 at the end.

I fell for Yury's charm a total of three different times spread out over a few months. Each time, after my indiscretion, Pastor Stonefish invited people to come to the altar to repent concerning things along those lines, with a warning that it could affect destiny. I missed my family life. It was filled with deceit, but I was thinking about some of the good times. I had no clue how God was going to work things out regarding Luca. I didn't even know how to talk to God about it.

I felt alone, confused, depressed, discouraged, heartbroken, and tired. I was numb. I'd heard various ministers say, "It costs something to follow God." My son and I moved out of our house and into our new apartment on April 29, 2017, since the buyers wanted the house by May 1, 2017. I kept a pleasant attitude to help myself cope with the way our lives were changing, and I had to be strong for Jasper. I didn't want him, Jillian, or Jaren to see me fall apart, because I was sad and felt as if I had had the wind knocked out of me. There wasn't time to be grief-stricken because my husband saw me as a burden and a snafu.

I didn't want to put fear or pressure on them, since children were supposed to look to their parents for answers and hope whenever uncertainties covered their lives. Annoyed with the whole situation, I started mouthing off complaints to Jaren about my spiritual battle, because it wasn't going the way I thought it should.

I said, "My February 14 prophecy didn't happen the way it was supposed to. God knows I don't do well when I have to talk to Luca at his concerts. I felt like I was going to throw up all over the table. I don't know what's going to happen now. God knows I'm struggling with the idea of women wanting to burn their Bibles if I marry Luca. I'm a private person. That's his world, not mine."

Jaren stared at me with serious, sympathetic eyes and nodded as I spoke. Then he said, "Mom, you said God told you to go there. When God tells you something, you need to do it with confidence. Do you know what you are supposed to do next?"

I said, "No, I haven't heard anything else lately."

Jaren exhaled and said, "Well, if God tells you to do something else, don't shrink back in confusion or fear. You are a soldier in God's army, so be brave, and complete your assignment."

I saluted Jaren and said, "Sir, yes, sir! Oorah! Semper Fi!"

After all three of my not-so-secret-in-God's-eyes rendezvous with Yury, I accepted all of Pastor Stonefish's invitations of repentance at the altar. However, in August 2017, after the third time I did the undercover tango with Yury, Pastor Stonefish announced, "Today is a very sad day for someone here. Your door to destiny has been permanently closed."

My heart sank. I imagined hearing the sound of prison doors slamming shut behind me. After the deafening, callous, ironclad clink, the reality of judgment set in, and regret took over.

Later, I heard the message again when I watched Linking Christians Inc. Someone said, "You have messed up big-time and caused your open door to close because of your actions."

Another person said, "Your mouth is getting you into trouble. By your words you are justified, and by your words you are condemned."

The person's statement echoed Matthew 12:37 NIV: "For by your words you will be justified, and by your words you will be condemned."

At that moment, I wished I could have melted and slid through the floor. Then Luca featured a short, temporary video message on YouTube informing me he was not my Boaz. I had an understanding of what rock bottom was. I hadn't even known it was possible to be spiritually dumped. It was another sad day.

First, I lost my husband. That was sad enough by itself, but God didn't show me I was going to lose the person he'd chosen for me too. From what I'd learned from listening to ministers, I knew that God took getting his will done on earth seriously. His methods of accomplishing his will didn't make sense to the natural mind. Faith and the apparent sense of his ways were opposites in the kingdom of God. For example, in the world, people were promoted through education and climbing their way to the top; however, in the kingdom of God, people got promoted by serving others. I knew I had wrecked the way God had given me to connect with someone who already loved him and served him. It was all a result of my own wrongdoing and sins. It was another bitter pill to swallow. I was trapped on a private journey that left me in a dazed existence that colored me fruity to those closest to me. I'd heard that a divorce felt similar to the death of a loved one, and for me, it was true.

At first, the pain was inconsolable and indescribable. After a while, it felt like millions of red ants continuously biting and stinging my heart with no relief in sight. It made me pray that my raw wounds turned into scars. It was like floating in dark, gloomy water with nothing but the heavy weight of sorrow pressing against me. It forced me to involuntarily glide through a seesaw of mood swings ranging from anger to hope, depression to joy, and despair to well-being. Then I experienced a moment of peace just before the process started over again.

It was also like the emotional bleeding, rotting, and death of what had been and the realization that future hopes and dreams with my former spouse had been blown to smithereens and crushed into thousands of pieces. It was basically like hell on earth.

This is my attempt to allow you to learn from my experience. If you want to avoid my despair, please avoid divorce and hell too if you can. Being in a marriage with someone I basically had to beg to love me the way I needed to be loved wasn't healthy for me. Even though being rejected by my own husband was mortifying, I believe God will bring something good out of my grief. That's why having a relationship with God matters. If I had to go through this kind of suffering without the strength that comes from knowing him, I don't know how I would have made it past the pain. I'm learning to give myself permission to recover from the darkness of heartache, misery, and mourning and simply call on and wait for the help that comes from the Lord.

Even though God closed my divine door in August 2017 with Luca after my immoral blunder, he allowed me to know he was opening another one for me. Unfortunately, my timing was off.

I was in the habit of faithfully going to church and watching my favorite lineup of ministers on Linking Christians Inc. One weekend in September, since Jaren was visiting Jasper and me while on leave from the marines, I allowed him to use our TV as he wished.

Our new apartment was smaller than the house we'd sold, and instead of having five televisions, we were down to having only two. Per our routine, I always watched TV in the living room, and after school, Jasper always played video games in his room.

That particular Sunday, I had recorded Bishop Wiseman's service and planned to watch it that night once Jaren got tired of watching TV. However, he kept asking me to watch various movies and shows he thought I would find interesting. Therefore, I never got a chance to watch Bishop Wiseman's service.

The next day, after I dropped Jasper off at his community college, I went to the DMV to pay the taxes on my vehicle. As I was leaving, in the parking lot, a man dressed in an oversized, loose, flowing bright red dress shirt with ruffles and bright yellow or orange pants walked toward me. He reminded me of a reject from the 1972 movie *Super Fly*. He stopped to speak to me. I thought our encounter was odd, but I wasn't afraid.

He asked, "Do you have any children?"

I answered, "Not little ones."

He said, "Are you looking for a job?"

I said, "No." I didn't know what was going on.

He asked, "Do you want a boyfriend?"

I said, "I'm married," thinking, *This is so weird.*

Then he said, "I'm just trying to help you."

I walked away thinking, *How does he think he's going to help me? Also, he has no idea what just happened in my life. I'm not going to blindly add anything or anyone else to it. To do so would only make it even more painful and complicated than it already is.*

Because Jaren was still visiting us, I didn't watch Bishop Wiseman's service until Tuesday evening. When I did, I heard him say, "Someone is coming to offer you a job. When the offer comes, don't reject it because you think it is too big for you."

Hearing those words made my spirit jump. It filled me with hope. I told my children what Bishop Wiseman had said. I was excited and filled with anticipation. Then, after I repeated Bishop Wiseman's words, it dawned on me: the man wearing loud clothes who'd approached me in the parking lot of the DMV had been the job offer he was talking about. If I had only watched his service when I normally did, I would have been prepared when the man walked toward me. I thought, *God, you know everything. Why are you allowing me to not understand what you are doing and to miss you when you do things for me?*

God was patient with me, though. He didn't flip out on me because my timing didn't line up with his. I continued getting encouraged through Bishop Wiseman, Pastor Stonefish, and many other ministers. In October, I was pleasantly surprised when Bishop Wiseman came to a church in North Carolina. He was the guest speaker at a local church.

While there, he said, "God wanted me to come specifically for someone. What you did a while ago that didn't work is going to work this time. You are not crazy. I know you are heartbroken. Everyone is not going to go where God wants to take you. God will bring the right people into your life. You need someone to help get you to your destiny. You don't get there alone."

I left feeling hopeful. I didn't know what was going to happen next, but I believed I would be all right when it came.

Then, in November 2017, Pastor Stonefish said, "I'm speaking to someone specifically. It's time for you to go after your destiny. You only have a small window of opportunity to decide."

I thought, *Oh my goodness! That means go back to Texas.* After church, I talked to Jillian, Jasper, and Yury together. I shared what I'd heard Pastor Stonefish say. Jillian was sitting on the couch. Her eyes dropped to the floor as pain swept across her face. Jasper was standing behind her. He closed his eyes and breathed ruggedly. Yury clenched his fists and turned his head toward the window. Sadness covered their faces, but my children didn't say a word.

Then Yury said, "I hate to see you go. I'm going to miss you."

I said, "I'll miss you too, but you don't want to serve God with me."

He nodded, saying, "That's correct. You've got that right."

Later, I texted Jaren, and he said, "Mom, you've got to do what you believe God wants you to do."

I wrote back, "Jaren, thank you for being more spiritual than I am and so mature about this whole situation."

"Mom, I'm a soldier in the United States Marines. When my commander issues an order, I don't ask questions. I just obey the order. It's the same thing when God tells you to do something. I get it."

"I'm proud of you. Amen!"

Saturday, December 8, 2017, was my target date to leave by airplane for Dallas, so I could attend church service the next day. I used my alimony and remaining money from the sale of the house, which wasn't a lot, to fund all my expenses. The movers packed up my apartment and placed my furniture and other belongings in storage. Then another moving company took my vehicle to Dallas for me. On Sunday, December 9, 2017, I planned to go to Great Is the Lord Church, which Bishop Wiseman presided over, for their 10:00 a.m. service.

The hotel I slept in was just ten minutes from the church. I called a taxicab service at 9:30 a.m., thinking, *Even if it takes twenty minutes for the driver to pick me up, I'll still get to church on time.*

My calculation was spot-on as far as the taxicab driver picking me up at 9:50 a.m. His GPS gave him directions, but he told me traffic on the freeway would be backed up with all the churchgoers. He said he knew a shortcut, so I said OK. As he drove, I kept my eyes on the time on his car's dashboard. When it showed 10:10 a.m., I asked the driver, "Are we getting close? You said this was the shortcut, right?"

He said, "It shouldn't be much longer. I'm trying to avoid streets with lots of traffic."

I said, "Oh, OK."

He kept driving. I was starting to wonder if he knew what he was doing. Then the clock showed 10:20 a.m. I wondered if he was trying to reenact the movie *Taken*, but then at 10:35 a.m., I saw the name of the street the church was on. We arrived at the church at 10:40 a.m. I came to the realization the cab driver had taken me the long way because he was motivated by greed; a ten-minute fare was much smaller than a fifty-minute fare. I was forty minutes late for the service. When I walked into the service, I could tell I had already missed my date with destiny because of what Bishop Wiseman was saying.

He said in an elevated, penetrating tone, "You mean to tell me you didn't come? That your date with destiny doesn't matter to you? You door is closed!"

He was mad. I sat in my seat, petrified. I wanted to stand up and say, "I'm here," but I didn't know the proper way to approach the situation. I had never seen a book called *Step-by-Step Instructions for Stepping into Your Destiny*, nor had I ever had a how-to conversation with anyone on the subject. That day, hearing Bishop Wiseman's tone took me back to my childhood and the way Mama had used her powerful voice to reprimand her daughters.

Her voice alone had done it for me. It had sounded like thunder and lightning. She'd never had to use any other kind of disciplinarian instruments on me. Still to that day, if someone made my mother angry, if she used that tone from my youth, it paralyzed me.

During the church service, I thought, *No! This can't be happening! God, I already left everyone and everything to come here!* After church, I met a couple of ladies who also had come there by faith. We talked for a little while. They had come from California. Then I went back to my hotel room. I didn't have a place to live or know what to do next.

That evening, I talked to Mom. She reacted the same way she had the first time I came to Dallas. The next day, I went to the Christian school where I'd applied for employment my first time in Dallas.

However, the next morning, while watching Bishop Wiseman's program, I heard, "The job God has for you is not what you are thinking."

Hearing those words let me know God didn't want me to go back to the school again. Then, a week later, I saw that Luca had gotten married. It was the first time in my life I had ever become suicidal. My brain felt as if it were going to snap in half. It was as if I were glued to never-ending hopelessness. I knew Luca had spiritually broken up with me, but I never had imagined him getting married so quickly. I thought about everything I'd told my children and family. Out of everyone, my children believed what I'd told them, and knowing I had lost any additional chances of correcting my mistakes was hard to bear. Just as Jesus wept in John 11:35 NIV, John 11:35, I wept.

That evening and then Sunday morning during the service, I heard Bishop Wiseman's voice say, "You are not to take your life.

God is not through with you yet. He still has a plan for your life. I rebuke the spirit of suicide!"

I needed to hear those words. They made me feel that God knew what was happening in my life. That Sunday, I also learned that because I hadn't revered what God was doing with my destiny, it would be three months before he would allow me to have another divine visitation. Hearing those words made me tremble inside and petrified me. Since it was getting closer to the Christmas holiday, I went back to Greensboro, North Carolina, to spend time with my children at Yury's house.

Even though I had just left about a week ago, he was kind enough to allow me to stay with them. While I was at his house, Yury was more distant than he used to be toward me. We still ate dinner together while watching TV, but he spent all his other time at home by himself in his bedroom. Except for talking about our children or the movie, we didn't talk.

I stayed until a few days after the 2018 New Year came in. During that time, being in the presence of people who loved me and once had loved me, plus continuing to listen to God's Word, words of hope, and praise-and-worship music, helped heal my mind. This time, I was able to keep myself from Yury's advances toward me. I'd learned a valuable lesson regarding how God viewed morality when he closed my destiny door with Luca. Plus, I was wise to the fact that Yury only wanted sex from me if I was willing to let him have it. He no longer wanted a relationship with me or to have me as his wife. He didn't see me as his good thing.

I also learned during my time with my family that Yury was keeping up with what Luca was doing, because he knew Luca had gotten married. Yury laughed and did his version of "I told you so." His words and attitude were poignant and bittersweet and burned my soul. Luca would have been my proof God was calling me—my miracle.

Once I returned to Dallas, I went back to the same hotel. That was where the moving company delivered my vehicle. The cost of living in the hotel was adding up. After staying there for a little more than forty-five days, I had run up more than $3,500 on my credit card. Since I was still getting confirmations that God wanted me in Texas, I knew I had to get an apartment, so that was what I did. I moved into my apartment on January 22, 2018. Then, in February, God moved on Mom's heart by calming her, so she no longer verbally attacked me anymore. She began encouraging me to follow what God was telling me. With the month of March drawing near, I began hearing Bishop Wiseman say, "God is working on something for you. You are going to step into your destiny. It's coming."

FIFTEEN

FROM WHAT I was hearing, I knew to expect something to happen at Thursday night Bible study on March 15. However, I didn't know what. Would flashing lights announce, "This is your destiny moment; if you are choosing to live in God's will, come to the altar"? Or would it be something similar to the man in *Coming to America* singing the song "She's Your Queen" but "It's Your Destiny" instead?

Since I was alone in a large, unknown city and surroundings, I was still struggling with fear. Again, that was the state of mind I was in that night. Bible study came and went, and there wasn't any kind of announcement. I left the church feeling disappointed. I knew I had missed it, but I couldn't figure out what I had missed.

Then, early Sunday morning, in a dream, I kept seeing a particular man and woman dressed in fancy ministerial robes whom I had seen in church Thursday night. They were visitors. God showed me if I had gone to the altar during the altar call, they would have helped me step into my destiny. They had come that night from another state specifically for that purpose.

After that night, God was gracious and gave me countless opportunities to step into my destiny. Unfortunately, because I was dealing with the anxiety of failure, confusion, and fear; was leaning on my own understanding; and did not know how a destiny moment should look or sound or the unwritten rules and because each date with destiny was totally different from the last, I blew them all. In terms of test anxiety, I would have fit into the severe anxiety group. I bombed each attempt I was given to cross over into what God promised me. I was frustrated and wondered, *Why would God allow me to go through possibly fifteen or more destiny failings and mistakes? He's all-knowing and knew I didn't know what to do or what to listen for. God knows how we feel.*

In August 2018, I was discouraged. I went to see a minister who operated in the prophetic as a favor to a friend God had placed in my life. I had no intention of letting that minister prophesy over me. However, once we arrived at the small church, which had possibly thirty people present that night, after the visiting evangelist took his seat in the sanctuary, I knew God was working.

Evangelist Jay Ford, who was tall and slim and had a kind face, sitting in the front row, kept turning back to look at Ward and me. I'd met Ward, whom I'd given the nickname Little Brother, while volunteering at Bishop Wiseman's corporate office. Ward's story was similar to mine. God had shown him who his wife was and had led him to Texas from Alabama by faith.

After Evangelist Jay Ford's fourth time of turning and looking back at us, I knew I had to let him talk to me during that designated time. At the end of the service, we were given the chance to have him prophesy over us.

When it was my turn, I stood in front of Evangelist Ford; he reached out for my hand; and while holding my hand, he rocked his body back and forth as he said in an informative, inspirational, rhythmic tone, "The picture I saw was like a flag, and you were waving the flag back and forth, and it was the American flag. And I just saw as you began to wave it that it was glory. As we know, the flag is called Old Glory, but as you held it before the king, you were holding the nation. And I saw and heard the song as if you pledged an allegiance of the king of kings. I saw you as a woman who began to lift up the nation. And as you waved the flag before the throne of the Lord, the Lord said, 'Many wave for others, but your wave is before me. Hold the nation, and hold it dearly, for you are not captive, but you are a daughter free and free indeed. You're free. You're free, for I have set you free. And the freedom shall counsel you.'

"The freedom shall counsel you. And the sincerity of the stand shall call you to where to go and where to move. It's a move. You will move in justice. As the move comes, you'll move in justice. 'And the justice shall be mine,' says the Lord, thy God. I saw you looking at the area of decisions. I saw counsel on the left hand and counsel on the right hand. And you look and say, 'What shall I say, and what shall I do?'

"These are decisions of judgment, and the Lord said the righteousness of the Lord's Word shall prevail. There is a preview and a harvest. He put preview in front of you. Words of knowledge that is yet to come. I saw him whisper to you, 'This is what I say. This is what shall come, and it won't be late. It shall have a time and a season, but it shall come forth. Wait on the timing, for it shall be perfect. In its time, it shall speak, and the time shall come forth, and you shall run.' It was season by season. But he shall speak to you of even the affirmation. I heard affirmations coming back. The words you prayed and the words you spoke were true.

"We didn't see, but now we see. We didn't understand, but now we hear. We perceive what God said. And I saw again as the Lord spoke to the gifting of the prophetic inside you. It was a portrait of words that were yet to come. The pictures shall be revealed before your eyes. You'll see in season, and he will eliminate your fears. Just speak what he speaks. He will teach you as you see. Ask the question, for he will identify your steps. He will organize with order, and out of order, you will know it by the spirit of God quickly. He'll bring your feet in order. And it is the justice of the Lord step by step, for the faith required is his faith. His faith shall be your faith.

"Even as a ring of covenant. The Word is his covenant and shall not fail. His Word shall be upon your lips. And you'll search the heart of the Lord, asking, 'What shall I say? What shall I do?' The to-do list is in front of you. It will be recorded, but with a merry heart, you will find an instantaneity." He struggled to say the word correctly. "*Instantaneity*—try to say that word. I'm making a new word, Lord. But instantly, you will find that things are coming very quickly. Things are being established that took years and time. It seems I had no favor—that God's favor overturned—and even for the now. Now.

"The season is coming. It's preference by season, but it shall come, as the Lord's favor shall rest upon you. Jesus grew in favor with both God and man.

"The Bible says, 'Seek first the kingdom of God, and these things shall be added to you.' As you grow in favor before God, you shall have favor and trust that is given to you by man. And God gives doors ordained by him. You'll go through the doors with gladness. And he will give you identity and the authority of decisions.

"The Lord said to make the decision mathematically. You will see. You will understand, and you'll perceive with wisdom. The knowledge of God shall be with you. Father, I thank you for her flight as one who runs but also as one who moves. Father, I thank you in the transition. The time of transition. The Lord said, 'It shall be for good, for my goodness is with you. Obey my word, and order my steps, for I have ordered your steps in my steps. And they shall be concealed as you step by faith.'

"I saw the first step. You said, 'God, I don't know where I'm going. I don't know what I'm doing. God, what am I even doing here?'

"And the Lord said, 'Step upon step, identify. I'll identify, and I'll bring order, and there shall be no confusion.' *Confusion*—a blasphemous word. You have no place near the daughter of the Lord. He said, 'By the Holy Spirit, let counsel come.' And you have arrived in the midst of counsel. God, cause a season with wisdom. A season with wisdom and counsel. The spirit of God will give you understanding. Daughter, this is a breakout. Daughter, this is a breakout. This is a breakout. Daughter, this is a breakout.

"For the Lord spoke, and he hid you from the thief. He literally hid you from the thief so the thief could not steal any more from you. I bless you. God, I bless the substance in her hands, which you have given to her. Because she gave you honor for all that she has. I bless her in your name. In the name of Jesus, rise up and walk. Amen! Amen! Bless you!"

I was amazed. I knew God had spoken to him, because Evangelist Ford knew I had been telling God I didn't know what to say or what to do ever since I came to Dallas. He knew I was struggling with confusion and fear and that God showed me glimpses of my future in dreams. Yes, God showed up for me. I would forever be grateful for that moment. I needed it.

When 2019 rolled in, I was still waiting. One Sunday, Bishop Wiseman prophesied that God had selected another husband for me. He said, "He's a doctor." There wasn't any doubt in my mind he was talking to me. I thanked God for that information. I asked God to bring my new husband to me in my everyday setting. Years ago, I'd had a turbulent time in Luca's surroundings and had been too nervous to face him, and I wanted the second time around to be different.

In March 2018, I was hired at Delish Dish Bistro in Bishop Wiseman's corporate building, but after I'd worked for one week, God used a minister on TV to prophetically tell me, "That job is your Ismael and not your Isaac. You have to let go of Ismael, and then Isaac will come." Hearing those words, I immediately turned in my two weeks' notice. However, since being at Delish Dish Bistro gave me something to do and a place to go, I decided to volunteer in the bistro until God brought my Isaac, my promised job.

Then, in early February 2019, the man Bishop Wiseman had prophesied about walked into the bistro for the first time. I knew it was a divine moment. My heart leaped for joy. He already loved God and was already serving God too.

He had kind eyes, a great smile, an inner beauty that saturated his face, and a voice that made me go weak in the knees. Instantly, I was attracted to him. I knew God had answered my prayers. For me, it was love at first sight. Leon Scott came in with a group of people. He had just started going to the same church I went to. Somehow, based on Bishop Wiseman's prophesy and my prayer for help from God, I knew he was the one God had sent. Leon and the group of eight people placed their belongings on a table and then got in line to view the food in the steam table and salad bar.

As soon as they entered the bistro, I was overcome by joy for my future, so I began waving my hands at him and smiling until my face hurt. Leon hesitated to get in line. He sat for a moment with his head turned in my direction. He rubbed his hands against his thighs a few times. His mouth was slightly open, and he displayed amplified, curious eyes.

Moments later, when he came to the steam table, after I served him, in an attractive, modulated voice, he said, "Hello."

I said, "Hi." I tried to refrain from acting like a schoolgirl with a crush. I wanted to rush over to him, put my arms around him, and say, "I'll take him, God! He's beautiful! Thank you for not forgetting about me!" I was ecstatic that I wasn't going to be alone anymore. In addition, I was overjoyed that God was giving me a second chance to have a family again. Leon Scott was handsome, smart, and tall. He made my heart sing, which was refreshing after all the pain I'd endured.

Then God showed me a dream in which my head was resting comfortably on Leon's chest. He gave me a picture confirming what I had heard Bishop Wiseman say in church. Since he was part of my destiny, from what I learned, he would only come into my life during my destiny moment, God's divine moment.

Leon was black, though I looked at a person's heart, not his color. In 2019, I had blown all the destiny moments God gave me, because each time was different, which threw me off. This time, God instructed me to invite Leon into my life. Most people probably would have thought, *That's easy. How could you possibly mess that up?*

However, I had been brought up to believe men were supposed to pursue women. Mama used to say, "Women who are tramps or hussies chase after men." Those words had been drilled into my mind since I was a child. So approaching Leon for the purpose of inviting him into my life was like facing a large bowl of snake soup in front of me at the dinner table. Imagine the bowl in the center of a charger plate to prevent spills on the fancy tablecloth; however, sautéed baby snakes had been placed meticulously around the charger, and eyeballs were swimming around in the soup. Then the chef said, "Bon appétit," but I was thinking, *Bon appé-yuck.* Most people would have gagged and thought of such a dish as grotesque.

Well, that instruction from the Lord made me gag. I had a hard time even figuring out how to do it. Inviting a man into my life was a foreign concept. I tried a number of times after hearing it was time to make a move, but my actions were awkward and didn't yield a good result. Plus, my timing was off.

During a sermon on a Sunday in May 2019, I heard Bishop Wiseman say, "God said he already brought your future to you, but it's up to you to bring it into your life."

Then, on Thursday, before Bible study class, I saw Leon sitting toward the front of the church.

I asked him, "Can I talk to you for a moment after Bible study class?"

He smiled and said, "Yes, absolutely!"

I said, "OK, thank you!"

The whole time during Bible study, my stomach shook, rattled, and rolled. It was difficult for me to relax, and my mind was in a fog. Once the lesson was over, I managed to come up with a plan.

I approached him and asked, "How can I volunteer for you?"

He scratched his head with a blank stare, narrowed his eyes, and said, "Let me give you my secretary's information." He looked in his phone and gave me her contact information. Then he said, "So is there anything else you want to ask me?" He watched attentively and pursed his lips.

Still not knowing what to say, I said, "No, not right now."

He lowered his head. Then a man came to talk to him. I walked away feeling as if I'd failed a major exam. I thought offering to volunteer for him would be a natural, unobtrusive way to get to know him, but it didn't work the way I was hoping it would. Days later, past the destiny moment, when I saw him leaving the bistro, I asked to talk to him about what God had revealed to me about him. My shift had ended, so I followed him outside.

I said, "I don't usually go around talking like this, but I'm sure I heard from God. I heard Bishop Wiseman say some prophetic words that I believe were for me. He said, 'God has already chosen another husband for you, and he's a doctor.'" Leon had a PhD in environmental science and engineering.

Leon leaned forward and focused on what I was saying.

I continued. "Then, days later, I saw you in a dream. My head was resting comfortably on your chest."

His eyes appeared the same size as the moon. He cleared his throat and said, "Wow! Really? That's something there. Well, that's something to pray about. Thank you for telling me." He shook my hand.

I said, "OK. Thank you!" I walked away, puzzled, thinking, *Thank you, I think.*

I was embarrassed, but I was also 100 percent sure I had heard from God and had heard prophetic words from Bishop Wiseman. I just couldn't figure out how or when to invite Leon into my life. I'd thought for sure that telling him what God had shown me and what I'd heard would have done it. It had worked on me with Kent thirty years ago. At that time, Kent hadn't necessarily been my type, but because I'd believed him when he said God had said I was his wife, I'd decided to be obedient. Plus, I wanted to please God.

In my mind, telling Leon what God had said helped me feel like I was not a floozy. That was another word Mama used. The words "Would you like to go out?" never came to my mind.

I knew that destiny moments only lasted for a short time and couldn't be done on your own timetable. Thinking about the short amount of time and not knowing how to fulfill the instruction had my mind and emotions in an adrenaline rush ramped up by confusion and fear. It was hard for me to figure out which way was up, so to speak. God had a minister talk me through my discouragement regarding the process and had him share with me that it was all about listening to what God was saying and following his instruction. That advice helped me transition from panic mode, but I was still messing up.

Then 2020 came in, and I missed a few of those moments again. On January 31, I had a dream. I dreamed I was in a nearly empty church. Only a few people were there. It was a large church, so the emptiness was eerie. I had three offering checks and asked the usher for three envelopes. After he gave them to me, I placed all the envelopes in the offering plate. Then, somehow, I knew a second offering was going to be taken up, so I asked the usher for one of my offering envelopes back.

Then the dream shifted. I was walking outside away from the church, which appeared to have been in the city. I kept walking and somehow ended up in the country. I was on a wet, muddy road. A white miniature horse was walking toward me. I had mud all over my tennis shoes. There was a small white house straight ahead. People, many of them, were outside in the yard, talking. I went inside the house. There were many people inside the house too. I went into the bathroom to clean my shoes. The bathroom was crowded too. There were people inside it and outside the window. I saw the toilet lid was down, so I sat on it. Moments later, Leon came to the door. It was a surprise.

He said, "Oh, excuse me!" and then he turned around.

I came out of the bathroom to go after him and said, "I was just sitting there. I wasn't using it."

He said, "No, I don't want to disturb you."

"It's OK," I said.

Then the dream ended. I didn't know what the dream meant, but I was still believing, hoping, and trusting God to bring about his promises in spite of my mistakes. As for Leon, I am trusting God to keep his promises and work things out for my good because he is a promise keeper. Therefore, I say by faith, a ray of sunshine is bursting in through the dark clouds in my life.

EPILOGUE

I have been meditating on the fact that God's Word is true, and he can't lie. Panicking and trying to figure out why something happened and how God is going to fix it has caused me to get in his way. My actions have delayed what he wanted done in my life. I'm reminding myself to relax and just say yes. God is for me, and even though his ways are unusual to me, he is not trying to hurt me. Plus, I have moved out of being petrified.

During my time in limbo, through the years, God allowed me to see Bishop Wiseman's and First Lady Wiseman's hearts. They love God and people. They help people learn who they are in Christ. Also, they encourage everyone to go after what God has called him or her to do. I'm no longer in a tailspin and no longer feel my life is topsy-turvy. With every new day, I am finally inching toward a peaceful state of mind and am reminding myself to revisit the love I know comes from God. During my storm, I forgot that. It doesn't feel as if God is punishing me anymore. I was reminded that I can trust his Word.

God said what he called me to be, so I am who he said I am. God told me whom he chose for me, so it is just as God said. God said what he wants me to have, so it's mine. If God said it, it's already done. Period.

As Christians and believers, we are in the army of God. God is our general. We take our orders from him. We don't get to make our own decisions independently. Our lives are not our own. The bottom line is, I know I heard from God. Do you know what I have learned from my own life's story? I have learned it's important not to just listen to or believe what people tell you with their mouths but to make sure their actions line up with their words. That may take time, so don't be in a hurry, or you'll miss important, truth-telling clues. I've learned not to ignore red flags.

If you observe actions or beliefs that conflict with your own or with God's Word, don't just brush them off and think you'll work on them later. You can't make others want what you want, love what you love, or be faithful if they have a desire to cheat. Don't get physical—sexually active—while dating. That will only cloud your judgment, and the Bible tells us to stay away from sexual sin and keep our bodies holy (1 Thessalonians 4:3–4 NIV).

I've learned it is important for a Christian to avoid dating and marrying anyone who doesn't already spend time with God by reading or listening to his Word, the Bible. Also, if that person is not already practicing living the way God instructs us to by going to church to be around other believers, paying tithes and offerings, and living a moral life, don't fool yourself into thinking things are going to change once you get married.

Yury's family and friends lived far away, and because of his color, Mom banned him from her house during our dating phase, so I didn't get a chance to observe red flags through the unbiased eyes of family and friends. Despite my going through the chaotic rigamarole in our marriage and learning he was a sneaky, lying cheater, Yury and I are still cordial toward each other today. I forgive him. I've learned that forgiveness is a choice and not a feeling. I pray you learn from my story and save yourself, your unbelieving spouse, and your children from the pain of having controversial, divided beliefs and from the torment of divorce.

I have learned that even though I was blindsided and bamboozled by my ex-husband's concealed agenda in the field of love, I shouldn't hate him or myself, beat myself up, or call myself a fool. I didn't fail because I gave my whole heart to someone who didn't consider me to be precious and irreplaceable. He was undeserving of my love. I know Yury wasn't coming from a callous, heartless, vicious place, but I believe he was strictly operating and driven by lust and his own fantasy. Recently, Mama told me, "Yury will never find another woman like you again. He couldn't see you were treasure for him. God will bring someone into your life who sees you for who you are and treats you that way." I want to share my mama's words as part of your healing too.

God's Word says in Isaiah 61:3 NIV, Isaiah 61:3, "And provide for those who grieve in Zion—to bestow on them a crown of beauty instead of ashes, the oil of joy instead of mourning, and a garment of praise instead of a spirit of despair. They will be called oaks of righteousness, a planting of the Lord for the display of his splendor."

PRAYER

Heavenly Father, thank you for who you are and for the love you have for us. I ask you to allow my story to inspire others who encounter pain similar to the pain I have experienced in my life. Let my experience point them to the power of your healing, love, and presence. Let my story prove true that we can take the good, the bad, and the ugly that life sometimes produces, especially when it catches us off guard, and turn our bruises into blessings for your name's sake. Lord, because you are God, let them experience your working everything out for their good. I pray and believe in Jesus's name. Amen!

FURTHER READINGS

https://kathysteinemann.com/musings/expressions

https://www.bryndonovan.com/2015/04/05/master-list-of-facial-expressions/

https://www.macmillandictionary.com/us/thesaurus-category/american/words-used-to-describe-fac

https://writinglikeaboss.com/how-to-describe-landscapes

https://jerryjenkins.com/powerful-verbs/

https://www.dailywritingtips.com/100-exquisite-adjectives/

https://www.bryndonovan.com/2015/04/10/master-list-of-gestures-and-body-language-for-writers/

https://www.nownovel.com/blog/ways-to-say-said-simplified-dialogue/

https://www.livewritethrive.com/2013/11/20/show-dont-tell-how-time-is-passing/

Printed in the United States
by Baker & Taylor Publisher Services